MY OCEANS

MY OCEANS

ESSAYS OF WATER, WHALES, AND WOMEN

CHRISTINA RIVERA

CURBSTONE BOOKS / NORTHWESTERN UNIVERSITY PRESS
EVANSTON, ILLINOIS

Northwestern University Press
www.nupress.northwestern.edu

Copyright © 2025 by Christina Rivera. Published 2025 by Curbstone
Books / Northwestern University Press. All rights reserved.

Printed in the United States of America

10 9 8 7 6 5 4 3 2 1

ISBN 978-0-8101-4837-6 (paper)
ISBN 978-0-8101-4838-3 (ebook)

Cataloging-in-Publication Data are available from the Library
of Congress.

In dedication,
to the endlings.

CONTENTS

ACT III. FATHOMS

AUTHOR'S NOTE

THIS IS NOT AN ESSAY *COLLECTION*; NOT A GATHERING OF things once scattered. This is a *book of essays*. Each piece born under the same moon. Fragments, yes. Because womanhood is fragmented, and motherhood is fragmented, and my understanding of my place in nature is as one of billions of faceted fragments. Motherhood is not a tidy or linear narrative. It's punctuated. I wrote this book between naptimes and mealtimes and bedtimes. I also wrote this book in pieces because it was *through* my fragmentation that the distinctions between Earth's oceans and my own receded. The shape, the movement, of these essays was always waves. Sometimes crashing, sometimes lapping, sometimes with riptides that pulled me into existential crisis and spit me out. I don't pretend to have answers. If my journey has taught me anything, it's to rigorously confess that I make mistakes—that we have all made the so-many mistakes that have landed us upon this eroding shoreline of warming waters, melting glaciers, and waning species. Scientific statistics and facts also move. I tried to anchor some, but they are elusive things, like deep-water squid—shape-shifting with time, distance, depth, and perspective. Please accept our watery nature. Following a growing consensus among many British organizations and the International Union for Conservation of Nature, I'm capitalizing the common names of species in English. This both disambiguates (a giant squid is not necessarily a "Giant Squid") and conveys the respect of proper nouns to genetically distinct populations. As for how to read a "book of essays," there is no one way. You can follow the threads of their undulating order, or reach for the themes that pull you. Humpback Whale songs travel ahead and behind paths of migration. When one whale learns the song of another, its own song evolves. As I have woven melody from my ancestors and teachers into these sentences, weave into your own story what resonates.

ACT I

SUBMERSION

tears have a purpose.
they are what we carry of the ocean,
and perhaps we must become the sea,
give ourselves to it,
if we are to be transformed.

—Linda Hogan, *Solar Storms*

BLOOD MOON

MY BED OFFERS ME NO COMFORT. THE SKIN ON MY ANKLES IS stretched so tight it might split. My belly is tiger-striped by my fingernails scratching an unreachable itch. My daughter is ten days past her due date and after a week's battering by waves of "false labor," my patience expires. Even if the prodromal contractions retreated, I would not rest. The eight-pound baby sits on my bladder, and on my ninth trip to the bathroom in one night—I give up. I yank a blanket from the bed, my husband unroused. I shuffle to the window, lean against cold glass, and am startled—by the wide-eyed rise of a near full moon.

It's the moon's muted light on my black lawn that makes me think of the Leatherback Turtle. She comes to me often when I am uncomfortable and restless. Through the window of the dark living room, within the craggy aspen silhouettes that mark the negative space of moonlight, I imagine her two thousand pounds bobbing in black ocean, waiting.

Once, this sea turtle fit into the heart of my palm. That's how I met her. Under the thatched grass of a conservation outpost on the Pacific coastline of Guatemala. In the hatchery, I recorded her width and put the slide rule down. When I held her up to my nose, my eyes crossed. She was a miniature of her mother, down to the white-ridged lines of her black shell. The hatchling's eyes, hooded, blinked back at mine. But she didn't stop paddling; her winged arms swam in my hand. I put her down and like a windup toy she paddled sand. She would not rest until she reached the sea. It made me wonder by whose hand this will to live was wound. But at age twenty-six, with the hatchling in my palm, the answer was still too big for me to fathom.

ON THE EVE OF A BLOOD MOON, MY WATER BREAKS. IN A dimmed room, between pummeling contractions, I crawl on a padded mat under a picture window. I don't make a sound, other than low rumbling outbreaths. I don't open my eyes for the doctor or my husband. But I find the full moon, framed between slow blinks, arcing across black sky.

My cervix dilates from two to ten centimeters as the sun, earth, and moon travel independently for four hours and forty-four minutes to align in total lunar eclipse.

THE PREGNANT LEATHERBACK TURTLE HAS, FOR OVER ONE hundred fifty million years, trusted her nest to an earth womb. But what she doesn't know is that today, Guatemala's black sand beaches have warmed to new temperatures. Lethal temperatures. A birthing sea turtle is in such a trance that she does not notice the humans behind her. She drops her eggs, covers them, and scoots back into the ocean without looking back. As volunteers, it was our work to unearth her eggs and rebury them in cooler sand behind protective wire.

The hatchling's instinct was sharp; when she broke ground in the nursery, the air was cool. By headlamp, I penciled in carapace measurements. I hugged the bucket with two arms as I walked to the high tideline. There, I lowered the lip of the bucket. As the hatchlings began their frenzied race, I strolled to the water, turned around, and laid down the beam of my flashlight. If it mimicked moon or horizon light, I wasn't sure. But the hatchlings paddled toward it.

If the Leatherback hatchling escapes the clutches of lizards and seagulls and trawl nets and plastic debris and coastal chemical runoff, she might swim into a phase of life that scientists call her "lost years." And if, in those ten to fifteen years, she evades sharks and engine blades and abandoned "ghost nets" and oil spills and plastic-bag jellyfish and the men who pull turtles from the sea to slash their white abdomens for meat, then she will be one in one- to ten-thousand that survives to adulthood. And if she finds a suitable mate from the males left—another one in one- to ten-thousand—if she decides not to shake him off when he nibbles her neck, if she lets him crawl onto her back, and if her eggs ripen, then maybe she will make the pilgrimage home. Which may take time. Leatherbacks travel as far as ten thousand miles a year.

But she is faithful. Faithful to a cycle unbroken for millions of years.

In faith, she swims home.

Male sea turtles paddle once into the sea and never return. But a female—by some unresolved scientific mystery—maps the land and her mother's phantomed path.

That she may find her way back.

UNDER THE FULL RED MOON, MY DAUGHTER IS BORN. I HOLD her in my arms, the beginning of this story. Ten toes and ten fingers, yes. But also six million possible futures nestled in her ovaries. Futures her body cradled before her own fingerprints formed.

With my daughter in my arms, I see reflected in her eyes my journey of pregnancy, labor, and birth. I look deeper and see my mother's journey and my mother's mother's journey. Like this, the planet lights up in moon-pulled tides and blood-pulling moons. I can't reckon a beginning. I wonder who held the beam of light.

With my baby's body nestled in my arms, sunrise comes. Someone draws the curtains of the window back. But I still see the moon framed. Burned in memory. A lingering shadow of the hours I was guided only by instinct and a single light in a dark sky.

I name my daughter Riva.
For one of its Spanish translations.
From the shore.

THE LEATHERBACK SWAM ON A PLANET SHARED WITH *Triceratops* and *Spinosaurus*. Today, the tracks of birthing Leatherbacks on Atlantic, Pacific, and Indian coastlines are scant. The headline I pull up says, "Leatherback Turtles May Become Extinct within 20 Years." This conclusion from 2013. Twelve years ago.

Maybe she's out there, my Leatherback ghost.

Bobbing in surf, paled by moonlight, waiting for instinct to tug her forth. Maybe she is waiting for the wave that will carry her closest to the only land she's ever known. To the shadow of her mother's path she has remembered and retraced. Maybe her hooded eye is looking.

But on the beach there are new lights. Resort lights and streetlights and restaurant lights and house lights and lighthouse lights and bouncing cigarette lights. So many lights she cannot discern the moon. And her belly, maybe it aches with contractions. Contractions that whisper of urgency. Of trance. If only she could reach land and close her eyes.

Out there, my Leatherback ghost bobs.

She has traveled so far.

She is full and aching.

TWO BREATHS

YOU WOULD NOT BELIEVE THE EXISTENCE OF A MANTA RAY until you've seen one. She's nearly a creature of mythology, with underwater arms that can span twentyish feet from tip to tip. The manta twists and turns by tilting the edges of her wings—her acrobatics accented by a dark dorsal topside and white-gilled underbelly. Her diamond frame and right-angled fins can encapsulate a three-thousand-pound mass so flat she might flash invisible when she turns vertical—like a nickel in a hand trick.

The Reef Mantas off the coast of Kailua-Kona congregate at night, when the bounty of planktonic creatures arise. So I organized a night boat. There were two options. My husband and I could snorkel at the top of the water, putting our masked faces under the sea's surface, looking for the tips of those steel wings peeking white and manifesting from darkness in our direction. Or we could don scuba tanks, weight belts, and four-millimeter wetsuits, and release the air from our diving vests and our lungs at the same time. Till there's no air left to buoy us, and our bodies sink to the sea floor.

This is where I find a nook among rocks to plant my knees.

Where we sway with Sea Fans—as we wait.

Down here, the waiting is quiet. There is the sound of my breath as I pull air from my tank. There is my exhalation, a knocking of air bubbles against each other like bamboo chimes. There is the scraping of a nocturnal creature's teeth on coral. Otherwise, it's black, and I am left mostly alone to the orbs of my thoughts.

My hand moves—as quickly as a hand can move underwater—for my husband's. He knows my quiet languages. He reads them in my eyes. Even behind the scuba mask he proves this literacy as he returns my hand squeeze—a little stronger than normal. Because he too is wondering what's going on with me. I, after all, am the expert. I am the one with the divemaster certification and dozens of night dives sketched into my logbook. I organized this dive with the manta rays. It was my idea. My wish. So what are these hooves now trampling in my chest? I know anxiety. But the slow kind that accumulates like tumbleweed through the night and is brushed to the side of the road by the velocity of day. I don't recognize this mob in my heart—all at once—scanning for an exit.

I look up. There's the surface of the ocean, only thirty feet above my head. I could take one breath of air from my tank and "slowly exhale and slowly kick" to the top and reach it just fine. I know this because it's one of the first diving tests I passed for my certifications. But there is danger. Equally silent and lethal danger. If I did not exhale as I made my "emergency swimming ascent," the air in my lungs would expand. And with nowhere to go, the air could break through the blood vessels in my lungs' tissues. The invisible pressure could rupture and collapse my lungs. Technically it's called "pneumothorax." Casually, it's called "burst lungs."

As I'm looking at the roof of the ocean, I'm thinking of this because I am thinking of what lives on the other side. This night dive is different from the last one I did with my husband, off a wooden Indonesian boat five years ago. The difference is our two small children, by now tucked into their beds by the babysitter. Two children who have no place even in their borderless imaginations to know their parents, tonight, are sitting on the floor of the ocean, swaying with Sea Fans, pointing flashlights at an underwater night sky of sparkling plankton.

Looking at the top of the water, I understand it is my distance from my children that makes my eyes wide enough to speak the quiet language of panic. Luckily, a scuba regulator functions much like a brown paper bag. I can hear my drag of air from the tank, see my exhalation in the rising bubbles. And I'm practiced at slow breathing. Especially underwater. In my dive-training months, on the occasions the divemasters could take the boat without clients, we would tumble into the water without briefings, maps, or dive tables. We'd take off our BCDs and turn them backward so as to "fly" underwater, with the tanks underneath us and our arms outstretched. And we'd play. Pulling a fin off a friend's foot, snapping another's mask, even turning off someone's tank as a prank. The playing wasn't always well received (especially by me), but it did make us all nimble for real emergencies. In those days, I was the last diver up. I was small and not as involved in the air-guzzling tumbles. Rather, it was my instinct to use my unrestricted time to hover. To make myself as still as a Sea Fan and watch what revealed itself from the dark nooks of coral walls. And because being a Sea Fan requires very little air, I was able to stretch my tank into the longest, safest, allowable dive.

I am at home in the underwater world.

After hundreds of dives, I did not expect to find this panic in it.

What was not my idea, my wish, was the new meaning of death upon the birth of my children. This was not mentioned in the shelf of motherhood books I read. No one told me about the heaviness. The Blue Whale weight of walking into the future with a baby on my hip and another child in velcroed shoes holding my hand. About how the small bodies add gravity to life. From the ocean floor, looking up, I feel this pressure. And I am not the only warm-blooded mammal in the ocean tonight with this anxiety.

A Sperm Whale births her babe in the sunlight zone of the ocean. Close to the surface is where she nurses her infant for two or more years. But the fat in her milk comes from meals consumed two thousand feet below. In frigid, high-pressure depths, where her babe can't follow. So while the Sperm Whale mother is foraging, she leaves her child to the care of an orbiting pod of related females who babysit, sometimes even wet-nursing the babe themselves. A "mother culture" it's called by whale biologists. While mom is below, she is still in touch with her offspring, sending messages via sonar clicks. Mom typically stays in the depths, hunting, for about an hour. Unless she panics. Peter Matthiessen once documented a whaling ship's chase of a Sperm Whale. The whaler's sonar pinged the animal at a thousand feet deep as it tracked her panicked flight, waiting for her to run out of air and into the crosshairs of the harpooner above. Matthiessen noted of the Sperm Whale's ability to stay submerged: "This time is rapidly decreased by panic."

I know the Sperm Whale's quick breath: The time I turned around at the pool and my three-year-old son was sinking in the deep end. My daughter's fall from a car seat teetering on the edge of a table. Five calls to poison control for the berries and plants and tubes of old medicines my toddlers put to their lips. Two swift Heimlich maneuvers. A broken arm. Midnight runs to the emergency room for spiking temperatures. My recurring nightmares in which climate disasters arrive.

Down in the high-pressure depths, with my body anchored by rocks and my husband's hand, I'm thinking about death. I do not ponder death as much as I did before I had children. I no longer have the time to meditate for two hours a day. I don't remember the dreams I used to prompt and record each night. I don't walk so close to cliffs of bodily risk anymore. Those were qualities of my pre-child life. Of regular earth-gravity living. Of nights uninterrupted by monsters, wet sheets, and the chills of fever. Motherhood breaks linear time. Life becomes instead—punctuated. By the unwavering eye contact of a nursing babe. By a small body shuddering with relief against my chest. By my son's outstretched arm, pointing to the moon.

Swaying with the Sea Fans, my husband squeezes my hand again. He has read in my quiet language that I'm OK enough to be daydreaming. Or water-dreaming. Or whatever one calls the cartwheels of the waking human imagination at nighttime on the floor of the sea. He sees, too, that I'm looking at the ocean's surface in a funny way. I squeeze his hand back, and a beam of light swings like a car's headlights into the fog of plankton. It points at the flicker of faraway wing tips, and though a diver is never supposed to hold her breath, I have no choice.

Our first visiting manta ray—an entirely nonviolent creature of one and a half tons—swims toward us as her ancestors have been swimming for five million years. She flies into the center of the flashlights illuminating the plankton of her midnight snack. Except night and day are not distinctions for those who live in swallowed light. Humans don't know if the manta ray sleeps. To the best knowledge of those who study her, she's a perpetually swimming thing. This manta now swoops in impossibly graceful loops in our light beams. I lean back. I would fall if the water did not hold me. *We are only guests*, I think. My sigh is captured in iridescent ovals, rising toward the ocean's top. Toward the land of my sleeping babies. Whom I have forgotten. Whom I can never forget. But whom I can hold even as I'm swaying with Sea Fans.

Long before I slipped into a black wetsuit, off a boat, and into the cold coastal waters of Kailua-Kona, Native Hawaiians observed the manta ray with due respect. Roxanne Kapuaimohalaikalani Stewart, a Hawaiian cultural specialist, says, "The name of the manta—hahalua—can be interpreted as 'two breaths' . . . 'ha,' meaning breath, and 'lua,' meaning two . . . When mantas leap [out of the water], their experience from below transcends into our sphere . . . Their transcendence speaks to things that we don't yet know."

I flip this image—seeing myself in the eyes of the manta as a land animal of too many lanky appendages, anchored among rocks, submerged in her ocean's sphere of preexisting laws and spirit. We are of different worlds, and yet we share viscera. We both have a heart. A stomach. Intestines. A gallbladder. Kidney. Liver. Uterus. Ovaries. Who would know the difference of our innards? And a brain! The manta has the largest brain of any fish, with developed areas for problem-solving, learning, communication, coordination, and intelligence. To the surprise of marine biologists, manta rays—in a "mirror test," widely used to gauge self-awareness—were able to recognize themselves.

I have forgotten my husband's hand. He has forgotten mine. Under the swooping manta, there's no room for anything but awe. My thoughts of my children are tucked away. Baby manta rays are born wrapped in their own wings like a blanket. There is a single set of images of a manta ray birthing in the wild. It was taken by Roberto Fabbri in the Red Sea in 1968. In the black-and-white series, a tidy bundle of wrapped manta bursts from its mother's body in a cloud of white. The photographer's caption—in tiny font—reads, "The manta ray was speared . . . It represented a big trophy." And if you squint at the photo of the mother mid-labor, you can see the man's murky outline in the shadow just behind her. You can see the long white glint of his metal speargun. He stands waiting, a few feet from her arching, birthing body. A few feet from her eyes.

Two breaths.

Female manta rays are pregnant for thirteen months. For the ten months I carried each of my children, I had two hearts, two brains, four ears, four legs, four eyes. My children came out of my body, and I was back to two legs, but not one heart. I know this because when my child's seashell ear is on my chest, my heart speeds up and theirs slows down. Female mantas might birth only one pup every three years. Their populations have a "low likelihood of recovery," yet in 2025 they are still harpooned, pulled from their home, and scraped alive of their gill rakers for fabled Chinese "medicines." Humans may not even notice their extinction. Whales were native to this planet forty-nine million years before humans arrived, and yet man, in less than a hundred years, disappeared three million whales—like a nickel in a hand trick.

Herman Melville in *Moby-Dick* (drawn from Melville's experiences aboard whalers) wrote of the Sperm Whale's mammary glands, "When by chance these precious parts in a nursing whale are cut by the hunter's lance, the mother's pouring milk and blood rivalingly discolor the sea for rods." In a Sperm Whale's fourteen tons of warm-blooded body, her blood is blue like mine. Red like mine when exposed to the oxygen in air or water. Her blood spills when her calf is born. Her blood leaks brown in the blue wake of her afterbirth, the way mine trailed on the linoleum floor between my hospital bed and the bathroom. Her milk may be flavored by squid the way mine is by garlic. Milk that drops in my breast by an ancestral song of DNA. A dropping of milk that feels like the cracking of ice, the crunch of snow. "Man" does not know this reflex. But I do. And if you call my empathy "feminine," that is my point. "Man" harpooned and dragged thirty-ton bodies onto boat decks until the oceans nearly went silent of Humpback song. Man thought that if he could kill it, he could own it. He spread the red viscera of warm bodies but recognized none of it in himself. Man looked into the mirror and saw *only* himself.

My husband and I ascend from the dive. We strip off our wet suits in the dark. Shiver in the cold of night. Towel off our transcendence from the womb of water.

At the house, I check on the children. I pull a blanket over the exposed limbs of my son. Tuck a pink bear under the arm of my daughter. Turn around with my lungs so full of hope they might burst. Knowing my tumbleweed of anxiety will not evade the velocity of day. That my children, tucked under covers, will face the consequences of all man's great failures of compassion and care. Holding my breath for a mother culture I can feel—but can't see.

I close their door, careful not to make a sound, still swaying with the Sea Fans under the silent and lethal weight of it all.

ONCOMING

I SEE THE BLACK CONCRETE COMING TOWARD THE WINDOW before I hear the tinsel pitch of cement fingernails on glass. But it's the shattering glass that makes sense of the concrete at my window. And so I remember the sound before the impact. Time is not obligated to logic in car accidents.

And then we are sliding. I'm in the middle of the row of seats behind the driver. Before the window broke into a thousand pieces, I was watching Portuguese cliffs blanketed with pink and yellow succulents go by. Steel-blue clouds had just overtaken the marigold of our beach day and first raindrops had unleashed notes of earth and ozone from the clay. I watched the clouds gallop in and drifted to sleep, right before the window turned black.

In between me and the shattering glass is Riva. Her caramel curls are coated in sand from the dune she rolled down before we noticed the approaching storm and gathered the plastic shovels and beach hats and damp towels into the mesh bag. When I moved her body from my hip into the car, her lids were half-mast; heavy enough that she didn't fight me when I snapped the second seat belt across her chest. Now, the plastic arm of this rented car seat is the only thing between the grinding black asphalt and the body of my sleeping child. I wrap my arms around her car seat, pulling her toward me. I think: *How long before the cement reaches her?* and push my arm between her body and the churning black gravel so that I will know first.

And then the car stops, and there is silence. A silence that fills the car, fills the rural highway, fills the farmlands on either side of us, twitches the ears of cattle who have lifted their heads at the sounds of shattering glass and five thousand pounds of metal sliding on cement. I don't realize the fickleness of this silence. My husband, in the front passenger seat, is thinking about the inherent danger of this second—about the oncoming lane in which the car has come to rest. But I am not. Because there is only one question in my mind.

I sweep my arm over the seat behind me, to the third row of the car, where Nash was in his booster seat alone before the glass shattered. I sweep for his body in the darkness of a window of cement and the darkness of a world where anything could happen. Where anything did happen. A world where the back of the car might not exist. With one hand holding back the panic barreling toward me, I reach for my son and command his name: "Nash. Nash."

The panic churns one sixtieth of a minute into the longest moment of my life. In this stretched time, I find his wrist, wrap my fingers around it. When he feels my touch, he says, "Mom."

NASH HAS A BOOK CALLED *THE PHOTO ARK* IN WHICH FULL-bleed photographs document "species before they disappear." The images in the collection are portraits, with the eyes of each animal in focus. The three hundred and ninety-nine pages offer more space, but less refuge, than Noah's famed boat.

The book's seams are frayed, worn feeble by my son's obsession. Nash paddles through pages with full palms. He stops on a photograph in which slate-gray wrinkles swirl around the foggy black iris of a Northern White Rhinoceros. He points to the caption. "Read, Mom." I tell him the picture was taken three days before the rhino's death. The last two of the subspecies are female, making the Northern White Rhino functionally extinct. Fossils suggest the lineage is over fifty million years old.

Nash glides through more pages. He stops on a White-Headed Vulture whose brow is furrowed under a backward tuft of ecru feathers. The bird has a wingspan of seven feet. In 2019, seventeen White-Headed Vultures were found dead in Botswana. The vultures had eaten the poisoned flesh of elephants killed by poachers for their ivory tusks. The poachers poisoned the flesh because dead birds can't circle and alert rangers to dead elephants.

Nash, next, uses both his hands to hold down a two-page spread featuring the turquoise scales, feathered white dorsal fin, and unicorn-ish horn of an Orange Spotted Filefish. The pop of impossible colors belongs to a species extra sensitive to warm waters. During one episode of higher-than-normal ocean temperatures in 1988, it disappeared entirely from Japan.

He palms more pages forward to the deep-set eyes of a Sumatran Orangutan looking into the camera at eye level. This orangutan is meant to live in tropical rainforests of Indonesia that have disappeared by bulldozer and fire for plantations, logging, mining, and roads. I recall a 2016 headline that warned, "Orangutans Face Complete Extinction within 10 Years." Nash will be thirteen in 2026.

This is the first year he's too big to sit in my lap, but he still leans his body into the envelope of my arms. He squirms, looks up at me. "Why, Mom? If we know it's going to happen. Why don't we stop it?"

I rummage for a calming, motherly answer. In the absence of one, I pull him closer. We turn more pages. I see through his eyes all the pieces of an inevitable future flipping toward us.

Before we close the book, Nash returns to his favorite page. It belongs to the Spix's Macaw. On this full spread, the cuffed ankles of two parrots of indigo plumage cling to a wooden perch. Neither of the birds look at the camera. One looks vacantly down. The other skyward with a half-mast eye.

"What does 'captivity' mean, Mom?"

"It means the last Spix's Macaws are kept in cages, Nash."

We have a window in our kitchen toward which Nash is always jutting a finger and shouting, "Red Tailed Hawk, Mom!" He has memorized the favorite prey of Turkey Vultures and the highest recorded flight speeds of Peregrine Falcons. But there's a line in the caption under the Spix's Macaw that he makes me read every night: *It hasn't been seen in the wild since 2000.*

"So there are no Spix's Macaws that fly around? Less than a hundred left, all in cages?"

He looks out the window.

It's black.

"IT STARTED WHEN I WAS PREGNANT WITH NASH," I TELL THE osteopath. "Early in the pregnancy, when I was still naive enough to lift a heavy chair. I felt something snap. And then a sharp pinch doubled me over." As I talk, my right hand drifts to my back, presses a thumb into the spot.

The osteopath doesn't wear a white coat and I wonder if all doctors trained in both Western and Eastern medicine have hung up their smocks and stethoscopes. She continues her review of my admissions interview. "And you've had this 'knot' in your back ever since?"

"Well, it comes and goes. But it has been really angry since the car accident . . ."

There's a frosted window in the doctor's office. I watch a granulated shadow pass by.

The doctor captures my gaze. "You were in a car accident?"

"Yes . . . a few weeks ago. My father-in-law fell asleep at the wheel. The car was totaled. But we all walked out of it. Well, technically, we crawled through a window."

She writes down a note and looks up. "You also list anxiety as something you're experiencing?"

I laugh a little. "Not like more than normal anxiety. Who doesn't have anxiety on this planet right now?"

She looks down, tilts her head at one of the symptoms I've listed. "Can you tell me about this recurring nightmare you're having?"

I rest my eyes on the white wall over the doctor's shoulder. "In the dream, I'm following a broken cement pier toward the beach. It's the Portuguese coast, so it has those impossibly arched sea cliffs carved of granite and red limestone. I see my children near the water, all bent knees and sandy elbows leaning over a hole they are digging from wet sand. And as I walk toward them, I notice the cliff walls are shimmering, then shaking, then quaking. And the walls begin to fall. I try to run to my children. But the ground shakes and chunks of cliff collapse into my sightline. When I reach the spot where they were playing, I see a swath of pink and yellow on the ground. I fall on my knees and wipe away the sand. It's my daughter's little swim shirt. It's the side that doesn't have the pocket. The back of her shirt. I scream as I dig. I pull her limp body from the earth into my arms. And I don't know why the dream lets me see this. But it shows me. My daughter's skin is ash. Her eyes are closed. Both her arms dangle backward as I pull her to my chest."

The doctor hands me a box of tissues.

She says, "Dreams show us unexpressed emotions. Can you name what emotion is underlying this dream?"

I look at the white wall over her shoulder. "Terror?"

She looks down. We both know "terror" isn't right.

When I stand up to leave, she hands me a color wheel with the names of two hundred emotions. She says, "Take it home. Think about it."

When I get into my car to leave, I sit still until I'm chilled enough to remember to turn the car on. Through my windshield, the cold blue Colorado sky looks vacant.

Nothing circles overhead.

I SEE A PHYSICAL THERAPIST TO WORK ON THE KNOT IN MY back. I tell her about the car accident. About my grief for the future of my children. I tell her I suspect I'm holding onto something I can't let go. She sets a glass of water with a lemon wedge on the table in front of me. I watch the water bead on the outside of the glass.

She looks over my left shoulder and says, "Sometimes when grief doesn't have a shape, something to see and touch— sometimes your body creates something so that you can know where to feel it."

IN THE MIDDLE OF THE NIGHT, IN THE DARK, I SIT UPRIGHT in my bed.

Helplessness.

The emotion is *helplessness.*

In the car accident, I found Nash's arm in the sweep of the row behind me and held on. And as I hung from my seat belt, hugging her car seat, my daughter turned her cheek to within an inch of mine and said, "Mama?"

With one hand on each of them, I looked into their eyes and repeated: *You're OK. You are OK.*

They did not cry. They did not scream. They braced themselves on my words, on my touch, on my confidence, on my instruction: *Nash. Papa is behind you. He's coming through the trunk. You're going to feel his hands on your back. Now Riva, I'm unbuckling you. But I have you. I'm going to raise you in the air. And do you see Papa up there? Reach for him.*

When their soft bodies were out of the crushed metal, I looked for their shoes. I knew there was broken glass out there, on the road, and I knew their feet were still bare from the beach. So I looked for their shoes on the floor of the sideways car. I don't remember how I found the shoes. Shock swallowed that detail.

But here's what woke me up in the middle of the night: *Where are the shoes I can give to my children for the broken world they will walk through?* I see the future sliding toward us. A collision of waking terrors and quaking homelands. Of poisoned waters and inescapable waves of heat. A photo ark of eyes turning their pages on existence. No Spix's Macaws fly free. Did I bear offspring with clipped wings? I chanted one mantra to my children in the car crash, while the opposite now circles in my head: *Nothing is OK. Nothing is OK. Nothing is OK.* The emotion is helplessness.

There exists for me a world in which another car came down the opposite side of that rural Portuguese road at sixty miles per hour during the same sixtieth of a minute that our car slid out of its lane. A world in which I sweep the back of the car and find it gone. That acute second of helplessness compacted a decade of anxiety into a moment of clarity.

My helplessness lodged into my back in the form of a knot I now call grief. Grief that plucks a chord of pain when I sit too long, lift without my knees, cradle a crying child. Grief for the assurance I can't give my children. Grief that crumbles midnight cliffs and chants: *How long before the future reaches them?*

The planet is hurtling through lanes it shouldn't, making nonsense of time. Breaking into a thousand pieces and eliciting a cement scream to which we barely raise our heads and stop chewing. I want to find shoes for my children. To lift them up through a window.

YESTERDAY, I FOLLOWED MY DAUGHTER ON A DIRT PATH along the Eagle River. She picked sagebrush, bromegrass, and cattails as we walked, and began a quiet discourse with the bouquet of dried seeds and blooms. I dared not interrupt. Over the hushed conversation between child and cattail, I welcomed the winter chill numbing my fingers. The reflection of sun on snow, whitewashing the world. The caws of black crows perched in naked cottonwoods. This is new: The gravity of all that's fleeting. Just as pain brings awareness of not-pain, so has my grief sharpened the details of the world.

Trailing my child by the river, not knowing the future into which she walks, I clutch one shard of hope with two hands:

that what brings us to our knees might command us to our feet. If the danger feels close enough—a cheek against ours—maybe we will move swiftly, collectively, with sharpened instinct, to put an arm between what we love and what's oncoming.

THE SMOOTH SIDES
OF DARKNESS

ONE WINTER IN INDIA, AMID MY LOST YEARS, I PICKED UP
the word *bardo* and put it in my pocket. There I thumbed the
cold, smooth stone—turning it over and over in unidentified
obsession. The word wasn't mine. I might have received it from
a Lama's teaching in Bodhgaya, the small town whose fame
rests in the shade of the Bodhi tree under which the Buddha
once meditated. It's likely there the word *bardo* was born along
with Buddhism, six millennia before the birth of the guy we call
Jesus. I put the word in my pocket because it was in the shape
of something I couldn't otherwise name. I held onto it. Rubbing
its smooth sides between my fingers, unclear as to my obsession with the term I was taught meant "the state of existence
between death and rebirth." Pema Khandro Rinpoche, a scholar
of Tibetan Buddhism whose teachings focus on the coalescence
of tradition and the modern context, extends the definition. She
describes the bardo as "moments when gaps appear, interrupt-
ing the continuity that we otherwise project onto our lives."

A man I once loved said to me, "There's something about the
way you leave." I had been looking for my socks under his bed.
I popped up my head. "What?"

He continued, "You know what it is? You never look back."

I paused my hustle, tilted my head.

He added teasingly, "I would know, I've watched you go enough times."

I laughed a little too hard, tugged on my boots, deposited a kiss on his cheek, and ran out the door to catch my waiting taxi. But looking through my reflection in the window of the cab, I thought long about what he'd said. About my ease in letting go. About my secret love for breaks in continuity, for the liminal places between here and there.

THE WORLD WAS DARK BUT IT WAS THE ONLY WORLD I KNEW. Dark was the womb and dark was January third in Anchorage, Alaska. On the night I was born, the sun set at 3:57 p.m. and rose at 10:12 a.m. I was due on the winter solstice in December, but my mother carried me fourteen more days into the year of growing light.

My mother was ready. She had waited for me for seven years after my older sister was born. She tells the story of How She Gave Up like this: She had a garage sale. She sold the stroller and the crib and all the things babies shake. She sold the box of toddler snow pants, boots, and winter coats my older siblings had shed. She sold it all and when it was gone from the house— only then—was I summoned: a heartbeat knocking in an empty womb. This is the story of my beginning, of the waiting place I was born from and of the eighteen hours and fifteen minutes of Alaskan night I was born into.

One night that same winter, a bitter cold of single digits reached from the coastal lowlands, through the window of my nursery. That night I unfurled from my swaddle of blankets and did not cry. That night my mother awoke, startled by a shake of instinct. She ran to my room and picked up my cold, quiet body. She willed me to warmth with the racing heart in her chest.

This is my creation myth. In it, whispers rattled from dreams, darkness reached through a window, and death came close enough to touch me—but I did not cry.

WE MOVED FROM ALASKA TO OREGON WHEN I WAS THREE. My first memory is watching the top of Mount St. Helens explode while propped by my dad's hands on the hood of a red Suburban. My second memory is standing near a fence outside my house, pulling my thumb out of my mouth, and deciding I was done sucking it. But it's my third memory from early childhood I want to retrieve. In it, I pulled out a sled from the garage and dragged it behind me. I didn't know where I was going. I know this because I have a five-year-old daughter and I watch her. When Riva nestles under the arms of the big blue spruce in front of our house, she does not "go" there so much as she is pulled. To that quiet place that fits only her, where she is enveloped in the underside perfumes of pine needles and cold soil. A hidden place between earth and day.

Like my daughter, I was pulled. But I was pulled—in this third memory—to the heart of the rhododendron bushes in the yard. Had my mother watched me from the deck, she could have tracked me by my sled-print into the bushes. Bushes that blushed red and pink in the summer, but did not blush on this day when they were sunk by a rare foot of Oregon snow. I centered the sled between the unblushing bushes and lay down with no intention to go anywhere. This will become my thing. Using things made to go fast, to go slow. Or to go nowhere at all; to hover in the midst. But I didn't know this yet. I was only five and just lay there, warm in my mittens and hand-me-down snow bibs. Watching snow fall, not sideways from the perspective of the upright, but watching the snow fall from under the snow. And this is what I remember distinctly: Looking for a source. Searching in the diffused Oregon light, that farthest edge of falling white, looking for what was beyond the gray camouflage of clouds. I was looking for the darkness I knew was on the other side. I lingered so long I remember no ending. I remember no one calling me back from the deck. I remember only the question in my mind: *But behind that?* I wanted to pierce it. To conceive it. *And what's behind that?* I asked, again and again. Darkness, I already suspected, a thin veil for something beyond horizons.

I REMEMBER THE GULLS. THE CALLS OF THOSE FLYING OVER-head but more the squawks of those squabbling over what the fishermen in rubber boots and gloved hands were tossing aside from the long metal counters where fish blood pooled. I was squabbling with the gulls because we were competing for the same goods. But I won because I was an adorable four-foot-tall thing with choppy black bangs wearing a sweater with a rainbow on the chest.

"Is it fish heads you're after, kid?" The salt-crusted voice came from a white-bearded man in rubber waders. "Here you go. Take 'em all." And to the squawking disappointment of the gulls, my little brother and I stole off with the plastic bag full of our good luck and headed toward the docks where the water was just dark but clear enough.

At the end of our favorite planks of splintered wood, we propped in cobra poses, hanging over the edge. My brother is only a year younger than me. There is no garage sale in his creation myth. My mother went to the doctor some months after my birth and said, "Stop the pregnancies." The doctor said, "Just a quick test first," and my mother dropped her wet face into her hands because she knew the test would only confirm what her dream had shown her the night before: a shock of black hair on a smiling baby boy.

Nine months later, my brother was born, a ball of sunshine and spunk. In his haste to catch up to me, he began walking at five months. That is his legend. And also how we found ourselves lined up like sardines on the wooden docks of southern Washington.

My little brother did everything I did, and I was squinting past my reflection, into the watery depths, where we could just make them out on the bottom of the ocean floor—moving sideways. The crabs were feasting on the pile of fish heads that the small gods, twenty feet above on the docks, kept dropping from the ocean sky. These sky gods, they tied the fish heads to tangles of discarded fishing line, but the small hands of the sky gods were bad at tying knots. So the crabs yanked the fish heads from the lines with ease and enjoyed the free lunch.

Like this, my little brother and I had been feeding the crabs for weeks. There was the rare occasion, of course, when a crab hitched itself good to a fish head. On this occasion we were so gentle in pulling up the line, the crab did not notice the ocean floor beneath him—sinking—and the light from that curious sky above getting closer. The faces of the sky gods above were both ecstatic and terrified because, after all, we were reluctant gods. What exactly would we do with the clawed thing once it was within our reach? How would we navigate those pinchers we had seen draw bright red blood from our dad's calloused brown hands?

Our reluctance shook the line. Enough for the crab to notice the sky light too close: It decided the fish head wasn't worth the journey to the other side. Sideways—the crab walked off the fish head. Down he tumbled through twenty feet of darkening blue bardo. Landing back on the sandy bottom of his existence. Knowing better—or maybe not—for next time. And I, I backed up on that splintering wooden dock with a love for murky floors, for backward-walking things, and for the mysteries of Pacific blue depths into which I had learned I could lower a line.

I WAS CHASING A WHALE SHARK. OR AT LEAST RUMOR OF one. The rumor turned out to be false, but it got me to the right place: to the wooden docks in the Bay Islands of Honduras from which I first submerged into the water underworld.

I was not born into the "sport" of scuba diving. But we did spend my mother's summer teaching breaks living out of a rusted-white trailer that sat permanently in a campground across from Oregon's Pacific Ocean. There I passed months in the crags of low tide: turning over snail shells and waiting for the claw of its hermit to unfold; marveling the returned rubbery grasp of a willowy Sea Anemone; sitting still long enough that my shadow merged with rocks until armies of Purple Shore Crabs emerged from seawalls. Like this I came to know the low-tide world—the difference between the smells of hot and wet sand, the poke of beach grass through my sweater, the curl of my hair touched by salted mist. But, as a child, I never fully submerged my body in the ocean.

I was twenty-one when I first pulled an ill-fitted pair of rented fins over my feet and a scratched scuba mask onto my face. When my heart stuttered as I shuffled backward into the sandy break so as to not—as I was instructed by a local—disrupt any resting stingrays. I was twenty-one when I reached that precise depth of Caribbean Sea where I could lift up my legs, turn my body over to the buoyant palm of the ocean, and lower my face—for my first look ever—into the wilderness of the ocean. I might have screamed. I shouted enough through my snorkel that my best friend on the beach fell over laughing. My whole body trilled with the shock of life and color moving under the *Mar Caribe*. The blue world simply turned on, like a lightbulb. And damn, if *it* existed—all along, right below my nose—well, what couldn't? What else could I see, could I find, in total submersion?

Whale Sharks. Or so I hoped when I chased that rumor of their migration to the Bay Islands of Honduras. The biggest fish in the world, with a white belly under checkerboard blue skin, could reach the mythical proportions of forty feet in length and over twenty tons in weight. My first week on the island of Utila, I signed up for an Open Water Certification course. The second week, my Advanced Diving Certification. Unable to leave the water, I asked a dive shop if they'd train me as a divemaster. I had no intention of ever working as a divemaster. I had every intention of diving every morning and afternoon, every day.

On one of those days I was on the boat with two other divemasters, one Swiss and the other Australian. Sixty feet underwater, I caught them in my periphery—chasing each other's fins, grabbing wetsuits, snapping masks, yanking tanks, somersaulting over each other—all in tryst over some hand-sized treasure seized from the sand. As we ascended, large air bubbles bottled my laughs and lifted them to the ocean top. Back on the boat, the tantrum tumbled toward me. "Look! Look! It's amazing! Look!" Each boy pulled from a sleeve of his wetsuit a fragment of what looked like delicate pottery. As they produced the two halves, one reached over to the other and smacked him across the back of the head. "Look what you did! I can't believe you broke it!" While the smack was returned, I took the two pieces, matched their hems together, and allowed myself only a half-smile. One boy returned his attention to me and exclaimed, "Look at the fine inscriptions, the delicate handiwork!" The other echoed, "Can you believe it? Do you think it's a Mayan artifact? It must be!"

Indeed, the most ornate and symmetrical looping flowers were stitched across the clay-like surface. I couldn't hold back any longer and cracked a grin. The boys' eyes narrowed. I shook off my smile and told them the story of the sea creature I knew well. One that had evidently evaded the closer shores of their own homelands. The boys passed the flowered piece between them. "Really? It's called what? A Sand Dollar?" The boys stashed their respective pieces back under the sleeves of their wetsuits. One thumped the other over the back of the head and said, "A Sand Dollar."

I distanced myself from their re-initiated tumble, but today I still hold the story close. Because I remember the marvel. The spell of sea treasure. The precious relic pulled from one world into another. I would chase the rumors of Whale Sharks to the coasts of four more continents. I've still never seen one. I don't care because I'm happy with the places the clues took me. Wrong clues, but keys nonetheless, unlocking my awareness of the 70 percent of Earth's body of unknown depths and indeterminate borders on maps. Clues that led me into chase of inconceivable wonders. The stingray veiled by sand, the fish of mythological proportions, the Sand Dollar pottery—they are spells of wonder for me still unbroken. Today, when I enter the ocean, when the water reaches the half line of my mask, at that moment when I see the world above the ocean and the world below at the same time, when I fall into the palm of the sea and hover in the bardo between the wavy-blue and blinding-white, that same first question arises again: *If this exists—what can't?*

AN ALBATROSS'S VIEW, HIGH ENOUGH, MIGHT RENDER IT flat. The ocean top of course is anything but, with crests pulled by tides and tides pulled by gravity and gravity pulled by the wane of a moon in orbit of Earth in orbit of Sun in orbit of a heart of stars at the center of the thing we call the Milky Way. The Waved Albatross knows the sparkling top is neither flat nor wall. She watches for the flash of scales, for switchbacking shadows, that she may punch her body from the world of air into the world of water and retrieve from it an offering. It is in this otherworldliness I'm interested. Below that first layer of ocean 200 meters from the top that we call the Sunlight Zone—a place I have traveled not even the half with flippers and mask and a tank of air on my back. Below the Twilight Zone where darkness also becomes day. Below the Midnight Zone at 1,000 meters and even the Abyssal Zone at 4,000. I am reaching for the Hadal Zone defined as 6,000 meters "and deeper." I want to know more about the "and deeper." It brings me comfort to know there is a place on Earth unnamed by man. A place where the pressure is lethal to colonizers, where sound and light move in different waves, where the same pressure that bars human entrance has evolved what lives at the bottom into soft bones and squishy bodies. Compressing life to its marrow.

My love for the bardos of slippery words and wave-less goodbyes and telling dreams and the sub-degree stillness of the Hadal Zone are still my secret. By day I deny it. I put on makeup and jeans and shoes like these layers will hold me back. I busy myself with holidays and Excel sheets and laundry, tasks that spin me into something that looks like perfect circles. When the great *cantadora* Clarissa Pinkola Estés Réyes recounted the old selkie myth in her story, "Sealskin, Soulskin," I reached in recognition and touched my own face. In the telling, a woman made of moon milk dances on a rock in the sea, naked of the sealskin by which she shape-shifts back to the ocean creature she is. A man on land falls in love upon sight, steals the woman's skin, and promises to give it back after seven years of companionship. They have a child, but the woman loses weight, her skin flakes and she becomes "palest white." Her child, one day, finds the hidden sealskin and the woman puts it on, grabs her son, and jumps into the ocean upon the call of "something older than she, older than he, older than time." Eventually, she returns the child to the land because it's "not his time," but only after reunion with her sea kin in an underwater cove.

At first, I felt sad for the child and for the woman: How could they bear this separation of bodies and spirits where the water meets land? But Dr. E translated the deeper lesson: The child was the one who brought the soulskin to his mother. He *enabled* her return home. And the spirit child is metaphorical: He is the union of soul and ego, belonging to neither land nor sea, but in between.

Maybe I am struggling with these awkward legs, my skin dried by too much time on land, and maybe I am thirsty, so thirsty, for submersion. The open window in the Alaskan room. The whispers between night dreams and mothers. The reach of an echoing existential question through a snowy Oregon globe. The "and deeper" of oceans where bones bend. What they have in common is a pause—and my longing to linger there—in the palm of that vulnerable unknown, between the seen and submerged. And maybe there is a rock in the ocean where I can dance between the worlds of mother-body and moon-milk-soul.

THE HUMPBACK WHALE HAS THE LONGEST KNOWN MIGRAtion of any mammal on Earth, some swimming five thousand miles just in one direction. The migration is informed by an inherited song, passed from ancestors, that may guide the whale to breeding waters or feeding waters or birthing waters or away from danger. My own pilgrimage of lost years was less graceful than the Humpback's. I am merely human with tiny eyes and infinite ego. I climbed peaks without destination, dropped into mountain ranges underwater, walked once across a country without a map. But like the Humpback fattened on krill and swimming south, I too fasted and shed. I shed family and culture and goals and money. And what was left was a new map, a new language, the sound of an inherited song, distant but vibrating in my bones. Linda Hogan wrote in her poem "Map": "This is what I know from blood: / the first language is not our own. / There are names each thing has for itself, / and beneath us the other order already moves."

Pema Khandro Rinpoche's took her definition of the bardo further: "If we appreciate these successive deaths and rebirths in our lives, then we can value the bardo for what it is—the pause that makes movement apparent, the silence that makes all sounds more vivid, the end that clarifies what exactly we will now be beginning."

I feel like it's catching up to me: my denial of my excitement for the things that strip us down, shake us up, stand us still, bring us closer to what's outside the window of square existence. That I have found my sealskin and a calling, older than time, to drop into the darkness of not-knowing and see what crawls sideways on its murky floors, to cede control to an oceanic underneath.

I stand here with the cold stone in my pocket—still turning it over and over. My reminder of my many small deaths, my as-many rebirths. My portal to the place deep inside where I hear the echo of that same old question I mulled under the unblushing rhododendron bush:

And behind that? What's behind that?

RED TALISMAN

IN SEPIA PHOTOS OF THE FLOWER MARKET, I PICTURE MY father: the back of his shiny black hair bent over buckets of blooms. I can see him, then, standing with maybe a bundle of pearl chrysanthemums or peach carnations in his brown boy arms. A child with the lodgepole spine of knowing pride would mean the difference between survival or not under the street-corner eyes of that City of Angels.

My big brother retraced my father's steps with a camera. He called his collage of ugly photos our dad's "street life": cement sidewalks, hanging traffic lights, squat buildings with short awnings, a white-rimmed sign with "WALL ST" marching across. My father isn't in the photos because no photos were taken of him. Dad was the ninth of nine children and only four years old when his mother died. His father went absent in grief before his own mysterious death a few years later. My brother was only putting lost puzzle pieces together. Overlapping the names of places he'd heard my father recall. Collaging a memory.

I also don't know how my father fell in love with the sea, having no one to inherit the love from. But every summer of my childhood, by gull's eye, Dad's aluminum dinghy was a silver speck amid the boiling white caps of the Oregon Pacific. He captained that dinghy from the sunken back of the boat, one hand curled around a Tab soda and the other stiff-arming the outbound motor. Us four kids folded our limbs inside orange life vests in retreat from the salty face-punching winds, as Dad's obsession crinkled the corners of his eyes. He could not have remembered his mother's arms; maybe he sought something that could hold him. In the dinghy, his eyes were always scanning for land we couldn't see.

One of my earliest memories is finding a dollar bill on a sandy coastal path. I squealed with thrill and folded and unfolded the dollar as my father whistled through his smile behind me. Years later, I learned to count via my father's coffee tins of nickels, dimes, quarters, and silver dollars lined from smallest to tallest in the pantry. We kids stacked the metal circles into gilded leaning towers and added them into tens and hundreds. My father would cup the coins and waterfall them into our hands; what we caught, we could keep. On Easter, my father masterminded legendary hunts in the acre of weeping green behind our house. Children under five plucked Susan B. Anthonys from behind the ears of white trilliums while seventeen-year-olds scrambled up Douglas firs pocketing sums that made neighbors gasp and my father giggle maniacally. What I did not grasp at the time was that my father was as generous in giving money to the casinos as he was to us. He detested smoke and drugs and didn't drink. Free of any stimulant other than the sound of coins falling, he dropped the family savings into a slot machine, rhythmically pulling down a barbed arm in search of alignment. At first, I thought it was an addiction to risk. Now I see it was his inheritance of loss.

Dad didn't often look over his shoulder at his orphaned childhood. When he did, he squinted. Dad had a way of seeing. He saw through his beautiful sisters who married up, leaving their first language, Latino surname, and the smallest of nine siblings behind. He saw through the street dealers who thought they could make good use of his quick brown legs. He saw, too, in the reflection of Wall Street windows, a boy with wits and chance. So he ignored the eyes of the streets—and sold flowers.

Maybe he sold roses. Red Talismans were popular in the '40s; crimson gatherings of fragrant petals on glossy green leaves, stems of new American dreams. Maybe he held the red blooms as he watched passing cars. Maybe he looked into the eyes of passersby and saw things people didn't think he could see. I inherited this seeing. This inkling for knowing more than what's shown. I see through bosses and politicians and my children when they fiddle with truth. I see patterns that make me turn away from inevitable futures. My best friend last week said, "You know what I never want? For you to tell me all the truth you see." And I did not know, until now, what I inherited from my father. Of his survival instincts. Of his love for white caps and salty winds. Of his hope and, also, his knowing.

What did those passersby pay, I wonder, for a dozen stems when a stamp was three cents and a gallon of gas, twenty? What did they pay for what they saw in the brown eyes of a brown boy holding bundles to his chest?

I kept my father's name.

For the unknown ancestors and lodgepole pride I inherited with my dad's brown eyes.

THE SEVENTEENTH DAY

STARS BLINK BACK AT ME THROUGH THE TOP OF MY BED-room window, but I feel dawn coming. I pat my night table just as my phone's alarm vibrates. I'd been waiting all night, my sleep fragmented in knowing I was not allowed to use the bathroom. My mouth, too, tacky with thirst. There was no water on my nightstand because the test instructions had forbidden it.

So as not to disturb my sleeping husband, I tiptoe to the bathroom and flip the switch, which starkly reveals the awaiting blue box from the Great Plains Laboratory labeled GPL-TOX Profile. In parentheses next to the acronym: *173 Toxic Non-Metal Chemicals.*

I am not new to this test. We have a history, a story I shelved but picked up again because I was reminded by the most unlikely of reminders—another female mammalian body swimming through the waters of the twenty-first century. Her name, Tahlequah. Global millions watched with me in 2018 as Tahlequah, the Orca known also as J35, swam for seventeen days, pushing the decomposing body of her dead baby through a thousand miles of Salish Sea.

Tahlequah is back in the news. The cetologists who spot her through heavy binoculars celebrate because Talequah has given birth to a new male calf. His official pod identification is J57 and his birth offers a spark of hope for the Southern Resident

Killer Whale population listed as endangered in 2005. In drone photos, the new babe frolics beside his mother. The celebrations, though, belie the weight of Tahlequah's story—and summon my own unfinished.

THE SAME SUMMER OF TAHLEQUAH'S "TOUR OF GRIEF," I booked my first appointment with a locally renowned osteopath. I was done with my pregnancies and my children had stopped nursing and toddled away, but my body no longer felt mine. I had symptoms swirling out of control: brain fog, hand rashes, weight gain, and recurring climate nightmares that woke me regularly in cold sweats. I saved over a year for the appointments my health insurance wouldn't cover. The first tests yielded no conclusions. No abnormal hormones or alarming blood numbers or parasites or excessive exposure to mold. Then there was the heavy metals test. I swallowed gray pills the doctor called *chelating agents* before that urine sample. Two hours later, I staggered to my living room and, steadying my head with one hand, reached for my phone to call my osteopath. "What's happening to me? My body feels heavy and slow, like I'm swimming, or sinking, in a black cloud."

I remember the pause on the other side of the line. Then I was assured the reaction wasn't dangerous—though maybe telling. That's when my osteopath added the test for 217 chemicals to my checklist. A month later I called.

"Shouldn't those results be in?"

"Oh, you're home?"

"Just arrived. I thought you said you'd upload those test results to my patient portal . . ."

The doctor knew I was prone to over-investigation of my reports. That it was my style to arrive with a binder full of color-coded and bullet-pointed questions penned in .05 mm ballpoint.

"We do have your results back," she said. "But we knew you were out of town and we thought it better if you came to the office to discuss them. Can you come in . . . today?"

TAHLEQUAH IS ONE OF SEVENTY-THREE "RESIDENT ORCAS" whose ancestors have known the Salish Sea of Washington State and British Columbia as home for over 700,000 years. Killer Whales (a name given to Orcas by ancient sailors) are identified by the unique swirl and color tones of patches on their back, right behind the dorsal fin, which functions like a fingerprint for the cetologists who take notes. It was this "saddle patch" that identified Tahlequah when she gave birth to the female calf in 2018. She had carried the babe in her belly for roughly eighteen months. It was the first birth in the J Pod family in three years.

I imagine the calf before she died. Her unblemished ink-black skin and white patches on her belly and chin mirroring those of her mother. Her tiny two-lobed whale's tail—a perfect replica of Tahlequah's flukes—propelling her small body to her mother's side for the half hour she lived. If we, those obsessed with her death, had accepted the reality of the statistics, we might have been prepared. In 2018, 75 percent of Southern Resident Killer Whale calves were dying. They called it the SRKW *Dead Baby Boom.*

I PEE IN THE CUP FOR THE FOLLOW-UP CHEMICALS TEST. IT'S a task I've mastered from the twenty-eight months comprising my four pregnancies (two successful, two not) in which each trip to the obstetrician began with a plastic cup and a permanent marker. But this time I'm not pregnant and the instructions for the chemicals test are concise: *The sample must be yellow in color.* Because this test is looking for mycotoxins that congregate in the urine of a dehydrated body.

I was supposed to get the follow-up test two years ago but didn't because, after eight months of detoxing, I gave up on the prescribed regimen. I was sick of the rotten egg smell of detoxifying glutathione slipping down my throat, out of funds to fill the pill box with supplements separated by morning, lunch, and night, and scared of the niacin that flushed my face red and made me feel faint. I was over the drippy cod liver oil packs wrapped with plastic wrap around my belly, done boiling coffee for enemas and locking myself behind the bathroom door, and over the paleo diet clashing against my vegetarian palate. The replacement of all my mercury dental fillings had put me into debt. I suspect I also quit because I didn't want to know the results. Afraid my money and time and efforts would amount to nothing. Or everything. Afraid of more evidence shaking in my hands.

WHAT MOST PEOPLE DON'T KNOW ABOUT TAHLEQUAH IS that she miscarried another baby in 2010. She might have lost more. Just as human miscarriages and birth defects and incomplete pregnancies are reserved for whispers, Orcas' perinatal losses go mostly unobserved. Many obsessed with Tahlequah also don't know that her sister likely died from birthing complications. Tahlequah assumed care for her sister's infant, J54. The young calf starved to death soon after. One could assume Tahlequah was new to death given her seventeen-day demonstration of grief. But she was already too familiar.

Though they tried, researchers could not find the body of Tahlequah's baby for the investigation they hoped would provide more answers. But I keep thinking of what we do know. That Tahlequah would not let the calf's body sink. She put her head under her infant's limp body and pushed it to the surface. I think of what it required to carry the sinking near-400 pounds of her dead baby for seventeen days. Unlike humans, breathing for Orcas is not a reflex, but a conscious act. Tahlequah had to ascend at least once every twelve minutes. She didn't just ascend. She made the decision to go up for air. She went up. She took her baby's body with her. She took a breath. And this gets me. She decided each time again: I'm not done.

AT THE OSTEOPATH'S OFFICE, IN OUR APPOINTMENT IN which they preferred to "review the results in person," the toxicology report shook in my hands.

The tests concluded my flesh was steeped in heavy metals and industrial chemicals. *Mercury, lead,* and *uranium* I could at least pronounce. I scanned only the acronyms next to the chemicals presenting dangerous levels in my body: MTBE, a gasoline additive; PGO, a styrene used in plastic manufacturing; PERC, a chemical used in explosives and fertilizers; DPP, a flame retardant; NAPR, a solvent used for metal and dry cleaning and foam gluing; 2,4-D, an herbicide that was part of Agent Orange used by the United States in the Vietnam War. Under something called 2-hydroxyisobutyric acid, a chemical associated with "hepatic and kidney system toxicity, peripheral neurotoxicity, and cancer in animals," there was a scale that started at 200 and ended at 7,000. My score was 18,971.

The small acronyms, together, were assaulting my body as neurotoxins, endocrine disruptors, human carcinogens, and central nervous system and reproductive toxins. It was, the doctor concluded, the likely terrain of brain fog, rashes, and anxiety disorders. It was also the territory of miscarriages and fetal birth defects. Both of which were checked on my chart.

The doctor explained that I couldn't take more chelating agents or "just burn fat" because if the toxins and heavy metals didn't have a clear path out of my body, they would recycle through my bloodstream and lodge in more dangerous places— like my brain. The other way fat is released from the female body is through breast milk. The "biological transfer of contaminants" is what it's called, this breastfeeding of toxins from mammal to infant.

I couldn't look up from the reports in my hands when I said, "I nursed my children, each, for a year. Were these metals and toxins in my body then?"

Despite the lack of eye contact, the doctor's answer still found me: "Probably."

When I recounted the abandoned metal mines I live near in Colorado, the well in Oregon I drank water from as a child, the smog in India I breathed for two years, the grandfather on my mother's side who I'd never met because he'd died too young of lymphoma after a short career spraying pesticides in basements—my doctor just shook her head. "I know this is hard, but I recommend you focus on getting the toxins out. The investigations rarely yield answers. The fact is, modern humans are swimming in environmental toxins."

I looked at my hands. The rash had started under my wedding ring as small blisters rising, burning, itching, drying, flaking, moving down the inside of my finger, then up to a patch under my cuticle. Then the subterranean blisters popped up on my other hand. Same finger. Different migration. This time it traveled south, to the outside of my palm, where it was kept in check only by a steroid cream prescribed by a dermatologist who offered nothing else but a shrug.

ORCAS KNOW TOXINS. OR MAYBE THEY DON'T. BUT THE pathologists who do necropsies on the bodies of Killer Whales have discovered that they often carry as many as twenty-five times the number of PCBs statistically known to affect health, mortality, and fertility. PCB is short for polychlorinated biphenyls. PCBs are usually clear or yellow, can exist in liquid forms, and have no taste or smell. They were manufactured by Monsanto in the United States until about 1977, the year I was born. But PCBs don't go away. They accumulate in the bodies of what or whoever consumes them, like plankton and Chinook Salmon and seals. PCBs accumulate most in the bodies of apex predators. This is something Tahlequah and I have in common: we are both apex predators.

It's no secret where an SRKW Orca gets her toxins. She gets them from the Chinook Salmon that run the rivers to the Salish Sea. And it's not a secret where the Chinook Salmon get their PCBs: from exposure to PCB-contaminated sediments and PCB-contaminated food in waters polluted by upstream shipyards, slaughterhouses, and manufacturing plants. PCB exposure is linked to birth defects in both female Orcas and humans. The most observed symptom in humans is rashes.

Orcas share original "resident" status with the Indigenous peoples who cohabitated with everything "living upstream" in a five-thousand-year-old heritage. That equitable balance ended with the arrival of white settlers. Though under researched, Native communities are today more at risk for toxic exposure than any other ethnic group in the United States. One Canadian study in 1997 revealed that some Inuit women have levels of PCBs five times more than the safety threshold.

I feel it in my breasts, when I find these words from Inuit mother Lucy Qavavauq: "The idea scares me. The more I think about it, the more scared I get," she said as milk slid down her grinning babe's cheek, "I know there is a possibility of passing on contaminants to him . . . I can't imagine not breastfeeding my baby."

I KNOW THE SMELL OF THE SALISH SEA. THE CHINOOK Salmon and I share range. From the Gulf of Alaska coming through my nursery window, from my childhood dropping crab traps and salmon lines off Oregon and Washington coasts, from the Northern Californian cliffs on which I perched as a college student—I know that salted coast breath of chilled kelp, low clouds, and wet pulverized shell. After her migration between the Arctic and Northern California, a female Chinook might swim hundreds of miles to return to her birth stream where she can leave up to 14,000 eggs in a nesting hole. There, she and her mate hover to protect the fertilized eggs. In this very act of guarding their future generations, the Chinook die—before the eggs even hatch.

My dad was obsessed with Chinook. Every April, he let me skip school to drive with him to the Bonneville Dam to watch the salmon climb the man-made fish ladder on the Columbia River. I remember the roar of the river above and the dank smell of concrete below in the fish viewing room with its dark window where heaving fish jaws came out of the shadows as frantic tails propelled bodies up cement stairs. My dad would dart his pointer finger from the sixty-pounders behind the window to the wall-mounted black screen with white numbers that up-ticked the official counts of each salmon species. In 1986, when I was eight years old, that spring Chinook count totaled 118,614. Today, two populations of Pacific Northwest Chinook Salmon are endangered and seven are threatened. The Southern Resident Orcas exclusively eat fish. They used to feast on Chinook Salmon from British Columbia's Fraser River. A test fishery there that's been tracking Chinook returns since 1981 reported they only caught seven Chinook in their nets in all of May and June 2020.

BECAUSE TAHLEQUAH AND I HAVE SHARED OCEANS AND RIVers, she made me curious as to my own level of exposure to PCBs. A PCB test requires a doctor's order. I explained to my osteopath, "I grew up twenty miles from a Superfund cleanup site in Oregon where PCBs were identified as a central contaminant. I learned to swim in the Willamette River. We jumped off the docks while my dad backed up his skiff on countless weekends. My father pulled from those waters the 'King' Chinook Salmon we ate for dinner. Would that constitute a likelihood of exposure?"

My doctor explained that PCBs store in fat and exposure is difficult to detect. I was fine with this. One less expensive test. Do I even need to know if I have PCBs in my body when it's already confirmed I carry dangerous levels of 2HIB, PGO, PERC, DPP, NAPR, and 2,4-D in my flesh?

Killer Whales should also not be confined to the PCB box. A necropsy on an Orca calf that washed up in Norway in 2017 revealed other chemicals in its polluted flesh, including brominated flame retardants (BFRs), pentabromotoluene (PBT), and hexabromobenzene (HBB).

So add my PCB exposure to my list of unknowns—the evidence of exactly what and how my body became toxic lost like Tahlequah's babe, to the blue depths of murky hearts.

ORCAS ARE SOCIALLY SOPHISTICATED. THEY SWAM, AFTER all, in Earth's oceans for millions of years before modern humans. Orcas live in matrilineal pods that include a dominant female and her close relatives who might span four generations. Female Orcas experience menopause and can live into their eighties, and we have only recently learned that it's these postmenopausal Orcas that guide their pods. The leadership, experience, and knowledge of these "grandmothers" has been shown to statistically boost the survival of grandcalves.

In an online presentation, Lori Marino, neuroscientist and president of the Whale Sanctuary, projects photos of the human brain next to the Orca brain on a wall. The human brain appears pink with plush folds of soft tissues. The Orca brain is not only much larger (5,000 grams compared to the human brain at 1,350 grams), but the folds look much more tightly packed. My son leans over my shoulder as I watch the presentation and points his finger at the Orca brain: "Wow, that one looks way smarter."

Even when body size is considered, the cerebrum of Orcas accounts for a larger percentage of brain volume compared to humans. With a laser pointer, Dr. Marino circles a part of the Orca's brain in the paralimbic lobe. This part of the brain, she explains, is associated with emotion, memory, compassion, empathy, learning, self-awareness, and abstract thinking.

"You see all this section here? All these intricate folds?" she asks the audience as she makes a circle with her red laser. "It's unique to cetaceans. Humans don't have it."

DURING TAHLEQUAH'S TOUR OF GRIEF, SOMEONE LIVING near Eagle Cove reported that at sunset, a group of five to six females "gathered at the mouth of the cove in a close, tight-knit circle, staying at the surface in a harmonious circular motion for nearly two hours. As the light dimmed, I was able to watch them continue what seemed to be a ritual or ceremony. They stayed directly centered in the moonbeam, even as it moved."

Tahlequah was not the only Orca in her pod to push her baby's corpse. After seven days, other members of the J Pod allowed Tahlequah to rest. Jenny Atkinson, director of the Whale Museum on San Juan Island noted, "She's not always the one carrying it; they seem to take turns."

The night before I terminated my pregnancy of a fetus with chromosomal defects, I composed a letter to the pod of women in my life. I chose the only words I could muster: "I'm losing the baby." I had miscarried once already the same year, and losing another baby—the anchor in my sea of grief—was too much. I paused before sending the email. Sharing my grief would force me to confront my shock and denial. But I was drowning. I hit send.

I did not expect to be hit back. Hit by cascading reverberations of collective shock and grief and sadness. Letters came back. Photos of lit candles. Lyrics of mourning songs. Images of altars I'd never seen. Poems. Tales of tears in the woods and fields and along rivers. A levity came over me—permission to be relieved from the grieving duty I could no longer carry by myself.

Tahlequah pushed her grief for seventeen days and she didn't do it for the world to see. I know this because I know grief. Tahlequah is a Cherokee word. It means "two is enough."

I still flinch at those who throw the pointed finger of "anthropomorphizing." But I am not interpreting Tahlequah's behavior through my limited experience of being human. I *am* tugging on the DNA strings that bind us but more than that, I'm recognizing the *limits* of my experience of being human. I don't feel big. I don't feel important. This connection with Tahlequah—it makes me feel like a tumbled grain of sand on a planet four and a half billion years old.

In my conversation with Ellie Sawyer, a naturalist who works, lives, and sleeps the Salish Sea, she slipped in a reckoning with such subtlety I'm unsure she even noticed the twisty breach of her own words. "These aren't human experiences, they are *animal* experiences," she said. Seeing myself in the eye of Tahlequah is more damning than anthropomorphizing. Orcas have large eyes that can focus below and above water. Tahlequah sees more than I do.

I PUT THE BOX WITH MY SAMPLE FOR THE FOLLOW-UP TEST into the overnight FedEx bag. The results won't be back for two weeks. I might get an updated detoxing protocol, but there will be no answers. Nothing that suffices or explains what we've done to ourselves. No answers for the global millions who may have brain fog or rashes or miscarriages but no access to the Great Plains Laboratory. I think so often of the families who hosted me while I worked in Varanasi, India. Of the smog I walked through in the alleys on my way to buy a toothbrush from the corner store or get copies of lesson plans made at the print shop. Smog levels that every fall and winter register in the "Hazardous" maroon level on the Air Quality Index (AQI) chart and indicate "emergency conditions for the entire population." Did I get some of the hazardous levels of toxins in my body from that smog? I have a hunch I did. But I don't know. I left Varanasi. The families that hosted me still live there. Along with 1.2 million others. It is their home.

ON THE SEVENTEENTH DAY, TAHLEQUAH DROPPED HER BABY'S body. She went up for air, and then she let the body of her babe drift away, to be reclaimed by the ocean's blue womb.

Toxins are an invisible villain; nearly impossible to see in the scope of a single mammalian life, yet lethal in reach and legacy. But the science is catching up. Latest research models predict Orca populations that live offshore from PCB pollution will collapse in under fifty years. Tahlequah and her family will likely be gone in one human lifetime.

My human lifetime.

A 2021 study evaluated samples of breast milk collected from women all over the United States. The tests concluded that all fifty samples of milk studied contained toxic "forever chemicals" (PFAS) at levels almost two thousand times what's considered safe for drinking water. Has the United States, like India, also silently ticked up in pollution levels indicating *emergency conditions for the entire population*?

"Who would want to live in a world which is just not quite fatal?" was a guiding question Rachel Carson, in 1962, borrowed from ecologist Paul Shepard for the opening chapters of her book *Silent Spring*. Carson's questions and investigations awakened awareness of the interdependency of health on this planet and made her a postmenopausal matriarch in the global environmental movement. But her tenure was too short. She died at fifty-six of breast cancer.

Have we reached it yet? The point where we circle up and take turns, holding and pushing a collective grief? The day we leave our denial behind and come up for air? On this dimming horizon, with everything on the line, can a matriline rise? Embracing a maternal instinct to protect lives beyond our individual fingerprints, willing to die in the process like the Chinook guarding their eggs? Can we gather like the J Pod and hold what is precious—centered in moonlight—even as the moon moves?

TO THE DELIGHT OF WATCHERS AND RESEARCHERS, THE NEW calf Tahlequah birthed most recently, in 2020, appears both lively and rambunctious. But there's a long swim ahead. Thirty-seven to 50 percent of Orca calves still die in their first year. A year when Tahlequah will nurse the new babe with the stores of fat in her body.

The "biological transfer of contaminants" is what it's called.

When Tahlequah's new babe, J57, needed a name, the Whale Museum put the matter to the public. When the votes were tallied, J57's name was announced: Phoenix—the mythical bird rising from ashes to live again.

My GPL-TOX results arrived this week. This time the doctor uploaded them to the portal. My toxic burden is down. Some of the chemicals in my body have been reduced to the thrilling "Not Detectable." Other toxins are down 50 or 25 percent; some have stayed steady; one toxin has doubled. Meanwhile, the rash on my hand continues to migrate. Today, the patch of blisters travels down my right palm, above the crinkling heart line, reaching for the cross of my head and fate lines. When the rash burns with impending outbreak, I have the curious urge to bite it.

"It's a long road," my osteopath reminds me during our follow-up appointment. The new detoxing regimen she recommends is beyond my financial reach. So the road will be longer.

This time in my consultation, I look into her eyes when I ask again—if it's likely I fed my toxins to my children when I breastfed them. On the Zoom screen she nods solemnly, says, "The bad news is that the largest toxin dump in a woman's lifetime is often when she breastfeeds her first child. The good news is that those new little bodies are probably better at detoxing than ours."

Probably.

Phoenix might actually have a higher chance of survival because a mother Orca offloads most of her toxic burden with her first baby and subsequent calves might not have as many toxins passed in utero and in milk. That metaphorical canary in the coal mine? The mines might be the bodies of mothers; the canaries—our firstborn.

ON JULY 16, 2021, I WENT TO THE SALISH SEA FOR THE FIRST time. I got on a boat before I even checked into my hotel. I saw no Orcas that day. I noted—with curiosity—that I didn't expect to. I was content simply riding choppy waves in Pacific-chilled winds.

"During those seventeen days, I knew where Tahlequah was," said the captain of my boat as he pointed over my shoulder. "She was right there. But I couldn't take people there, so I took them everywhere but to her." Over the roar of the boat's motors, I had stepped close to the captain to hear him disclose this detail. When I registered his words, I stepped back. He kept his eyes on the sea so I'm unsure if he saw me swiping my eyes under my sunglasses. But it's what I needed in this story: proof that we can stop what we're doing and change course in response to grief. In an act of dignity.

Ellie, the naturalist on the boat, asked me, "Did you know there was a 'superpod' gathering and 'greeting ceremony' the day after Tahlequah gave birth to Phoenix?"

When she saw my jaw drop in dismay she continued. "It was the first superpod recorded off San Juan Island in four years. All seventy-three of the Southern Residents were identified." Ellie recounted how the whales from all three pods swirled around, diving and rising to the surface, slapping fins and flukes, and breaching "like popcorn."

"I don't usually cry while I'm working," she said, "but that day, I sobbed."

Over the radio later that day they heard that a new calf had been photographed in the middle of that superpod, at Tahlequah's side.

That calf was Phoenix.

The super rally of pods—of distinct Orca families who have different languages and different diets and different cultures, all communicating by some shared code with the collective objective to gather, meet, and honor the next generation—gets me thinking. Makes me curious as to what lives in those intricate folds in the paralimbic lobe of cetacean brains that Dr. Marino circled with her laser pointer. Makes me wonder how long it took for those folds to evolve. If it was slow or swift. If we humans have hope . . . for new undulating pathways that can breach in sudden comprehension.

THREE DAYS AFTER MY TRIP TO THE SALISH SEA, THE ORCA Behavior Institute posted an image of a calendar with a hundred red Xs through the months of April, May, June, and July. The image linked to a press release that reported "July 19th marks the 100th consecutive day without J Pod visiting inland waters, a grim milestone . . ."

Maybe I didn't expect to see the J Pod during my days on the Salish Sea because I subconsciously knew that, more important than the presence of the "residents" in this story, is their absence.

Tahlequah, Phoenix, and their family did make an appearance in the Salish Sea this summer, but only after an unprecedented consecutive absence of 108 days. Their first visit was brief and they were soon again spotted heading back toward the outer coast. Was the pod checking in on the missing Chinook that fed their ancestors? Has their traditional migration pattern changed? Might they be forced to relinquish their 700,000-year-old heritage as "residents"? In Latin, *Orcinus orca* refers to "from the underworld" and there are lessons here. Messages from a blue world, and a future world, and a range of under- and possible worlds, if we care enough to listen. Care enough to act.

"Public will is political will," Ellie told me. "This isn't just a fight for the salmon or for the Southern Residents. It's a fight for a *shared* ecosystem."

This week I tuned in to the live, streaming soundscape of a hydrophone dropped into the ocean by Orcasound Lab. The microphone rests in the Haro Strait, under a kelp bed about a hundred feet offshore and twenty-six feet deep. I had been listening to the fuzzy white noise of the ocean for hours when suddenly my empty kitchen was filled with snappy clicks and bright whistles. It was the first time Orcas had ever passed by the microphone while I was listening. I turned the volume all the way up and leaned back in my chair, filled with stupid joy. Later in the day, the Orca Behavior Institute posted a photo of a mother and calf under the headline *This morning all of J Pod came back into Haro Strait*.

Rachel Carson once wrote, "There is something infinitely healing in the repeated refrains of nature—the assurance that dawn comes after night, and spring after winter." Nature's persistence, Carson's persistence, Ellie's persistence, and the persistence of every person who pushes for truth despite the stakes—they summon for me the resolve of Tahlequah: *She took a breath. And this gets me. She decided each time again: I'm not done.*

THE ENDLING

IN 1994, A NEWBORN VAQUITA PORPOISE WAS FOUND TOSS-
ing in a break in the Sea of Cortez, sixty miles south of the
US border. The man who found her wore black sunglasses
and a gray shirt with ARIZONA stamped across the chest. In a
photo, he cradled the Vaquita as he would a baby—with one
curved arm. The calf had a patch of white that started under
her belly and stretched to her chin. I found a single video of her
paddling shallow water in a plastic tub. The footage was pix-
elated, shaky, with the gray tones of an ultrasound. The voice
of a little girl narrated the video in first person as the camera
cut to the Vaquita's underbelly: "Todavía puedes ver mi cordón
umbilical." English captions translated: "You can even still see
my umbilical cord." The camera panned to the Vaquita's small
flukes, splashing and propelling her nowhere.

In the last thirty seconds, the ending of the story scrolled on a
black screen: *Desafortunadamente, la vaquita recién nacida no
sobrevivió* (Unfortunately, the newborn Vaquita did not survive).

I found the video in my search for updates on the endangered status of the Vaquita. *Vaquita* translates from Spanish
to English as "little cow," and these smallest of porpoises are
nicknamed so for their pretty face markings evoking the bat-
ting lashes of bovine. The Vaquita is Mexico's "national marine
mammal," and given both the Vaquita's emblematic fame and

53

striking cuteness, I wondered if there were less obvious reasons the international news wasn't picking up the story—if other stories were more important—or if the tragic story of the Vaquita is one no one wanted to hear.

I remembered this phenomenon from when I studied Spanish in Guatemala. Spanish was my father's first language, not mine, but I felt in it a link to my unknown ancestors. My Guatemalan teacher, two mugs of instant coffee between us, looked over my shoulder as she spoke of the genocide that took place in her mountains during my lifetime. Of massacres in which her uncles and aunts disappeared. When she linked my country's roles to her country's wars, I pressed a finger to my temple, "Espera, no entiendo." Which wasn't the truth. I did understand. I had the Spanish comprehension skills. But I needed her to slow down—because it hurt to understand. Perhaps the Vaquita is not in the news because it hurts to read about her.

Bycatch is a term for marine life caught in the path of undiscerning industrial fishing nets. A gill net is a wall of netting, often a mile long and a hundred feet deep, that hangs vertically in the ocean with buoys on top and weights on the bottom. This netting is designed to trap the body of anything passing through it. A Vaquita's first instinct when she touches a fishing net is to roll. Panic shortens her breath. Death is swift. Most of the Vaquita bodies deposited on the beach by tides show the rope-burned evidence of death by entanglement. It is widely known that illegal gill nets are to blame for strangling the species to death.

More complex are the above-water variables: the Chinese demand for the "aquatic cocaine" of bladders belonging to the endangered Totoaba fish caught in the same gill nets, the lucrative black markets of Mexican cartels, the broken promises of presidents and politicians, the American appetite for shrimp pulled by similar nets from the same water, and the local fury with international efforts that don't fully recognize community hardships. San Felipe fisherman Jorge Machuca explained, "If you see your children crying, what are you going to do?" Thus, the Vaquita is also caught in the bycatch of blame.

THE VAQUITA WILL, BY MY OWN GUESS, SOON BE POSTHU-mously declared as disappeared. Her wakes of existence flatlined in the years when my daughter learned to ride a bike and lost her first tooth. Years when you maybe graduated, or birthed a child, or retired. Because human life marched on—while the Vaquita disappeared.

There might still be, at this moment, a few Vaquitas left. Maybe a single mother and her calf. Maybe two sisters. Maybe one small pod swimming together. Or maybe one last Vaquita navigating gulf waters around the gill nets that drowned her grandparents, her brothers and sisters, maybe her calf, and definitely her ancestors. But what no one says is that she has no chance of recovery. That if she is out there, she is among or *is* maybe the last.

There is a name for the last of a species: an "endling." An endling gives a face to extinction. In the case of the Vaquita, one amplified in coloration that makes her eyes look large and unblinking. The better for us to see what is about to flicker into oblivion.

Not that it wasn't avoidable. The scientists warned us. This ending was no surprise. It was predicted thirty, twenty, ten, five, and two years ago. It was the conclusion we marched toward—maybe because we refused to look. Many of the local fishermen in San Felipe still insist the Vaquita "is a myth." They have families to feed, and some myths—like my inability to grasp history in Spanish to English translation—are convenient.

The Vaquita's lone protectors still believe in her. Sea Shepherd's band of eco-pirates have had a fully crewed vessel in the Mar de Cortés since 2015. This mission to save the Vaquita was named Milagro, perhaps for the divine intervention of the *miracle* needed to win the fight against the Vaquita's extinction.

Sea Shepherd's ship haunts me. I think of it always in the middle of the night when my eco-grief catches me. In the dark, I imagine a crew member at the helm with the "big eyes" binoculars, searching for the Vaquita's petite gray fin cutting through water—a thin sign the miracle mission isn't dead.

NEITHER THE INTERNATIONAL OR LOCAL NEWS OR OONA Isabelle Layolle—who created, mounted, and captained Mission Milagro—will declare the Vaquita extinct. Captain Layolle is the only person, in my opinion, who deserves the right to not talk about it. I watched all the documentaries featuring Layolle's mission before I sent her a note titled, "A Too-Long Email."

"Not sleeping," Oona Layolle answered when I asked over a video call about the hardest part of captaining Mission Milagro.

I thought of my own experience of losing sleep to recurring nightmares of climate disasters before I understood she was being literal. Layolle was talking about working night shifts: the hours when Sea Shepherd hunts for *pangas* (boats) dropping illegal nets under the cover of darkness. After the pangas flee, Sea Shepherd snags the nets and pulls them in. These scenes in the documentaries made me wipe my eyes with the back of my hand and turn toward the window. The net winching is a procession of death: collapsed sea turtles, limp stingrays, strangled sharks, and countless un-flopping fish. The dead bodies make me put a hand to my chest, but the crew themselves—thick gloves swiping tears streaming down chapped faces—make my breath stutter.

Layolle confirmed the grief was too much. "To be there protecting something that is always dying in front of your eyes, it was hard. After I left, I didn't speak about it for two years." My guess is Oona Layolle knows whether the last Vaquita is already dead. But she did not tell me so and I will not ask her. I know this inability to conclude. I once held a porpoise as it died beneath my palms. I still marvel at what synchrony found me knee-deep in the Pacific Ocean at sunset, at that same moment a beached porpoise stopped thrashing its tail and turned its eye skyward. Its bowels broke and the water around me blackened with waste and blood. I've turned this moment over and over for years. It resurfaces every time I write past three pages in my journal, returning only when my sentences turn lyrical. And here I am, still chasing the poem I can't finish.

My kids are still learning to swim, so I am familiar with the term describing the deaths of children who crawl, tumble, or slip footing into backyard pools and drown: "the silent killer." And my obsession with the last Vaquita, with broken ancestries, with the blackened waters of a beached porpoise, with my children born into the quick-breaking waves of ecological crises—they have this quiet violence in common.

The Vaquita will not be the only marine mammal to go extinct in too-recent memory. The Baiji, a Yangtze River Dolphin, disappeared in China in 2006. Scientists similarly predicted the Baiji's death thirty, twenty, ten, five, and two years before it went extinct. It was the conclusion we marched toward—and past. And here's the thing: if we sat and watched or intentionally not-watched the Baiji disappear, and if we sit here, right now, and watch-not-watch as the last Vaquita dies, what else will we let die—as we sit?

In 2019—seven years after the birth of my son and four years after the birth of my daughter—145 experts in a United Nations report estimated a million species will disappear in the coming decades. Ecologists called it the sixth mass extinction and yet it—like Guatemala's Indigenous genocide, like the critically endangered Vaquita—made few headlines. One of the rare cover stories I did find focused on a violent encounter between local fishermen and Sea Shepherd in the Vaquita Refuge. This is the emblematic problem I fear: a fight between marginalized communities and marginalized species over disappeared resources. One grandson of a San Felipe fisherman, Alan Alexis Valverde, said (in the film *Souls of the Vermilion Sea*), "Realistically, it's the essence of San Felipe, there's nothing else to do but fishing. But the essence of respect for the sea has been lost. The harmony between man and sea is lost." This microcosm hints at the global violence heading our way in battles for clean water, safe food, and livable land. Battles in which the Vaquita, a million species, and my own children will become the bycatch of the undiscerning industries of man.

General Efraín Ríos Montt's scorched-earth campaign in Guatemala in the early 1980s massacred over 600 Indigenous villages, "disappeared" 200,000 people, and displaced another 1.5 million. That I never learned in school about this genocide just south of my country's border makes sense of its nickname: the Silent Holocaust. We don't have more time to *espera*—to avoid understanding. Biologists call it *extinction denial* and I am guilty. As a child, I made long road trips with my family down Highway 1 on summer breaks. Because it was at my eye height, I remember so well the battalion of wings and legs and juicy bug bodies stuck to the grille of our red Suburban. I remember, too, the multiple stops my parents made at gas stations to squeegee the windows. But as an adult, I can't recall an instance of needing to pull off the road to clean my windshield. This anecdote is so relatable for people born in the 1980s, it's called "the windshield phenomenon" and describes that common moment by which people awaken to the massive disappearance of insects in only a few decades. I learned about the windshield phenomenon while listening to an audiobook as I pulled into the parking lot of a grocery store. I nudged my small car into a narrow spot in the middle of the lot as I collapsed in my seat and took in the hundreds and hundreds of cars that surrounded me—all featuring flawless, sparkling glass.

My husband is an intelligent man. He listens to experts daily on podcasts that keep him well informed. Variables and economics figure smoothly in his dyslexic mind. But when, at the dinner table, I explain to our son that polar bears will likely disappear in his lifetime, my husband tilts his head. My son looks at the ceiling and my daughter sets the cucumber she was nibbling back on her plate. They are still thinking about polar bears when I tell my husband a million species are, right now, on the verge of extinction. I watch him do the math in his head.

"That can't be right . . . that would mean dozens of species go extinct every day."

I nod to his phone. "Look it up."

While he picks up his phone, Riva looks at me with tears in her eyes. "Will pink bears go extinct too, Mom?" Pink Bear is the name of the stuffy Riva has nuzzled for the last 1,500 nights. Her question stabs me. It's unfair, what our man-made realities break in my daughter's old-growth imagination.

My husband puts down the phone. I can see in his slow blink he's confirmed his own math.

If I can find extinction denial in a grocery store parking lot and in my smart husband's blank eyes at my own dinner table, where else is it rife?

THERE IS A REASON NO ONE WILL DECLARE THE VAQUITA extinct. Conservationists call it the "Romeo Error." Romeo took his own life on the assumption his love, Juliet, was dead. When Juliet awoke to the corpse of her lover, she thrust a dagger into her own chest. Herein is the warning: If we give up hope before we wake, it might all end in bloodshed.

Imagine Juliet had woken a minute sooner, shaken off her poisoned slumber, sat upright, and made eye contact with her love. Because the timing here is important. If she hasn't already, the smallest porpoise on Earth may soon stop swimming forever, and when she does, she will be one of likely 150 species disappearing from the planet every single day. Can we behold this future? Where the Vaquita is gone and the bedtime books we read to our children feature animals with no footprints left on Earth? If the endling Vaquita is out there, can we face the eyes of what, of who, we are losing?

Elizabeth Woody, an American Navajo Warm Springs Wasco Yakama author, had a recurring nightmare as a child in which the earth shook, trees snapped, and the animals all disappeared. She wrote, "It was the loneliness and silence without the animals' lives that hurt the most."

A silence, an absence, that hurts. That's what I feel. Pain. Because this is not just a sad story. This is a love story. A tragic love story—the most epic, tragic love story of all . . . in which there are still two endings. And to avoid awakening only after what we love is pronounced dead, we need to sit up. To sit upright and shake our pain awake—until it hurts us into action.

LAST NIGHT AS I TUCKED THE COVERS AROUND MY DAUGHTER in bed, I watched Riva's eyes searching beyond my shoulder.

"What are you thinking about, love?"

"I'm thinking about polar bears."

"What about them?"

"I'm thinking about how they are disappearing."

Her eyes scanned behind me, searching mental corners I couldn't see.

"What else are you thinking?" I asked.

"I was wondering if there was a place where I could leave all the animals a note. But if I left a letter in the woods or in the water, it would probably fall apart."

Riva just learned to write her first sentences. Her three-word notes are taped to doors, left for night fairies next to her bed, and flutter loose-leaf around the house. I imagined one of her craggy fat-tip marker notes taped to an aspen in the grove behind our house.

"A note to the animals? What would it say?"

"I'm sorry. And I love you."

RIVA, FROM THE SHORE. RIVA, WHAT CAN WE DO TOGETHER? Me and our new reality. She and her first sentences. With her little hand and future generations in mine. What chapter do we write together that begins with a love note to a world of endlings?

ACT II

MIGRATIONS

There is yet one place to go: beneath the surface.
A catabasis into the under-realms.

—Dr. Báyò Akómoláfé

FOUR CIRCLES

I

First Pregnancy: Confirmation

I AM STRIPPING OFF SWEATERS IN COOL ROOMS. BY MY warmed blood, I know I am pregnant. But my husband and I whisper with optimism only after I have presented him with the dark finish line on the plastic test strip. I stow the proof of the otherwise invisible on the top shelf behind the bathroom mirror and, in quiet moments, I pull the secret down with one hand and press an open palm on my chest with the other.

Days later, my enthusiasm collapses in hormone-induced nausea. I know it's "a good thing" and cling to the promise like a buoy. I fill the bed with toast crumbs while reading Tolstoy and take naps in hope of a spell of unconsciousness to black out the high seas cresting from my belly to my throat. In hamburger, I smell the barn of the cow. In frying chicken, the scratched dirt of calloused feet. In bacon, the manure the pig bathed in. When I'm in a good mood, I call it *my pregnancy superpower*. The rest of the time, I shove plates away as if I have been insulted. If anyone takes offense, I do not notice, for there is nothing in sight beyond the cage of my body. I am fickle, shedding overflows of hormones through tears and, sometimes, a real fit of rage. My husband's steady hands begin the practice of diffusing my explosive shells. I, meanwhile, pick up a pillow habit: filling the trenches between my body and life with white walls of cotton and feathers. I cannot get warm enough. Only when I'm buried under all the blankets does the chill of a bitter inner cold smother. But at dawn, I reach across the divide to touch my husband's hand. His fingers crawl to mine and clutch my hand back. That the squeeze is subconscious means more.

Because it's still too early and taboo or damning or dumb, we do not share our radically new state of existence with the world. Rather, we hunker down in separate rooms of our house; my husband in the living room, me in the cave-bed.

Second Pregnancy: Confirmation

IN TWISTED SHEETS, I WAKE UP STILL STAMMERING THE words left from the fleeting dream: *I can't find it.* My heart slows down from a gallop and I pull back on the retreating clues. What was it that I couldn't find? I was in a car, crawling from the front to the back bench seat, digging my fingers into the leather cracks. *I can't find it. I lost it. I lost . . .* I sit upright in bed. My husband rolls over, senses my heavy presence, and murmurs a closed-eye instinctual prompt of concern. He's already downshifted to pregnant-wife gear. We already know how the catalyst in my womb shape-shifts me by chemical reaction into a stranger. His warm hand touches my elbow, disturbing the layer of cold shock left by the sly dream. I finally stammer: "I dreamt I lost the baby."

I make a "confirmation" ultrasound appointment. In the tomb-sized room, the obstetrician assures us that embryos are surprisingly resilient. And in proof of this fact, she rolls the Doppler across my belly and the room is gloriously filled, 160 beats a minute, with the sound of a heart that built itself, cell upon cell, within the past seven days. A kidney-bean body houses not only atriums and ventricles, but webbed fingers, eyelids, a nose, and even neural pathways. The harmony of the drumming heart floods us with relief.

Third Pregnancy: Confirmation

SILENCE. THAT'S ALL I WANT. A VACUUM OF GRAVITY. THE tastelessness of water. A neutral buoyancy where I might finally cease to exist. The rest: let it all go the fuck away. Especially those sweet inquiring texts from my light-footed best friend. I text her back: *I can't do this right now. Can you give me a break from this friendship?* We won't talk again for months, reconcile fully for years. At some later point, I will take an online test and check fourteen of the fifteen boxes describing the symptoms of prenatal depression. But right now, I have only enough of a notion of my need for help that I pick up the phone and stare at it. Finally, I dial a friend who has spent most of her life living with the checked-box symptoms ranging from insomnia to suicidal ideation: one who has carved the stories of her survival by inked needle across her shoulder blades, behind her ears, down her calves, and in cuffs around her ankles. I start with an apology: for my busy blindness to her everyday hell. She forgives me with a shrug—resignation of expecting true empathy apparently a stage of her recovery. She knows what I need and offers me the all-accepting embrace that she stopped asking for when she gave up the life in which she gave a fuck.

Fourth Pregnancy: Confirmation

THE SKINNY, PURPLE-LINED STICK JOINS THE STACK, WITHout ceremony, on the top shelf behind the mirror. An echo of old hope tempts me to pick up the test strips and fan their secrets out like a deck of tarot cards. Instead, I close the cabinet and crawl back into bed. Under the heavy comforter, with relief, I drown in fatigue. But I am snapped back to my physical body via a tapping in my abdomen. Phantom kicking. I pull my knees over my haunted womb.

I book an appointment with a massage therapist referenced to me as "the magic worker." Her name was whispered around in a way that required a booking months in advance. But the day before our planned session, she sends an email explaining that she has injured herself and must cancel. She mentions, as an aside, that she can do something called *craniosacral work* if I would be interested in a therapy that involves no physical pressure. I say yes. I'm petting her chocolate Lab in the hallway the next day when she hands me a glass of water, looks over my left shoulder, and states: "You're pregnant." My knees give just enough that her practiced forearms catch and lower me to the couch. I have barely whispered of the pregnancy with my husband. But now the world spins as my denial grows weak-kneed.

"You don't have to worry. This one is going to be OK." This most important prophecy of my life she delivers while kneading the scruff of her chocolate Lab.

She continues, "And you're right, you know. She's come back. She's telling me she doesn't want you to cry anymore."

II

First Pregnancy: Week 12

OUR DOCTOR IS A RETIRED SKI PATROLLER. SHE'S NATIVE TO our valley in the Rocky Mountains and as practical as her short salt-and-pepper hair. As she pulls the ultrasound screen to the bed, I realize I am ready for something to show for my un-showing belly. With a squirt of cold gel and exploratory pressure, from out of the storm on the electronic screen, a beacon pulses.

It's my baby's heartbeat; a hurried drumming under which my husband and I will bask for days in a spell of infatuated love-at-first-sound. An easy week later, the nausea subsides. As the tide of the first trimester recedes, my husband and I revel at the sparkling canvas of sand left behind, into which we begin building the castles of our inevitable fortune.

Second Pregnancy: Week 12

ON A WORK TRIP IN A CALIFORNIA MOUNTAIN TOWN, I descend scuffed stairs to the basement of a bar where I know a cramped single-stall bathroom hides. I shuffle the elastic band of my maternity jeans down over my already-swollen belly and am confronted with rusty spots of blood. The chatter of the world silences and a refrain begins: a whisper of *no-no-no* and *please-please-please* that grows into *god-god-god*. It is the first pleading lines of the mantra that will become my mourning song. And in seconds, it eclipses all the light in my life.

I step into more bathrooms as I travel back home to Colorado. It seems unfair that the bathrooms are public. I remember little of the trip other than the scratched metal partitions and the blood and the incessant chanting of the *denying-pleading-god* song. Over the emergency hotline, my doctor reassures us bleeding can be normal. But she gives me her personal cell phone number.

Two days later, my husband is still forcing a smile and I marvel at the perspective I have to pity his hope. I woke up calm that morning; felt my body gearing up for the animal mechanics of what needed to happen. Now, I coldly calculate my need for space and politely instruct my husband to take an unfortunately timed international house guest on a day-long fishing trip. After they leave, I call a friend who I know to battle nightly in the underworld in her quest to live in this one. This is what she advises: *Feel the pain. Feel it completely. Connect with your loss through the pain and release your grief through it.* I have no history of masochistic instincts. They are simply not in my black Lab DNA. But I understand them now. As the erratic cramps slowly churn into regular contractions, I hunger for them, doubling over from their satisfying punches. Between the bed and bathroom, I wring and wither on the floor in pools of labor sweat, tears, and dark leaking blood. The contractions pummel me until, at the edge of both my need and capacity, the pain disappears. I know this pause. I know where the pain has gone. What it is retrieving. I limp into the bathroom and sit down. I do not push so much as I let go. And I feel the last contraction ushering the baby through me. In an instinct that shocks me, I stand up, thrust my arm into the bowl of blood and scoop up the tiny sac I heard fall into the water. In my palm, the amniotic sac disintegrates like a swept cobweb, revealing a tiny corpse and all its perfect miniature parts: feet, legs, spine, arms, fingers, and nestled head, with black dot eyes that will never, ever leave me.

Third Pregnancy: Week 12

MY DOCTOR SUGGESTS ADDITIONAL DIAGNOSTICS IN CON-sideration of my "advanced maternal age" and recommends a new genetic test by which an embryo's fetal DNA can be read like a book between microscope slides. There's a subtle nod of agreement between me and my husband.

On my way to a writing workshop in California, a nurse from the hospital calls and explains that my blood sample was mislabeled and that I'll need to return for a new blood draw. This clerical error sets back the results three weeks, frustrates me for a minute, torments me for years. When I arrive at the retreat center, it is buried under an unseasonal layer of snow. In response to the writing prompts, I put my pen to paper but my sentences, one after another, flatline. In the middle of the night, I chronicle dreamscapes of black bears crawling through windows, great-grandmothers speaking in tongues, fear of a foreign border I must cross alone, and a life elixir that combusts if not kept in constant motion. I have since learned that my future often whispers to me in blank-day-pages and night-dream-tongues.

Fourth Pregnancy: Week 12

WITH MY BLADDER UNDER GROWING PRESSURE, I AVERAGE three trips to the bathroom an hour. In each enclosed room, I sit down, hold my breath, and inspect the porcelain and tissue for blood. When I see white, I swallow the breath I was holding. Looking down the hall of the remaining six months of my pregnancy, it's a bathroom horror hall of mirrors.

III

First Pregnancy: Week 15

I'M SENT FROM THE MOUNTAINS TO THE CITY FOR AN ULTRA-sound. I wrap my arm around my husband's as we pass through the sterile corridor of the hospital. My angst falls away when out of the static appears my tiny child, disturbed by the probing ultrasound transducer, kicking and punching tiny femurs and forearms in protest of the rude awakening. We did not expect this type of connection from a fuzzy picture on a black-and-white screen. We can't look away. In her practiced voice, the sonographer goes through the measurements one by one: heart chambers, crown-rump length, biparietal diameter, nasal bone, nuchal translucency, and other microscopic human dimensions. "Everything in perfect order, measuring exactly to date," she sums up. The power of her gavel in this verdict does not escape me. But she interrupts my consideration of parallel universes with a back-to-earth question: "Do you want to know the sex?" For the two hours that we wind through the mountain valleys on our way home, my husband and I alternately grasp each other's hands, whispering incredulously: *Boy! . . . A boy!*

Second Pregnancy: Week 15

MY HAIR FALLS OUT. THE WEIGHT I GAINED DURING THE pregnancy sticks to me. It seems a cruel addition to my suffering that my body will go through these standard postpartum stages when the normal light at the end of this symptom-tunnel is buried in the corner of my yard under a Buddhist dharma wheel. Four weeks past my miscarriage date and I am still bleeding, but it takes me still four more weeks before I ask myself if I might be attached to the bleeding; the last evidence of my unwitnessed trauma, and the trailing red proof of my subsequent existence.

Third Pregnancy: Week 15

SOMETIMES I WONDER HOW MY DOCTOR PREPPED HERSELF for the call. Did she shut the door to her office and stare at the phone while she held my heavy fate on a flimsy paper lab report? Did she take a few minutes to consider how to make her tone of voice neutral of the politics involved? Did she know the call would bring me to my knees faster and harder than my mother's description of my father's last breath? I'm sure I made her repeat herself. The test results. What they meant and with what degree of certainty. I wonder what she did with her hands in the silence that caught me up to her facts. Did she put a hand to her forehead when she heard me choking on the air needed to end the phone call?

I don't hear my husband come through the front door. I don't feel his arms around me. I don't recognize the sounds coming from my mouth. I don't know how long we sat with our jaws slack in shock. But the nailing of the verdict into my bones will tremor back through my body every three months for a year.

Side by side on the couch, the negative space between us feeling vast, our life paths veer out in front of us. In one, I fill my life mourning a baby lost in childbirth. In another, I spend months in a neonatal unit, extend a hand through a glove and wait for my baby's hand to curl around my finger. In yet another, I end my career, leave my little boy at home, and spend my days driving over mountain passes to reach the city-based specialists that will give my youngest child the best chances of worst cases. On the most optimistic of all these paths, my child outlives me and is left to unknown caretakers on a faltering planet. I voted, donated, and was actively pro-choice. All the while, I discreetly held the belief that I'd never personally choose to terminate a pregnancy. I was wrong.

We learn the pregnancy is already complicated and the doctor wants me under general anesthesia for the abortion. For once, the medical establishment and I are in perfect consensus: I want obliterating numbness and push my naked arm at the anesthesiologist. Thus, there is no physical pain in, or memory of, the procedure itself. It's only my acute understanding of exactly what I'm doing that pushes me against a wall. Do not, dear reader, misidentify my horror, my shame, my profound mourning, as regret. There's no regret in this story. This is me, bloody-kneed, on the knife's edge of grief and gratitude. As I go under and come out of the anesthesia, I am drunk in expressions of appreciation to the nurses and doctors who visit my bedside. I cling to their hands with both of my arms: *Thank you for being here. Thank you for holding my hand. Thank you for working here. Thank you. Thank you. Thank you.* Which upon reflection, I translate to: *Thank you for accepting me before I've accepted myself.*

Fourth Pregnancy: Week 15

I'M A PALE VERSION OF MYSELF FROM HOLDING MY BREATH when the thoughtlessly named "anomaly ultrasound" appointment arrives. By this time, multiple affirming test results have been delivered to us with white-smocked confidence. The consensus: this baby is healthy. But I still haven't exhaled. As the monitors are rolled up around my reclined body, my husband coaxes laughter out of the stiff ultrasound technician. She's the same specialist who ran through all these vital measurements with us a month ago. At the time, she included a 95 percent–sure prediction that the baby was a boy. My husband, more inclined to accept an ultrasound technician's prediction over an empath's, had already spread the word in our community. I'm pretending to appear distracted by the small talk, but my body belies my focus as it leans toward the picture on the screen. And it becomes obvious that I'm not the only one faking aloof when my husband shouts: "Wait a minute! That's a girl!" The technician has forgotten her previous prediction and is as cool as the metal probe when she states: "Yes. It's a girl. Didn't you know that?"

IV

First Pregnancy: Week 40

WATER ESCAPES MY BODY IN A CORPOREAL MOVEMENT THAT is shocking in its complete lack of my volition. I slow-step through a day of contractions on my way from home to the hospital. In the twenty-ninth hour, my body awakes like an alarm clock. Buzzing, I roll off the bed onto a birthing ball. I feel my husband's eyes watching me. But where I've gone, there is no return for such a human gesture as eye contact. Over the next three hours, I travel so far inward that I have bobbing, geographically impossible glimpses of the theater from above. In one of those downward glimpses, I see the fear in my husband's downcast eyes as he watches his wife withering on the thin mattress, a fetal monitor displaying numbers that make the nurses steal quick glances at the door in anticipation of the doctor. The doctor arrives and I am able to surface enough only to whisper: *I can't anymore.* The room grows heavy with my expressed defeat. The doctor lifts the maternity gown and, shedding all white-coat composure, shouts, "This baby is here!" There's a flurry of footsteps, cart-rolling, and hand-grasping, and through tiny slits I watch my doctor's legs shove into sky-blue scrubs. I close my eyes and hear my doula whispering in my ear: *Now the baby will give you a break. There's always a break right before the baby comes.* And the pain stops. Completely. I do not push so much as I let go. And my doctor's athletic arms catch my child from underneath me. I awake to a silent film: my husband's muted exasperations, my doctor's lips moving with confident commands, and my son's open mouth from which there definitely comes crying. But I hear nothing. I see his flailing limbs finding a new swaddled womb in my arms. Blue gloves make everything soiled disappear. The world swirls, but I sit still in white-towel tunnel vision from my eyes to his.

Second Pregnancy: Week 40

YOU KNOW WHAT PEOPLE DIDN'T TELL ME ABOUT? THE INTImacy of tragedy. The collapse into the lap of my lover: not in elated exertion, but emotional exhaustion. The speechlessness: not of direct eye contact, but downcast mutual understanding. The timelessness: not of unrelenting focus, but utter absence. The hand squeezes: not confirming secrets, but in warning of the pain that is either coming or going. The insomnia: not of a racing heart, but a stumbling spirit. The infatuation: not with he whom I've elevated with unrealistic expectations, but for he who trudged his way to the top of my pedestal in cold-earned respect. As I surface, now, from this trauma, I'm experiencing all the symptoms of a romance-hangover. And I'm left with the realization that I have fallen more in love with my husband through the intimacy of our loss.

Third Pregnancy: Week 40

ONE DAY AFTER ANOTHER, I GO THROUGH THE MOTIONS OF domestic life, sometimes at best only haunting my body. But my little boy brings me through. The best thing I ever taught my son to do is watch the sky. Something about the clouded perspective of adulthood means I never catch him in the act of searching, but only take note when his arm is outstretched across my domestic agenda like an exclamation point. He'll declare, "Mama. There's the moon right there." At his command, I'll drop all my busy thoughts and look at the sky. And there it will be, just the palest crescent hanging delicately in a hazy horizon of blues and whites. His life is also full of the rituals I need: spiced apples churned to sauce; rock-tossing trail walks; underdogs in swings; threats of tickles to rein him in the right direction; and book after book after book that end in sweet dreams. With no other option, I step into his world as a way of passage back to mine. Sometimes I wonder if he will remember this caretaking; if he will be mysteriously called in profession or partnership to the duties of lifeguarding he practiced in pulling his mother above water.

After a season of habit-haunting, my husband one day makes a joke and I laugh. It's a small, but honest, chuckle. He stops in his tracks, "Wait? I'm funny again? It's been nine months since you've laughed at one of my jokes. Look at that . . ." he says more to himself than to me. Accustomed, perhaps, to my absence.

Fourth Pregnancy: Week 40

I'M TOO UNCOMFORTABLE TO SLEEP, SO I SEW THROUGH THE middle of the night. I appliqué a tree with heart-shaped leaves onto a blanket and in its center, I hand-stitch a pale yellow heart-leaf with Terry Tempest Williams's words, "Once upon a time, when women were birds, there was the simple understanding that to sing at dawn and to sing at dusk was to heal the world through joy." I hope the stitches will hold down what threatens to flutter away. Ten days past her due date, I check into a hospital at capacity with a wave of other women pulled into labor by a full blood moon that NASA described as "when the edge of the Moon first enters the amber core of Earth's shadow." My roused stage of bouncing on the birthing ball does not last long. In a single breath, I close my eyes like the blinds and my puppet limbs go limp. My body crawls through animal and child poses on a blue padded mat on the floor. In the short pauses between intensifying contractions, I lift my eyes to the window where the moon traverses the night sky into eclipse. The pain finally obliterates all consciousness. Then blows out like a candle. I hear the room sigh and awake to my daughter's purple, screaming body being placed on my chest. I cradle her in trembling arms. Sweat, blood, and vernix mingle and my heart cracks along the seams of scar tissue. The hospital staff writes her name on the nurses' whiteboard: *Riva*, which has Latin roots meaning to "regain strength" and "renew." Later, I will reread NASA's description of the rare lunar eclipse that occurred in perfect alignment with the arc of her birth: "You might expect Earth seen in this way to be utterly dark, but it's not. The rim of the planet looks to be on fire! As you scan your eye around Earth's circumference, you're seeing every sunrise and every sunset in the world, all of them, all at once."

THE SILENCE OF THUNDER

THE PRESCHOOL TEACHER POSTED THE PICTURES FROM MY daughter's classroom online. In one image, Riva stacked ashwood blocks. In another, she wore a white smock and painted a blue ocean. Next, she swept pink rose petals into a dustpan with a hand broom. In each photo my daughter was wearing a pair of blue headphones I had neither purchased nor ever seen.

One day when I picked Riva up from school, I asked the teacher about them. She answered in her always-storytelling voice (as well received by parents as by preschoolers), "Oh Riva loves the noise-canceling headphones! Many days she puts them on right as she walks through the door!"

I buckled Riva into her car seat but kept thinking about the blue headphones. It did make sense; I had, myself, noted my daughter's recent mastery of the conjugations of "distraction."

"Mama, please turn off the music. It's distracting me."

"Can you tell brother to stop talking? I'm distracted."

"Mom, I can't focus. There are too many distractions."

As we drove home, Riva looked out the car window and I recalled my own life of seeking views through my reflection in windows. I am not just any introvert, which *Merriam-Webster* defines as: "a reserved or shy person who enjoys spending time alone," but the rarest kind: an "INFJ" according to the psychological researchers Katharine and Isabel Briggs. Though the famous Myers-Briggs personality model has been critiqued for its dated lenses, it still offered me the most revelatory of insights in its description of my personality as one who "presents as an extrovert" when—often to their own dismay—is the truest of introverts.

Until that point, I had assumed I was just a very-and-always-tired extrovert. But it made new sense of my twelve-hundred-mile pilgrimage across Southern Europe. My path had been different from other pilgrims. My route wound under bridges, chased rumors of waterfalls, rested under trees, and it was always just odd enough to circumvent the stiff boots and daily mileage chatter of passing pilgrims. I found all the company I wanted in conversation with clouds and creeks, and as Myers and Briggs might have hypothesized: I was alone but never felt lonely. Silence energized me.

It was a relief to come to this self-understanding. To stop putting on the forced smile and million-question game of extroversion and instead find my favorite place near windows on planes, along walls at reunions, and near the doors of gatherings of any number more than four.

Motherhood would, of course, dwindle the sands of my quiet time. I plummeted into the truest depths of my introversion during pregnancy, nestled under layers of quilts in bed through four years of turbulent gestations. In reflection, I think I needed the silencing of the entire world to grow the fingernails and eyelashes in the globe under my ribs.

To my surprise and delight, though, it was the natural inclination of my newborns to be introverted! To sleep as many as twenty hours a day, wanting only eye contact and caresses by way of communication. To require my one-on-one presence in the bedrooms of relatives' houses, where I stole away from holiday gatherings and found a door—to close—between me and the small-talk world. With the noise of the party muffled, I unwrapped my infant, curled up on the bed, and nursed my quietest best friend.

Not until my first child took ten steps at ten months did I comprehend the trouble I was in. The years that followed were full of sippy-cup curveballs, oblivious bodies running toward busy streets, the wails of bedtime refusal, and squat fingers under closed bathroom doors behind which I cried during "Mama time-outs." The volume of raising toddlers crashed against my every attempt at sequential thoughts. My bookmarks didn't move. Every sentence in my journal flatlined.

As the children grew, so did the social calendar.

"Christina, don't you want to float the river with us? All our friends will be there. It will be so fun . . ." my husband asked as he inadvertently corrupted his own case.

I like boats. I like rivers and deserts even more. But I want to sit and be still with them. I want to watch canyon shadows shift with coming and going light. I want to see the Osprey return to her nest and hear the call to her hatchlings echo off red walls. I want the poetry of crickets to the slow time of stars blinking open a black night.

But those are introverted things.

They are not the realities of a river-camping trip with six families and twelve children under age seven.

Anthrophony is the soundscape of noise created by humans, such as cheering, engines, sirens, highways, buzzing and beeping appliances, even music. *Biophony*, by comparison, is the sound of animals: cats purring, birds chirping, frogs singing, dolphins squealing. And *geophony* includes compositions made by nature: crashing waves, falling rain, cracking ice, a murmuring brook. These distinctions are new and essential to me! For, as it turns out, I'm not averse to all sounds. My heart raced when I read this line of Dr. Clarissa Pinkola Estés Réyes describing *Women Who Run with the Wolves* in her book by the same title: "For her, the sound of wind through trees is silence. For her, the crash of a mountain stream is silence. For her, thunder is silence."

Which recalls, for me, one of my favorite elements of scuba diving. I used to say it was the "silence" underwater I loved so much. When it was not only the retreat from human chatter, but also the biophony and geophony that stepped up their octaves when the anthrophony was silenced. Sixty feet under the sea, it was the scraping of an Olive Ridley Sea Turtle's teeth on coral, the crackling of Snapping Shrimp, and the clicks, purrs, hums, barks, and rattles of fish talk that lit my obsession with hovering in the womb of the sea.

Anthrophony can be a serious hazard to the human body. Man-made sounds can trigger rising blood pressure, slow digestion, and pump adrenal glands. Every night I shut my bedroom window to muffle the sound of the diesel-chugging eighteen-wheelers crossing the country via the interstate that cuts through my valley. I close the window, but the disconcerting lullaby of I-70 is still the soundtrack I begrudge as it lays tracks into my dreams.

Anthrophony is an even more serious hazard to whales. The bang of an air gun fired for oil and gas exploration—comparable in decibel to a rocket launch—can travel in water for months. A baby's scream (famous in the CIA's history of torture tools) registers at 130 decibels, but underwater sonar blasts by the US military generate slow-rolling sound waves that can reach 235 decibels. The persistent drone of shipping vessels—equivalent to a loud rock concert—doubled between 1950 and 2020. All this human noise is lethal to marine mammals who use the water the way humans use air. Man-made noises underwater shift migration patterns, affect animals' abilities to hunt, break communications between mother and calf, and disrupt navigation systems leaving some marine mammals lost. One study documented that noise pollution was reducing Fin, Humpback, and Minke Whale communication range by as much as 82 percent. I imagine my house 82 percent closer to I-70. The rumbles would shake my windows, pump my adrenaline through the night, and leave me anxious and insomniatic.

I-70 doesn't only bisect the two sides of my little mountain town. It runs through another nine states. Similarly, noise pollution doesn't only affect introverts. A recent study concluded one in three people are regularly exposed to excessive noise levels and the principal researcher warned, "Noise has long been ignored as a pollutant in this country and around the world."

My favorite white noise—the sound I use regularly to smother the anthrophony both outside and inside my own home—is the composition of biophony and geophony collected by the hydrophones dropped by the Orcasound Lab into the Pacific Ocean. I can listen all day to the pops and bubbles, whistles and hoots, rattles and tinkles that come through the underwater microphone. At times, I jump from my seat in shocked wonder when the song of a Humpback or the chatter of Orcas passes by.

But then there is a boat. I can't see it of course, but the boat is impossible *not* to hear. A single carrier ship on a marine "road," with its diesel propellers and generators, can have the same acoustic profile as an airplane. Multiple times, in response to the obliterating noise of a ship engine blasting from my computer speakers, I have slapped the lid of my laptop down. In the relief of the quiet that follows I think of the whales—with no volume control, no laptop lids to shut.

One day after I picked Riva up from preschool, I asked her about the blue headphones.

I watched her face in my rearview mirror as she looked through her reflection in the car window. "Sometimes I cry when people don't give me space."

I choked on this. It's not just the headphones. Riva recently instructed us she does not want a birthday party. She puts herself to sleep when house guests stay late. When my husband bounced out of bed one fall morning and sang, "Who wants to go to the Avalanche hockey game at the stadium in Denver?!" Riva jumped on the couch and sang back to him, "Noooooooootttt meeeeeee!"

My small daughter could boldly express needs for quiet that I still stuttered on as an adult. When had I shelved my needs for some quiet hours in my house, for a day lost in the pages of a book, for twenty minutes staring into a rainstorm?

When Riva confessed her need for silent space, I had to restrain my arms from swooping my daughter up and suffocating her in love. Because I know the life of keen observation and noise overload she walks into. I know the rooms with windows she will seek in her life. I know the guilt she will face for wanting to mute a "modern" world that's always too loud. I want to swoop her up because it is so much easier to unconditionally love my child than myself.

Noise is only one interpretation of the word "sound." *Sound* also means "entire or unbroken," as in, *sound of mind*. And though I have already defined the term *introversion*, the origins of the term are rooted in the mid-seventeenth century when the word was a verb to describe the action of "turning thoughts inward in spiritual contemplation."

I like these definitions. The *wholeness* of *inward thoughts* suits the quality of my mind when I am sixty feet under the ocean, moving not even a fin as a current drifts me along a wall of coral reef. It suits the dimmed rooms where my babies metamorphosed from womb-swimming to air-breathing things. And my love for a blinking black sky over red canyon walls. The definition also fits my daughter, with the blue headphones that might help her hear what's under the noise. I think she has something to teach me: about self-respecting my love for what rises only in quiet. Terry Tempest Williams offers perfect imagery for this rising: "Silence introduced in a society that worships noise is like the Moon exposing the night."

There is a sound, also, to recovery. A coral reef in Indonesia that was decimated by decades of dynamite fishing today hosts a restoration project in which "reef stars"—made of metal frames reseeded with live coral—were nestled into the degraded area. Researchers dropped hydrophones to record the sounds of the marine landscape recovering and described what they heard as: "whoops, croaks, foghorns, and growls." Lead researcher

Dr. Tim Lamont wasn't even sure exactly which animals were responsible for which sounds: "For me, that's part of the excitement of this whole field—the joy of knowing that you might hear something that nobody else has ever heard before."

The cacophony of American motherhood and modern culture still assault me. But taking a cue from the confidence of my daughter, I have changed my tune. I'm the mom at soccer practice with a book in a patch of grass too far outfield. At school meetups, I seek out the other parents on the outskirts, shamelessly introducing myself as the "awkward introvert." I celebrated my fortieth birthday alone in a bamboo hut with only the sound of waves crashing against the cliff beneath. When it's ten minutes past bedtime, my kids effectively aim for my Achilles heel: "Mom, if we read quietly in your bed, can we stay up later?" The sounds in my bedroom from 8:30 to 9:00 p.m.— chamomile tea sipped, paper pages turning, the cat purring, rain tapping the window—those are the sounds of recovery in my house.

Last weekend, as I tucked Riva into her sleeping bag in the camper, she closed her eyes and whispered, "I like dark better than light because it's quiet." I put my nose into her hair and whispered, "You and me both." As I have learned from her, I'll also ensure she retains this innate yearning. To love silence. To ask for space. To mute noise. To delight in the quiet of birdsong and snowfall and wind onsetting storm. To attune to what whispers underneath, maybe even hear something never heard before. Let an unflinching affection for quiet be what my little girl inherits from her mother. A little girl—who is the same inside as me—with a love for a canvas of thundering silence.

ANATOMY OF A SEAGULL

(Content warning for sexual violence.)

Lungs

*In addition to lungs, seagulls have air sacs
throughout their body that reserve air and
permit the continuous flow of oxygen that allows
flying and breathing at high elevations.*

MY HANDS MASSAGE THE SILKEN HEAD OF MY SIX-YEAR-OLD
daughter as she floats—eyes closed, cheeks puffed—on her
back in the bathtub. I have taught her how to lengthen her
inhale, how to fill her lungs with air, how to allow herself to
rise; that her body is made for elevation. But trust is not my
daughter's inclination. That she lets me cradle her head—it's
no small act. She will not let her father push her on the pedal
bike. She will not let her big brother touch her wiggly bottom
tooth. She will not high-five the man who greets her dad on
the sidewalk. She has watched most of her life from my hip;
untouched by the unwanted, unbroken by trauma, un-visibly
marked by the legacy of her mother's and mother's mother's
body. Except she has watched carefully, or she has felt carefully,
because something has transferred. In the bathtub, I sense this
caution and what she must let go of to starfish her bare body
and close her eyes. To let me thumb the shampoo suds from

her soft temples. She lets down her guard because I am her mother and because there is a special agreement about trust between two people who are inclined otherwise. In the quiet of the small, walled bathroom, I think of all the scattered, broken, untold pieces of my own girl body. The deconstructed parts I've never quite put together . . .

Wings

Seagulls have a wing shape called "active soaring," designed to allow a bird to fly without flapping, but also dependent on wind currents.

MY FAVORITE BOOK AS A CHILD WAS *JONATHAN LIVINGSTON Seagull*. The sky-blue cover featured the fuzzy gray silhouette of a seabird, and the seams of the book were cracked white from the pages my mother turned and turned and turned upon my insistence. I don't know why I loved the little outcast bird and his quest to fly higher and faster so much. Maybe it was that he made his own rules and broke them too. Or maybe I saw something of myself in the little gull who was certain there was more to life than scavenging. Author Richard Bach described the distinction between Jonathan and his flock: "For most gulls it was not flying that matters, but eating. For this gull, though, it was not eating that mattered, but flight." Flight, as I aged, became my theme. Flights to leave flocks I didn't fit, flights to leave lovers who wanted me to nest, flights to leave my country and its values with which I sparred. Flying, not always to escape, but just for the perspective from the sky. Wind currents, though. Those caught me unsuspecting.

Greater Covert Feathers

*A set of feathers located on the upper surface
of the wing, covering the base of primary
feathers. Coloration may help seagulls blend into
surroundings and communicate with other gulls.*

I WAS JUST OLD ENOUGH TO WALK TO HER HOUSE BY MYSELF.
At her front door, I knocked and asked if she could play. Inside,
we brushed the rainbow manes of plastic horses. But I always
kept my distance from her parents' door, down the hall, because
I knew the bruises we got on our knees from falling off our bikes
and the low limbs of trees, but I did not understand the brown
and yellow edges along her mother's hairline. The markings
that surfaced when her mother's makeup wore thin. I would
not comprehend until I overheard adults whispering of secrets
revealed by the divorce filings. But those bruises were my first
impressions—of the currents that can punch from overhead,
and what it can mean to live in the shape of a woman in a house.

Beak

*Seagulls' beaks are sharp, pointed, and well
suited for grasping and tearing prey; also used for
preening. Beak colors vary with species and age.*

ONLY A CAR DOOR SEPARATED THE GIRL FROM THE UPPER-
classmen. She was sixteen and her sin was being too pretty. But
it would be the girls of the flock who punished her. When the
keg dried up at the party in the woods, bold stares tipped into
threats and the young girl took shelter in a car. She locked herself inside. There she huddled in 360-degree view of the pack
of senior girls throwing fingers and squawking insults. I can't
remember if I was there, or somewhere deeper in the woods, or

if I heard the story from a friend later, but decades have passed and I'm still haunted by the image of the terrified too-beautiful girl, her horror caged behind tempered glass in a midnight forest of oblong faces. I learned from those taunting ghosts something subtle—something about the fate of girls with vibrant plumage, and about what women do to women who fall under the wants of men.

Nape

The rounded back of a seagull's neck.

THE LAKE WAS CONSIDERED A "MUST-SEE" IN GUATEMALA and I went alone. It was a weekend, a day off from my volunteer work in the city. Two young women colleagues who had just arrived, whom I had not yet met, went to the lake that same weekend. I never saw them. I only heard about them later. We'd had the same idea. We stayed in neighboring hostels, perched on cliffs over the same aqua waters. At our separate hostels, we filled our water bottles and put snacks in our backpacks and laced up our boots for a trail we were all told was muddy but full of volcano vistas. The difference between their path and mine was that as I walked out my door toward the trailhead, I passed a local who lifted their chin and whispered, *Cuidado*. I stopped and made enough conversation to understand that the command to "take care" was not in reference to the mud, but to the under-reported assaults on women hiking the path. Deflated, I went back to my room, unlaced my boots, and sat on the deck. I read a book that day. Only on my bus ride home did I hear what happened to the girls. They were found unconscious in the bushes alongside the lake path, rushed to the hospital where they awoke to bodies broken by men. Trust severed at the nape. The difference between our paths—a whispered *cuidado*.

Orbital Ring

*A ring of bare skin surrounding a gull's eye, in colors
that can range between pink, yellow, and red.*

THE BODIES BEHIND THE THAI MAN SPINNING FIRE WORE
bikini tops, cargo pants, and Red Bull T-shirts. It was 2005,
before the trending yellow and pink body paint of today's Full
Moon Parties. The beer I sipped that night on the tuk tuk to
Haad Tien Beach did not, as I'd hoped, make me extroverted
enough for the party. I twisted around billows of Western
accents, Thai English, and cigarette smoke and elbowed onto the
counter of a bamboo shack thinking another drink might buy
me an ounce of carelessness. Still unable to muster enthusiasm, I ambled back to the tuk tuks driving across the island and
that's when it started: the end of my remembering. My head
bobbed from the nook of my arm holding the overhead bar in
the taxi. I remember a flash of yellow and blue light. Nothing
more. I woke the next day, in my bungalow, with no recollection of how I got there. My head flashed sheet lightning when
I sat up and stumbled to a hammock. My hangover lasted three
days. I'd never had a three-day hangover. I'd never blacked out.
I blamed poorly mixed alcohols and the rumored amphetamines
of Thai Red Bull. I didn't wonder who might have been watching me that night. Who might have stood up and looked for me
when I slipped through the crowd like a minnow through a net.
A few years later, I happened upon an article about a girl raped
and murdered on the same beach under the same full moon.
Someone put something in her drink. I found article after article reporting similar incidents, different girls. The problem is
the druggings aren't remembered—there aren't reports for
the girls with missing memories. I reexamined my blackout
and three-day hangover from two drinks, but I didn't tell anyone. Not my best friend. Not my boyfriend. Not my mother.

I turned it off—like a light in a closet. I didn't have to look at what I couldn't see.

Flank

*Located between the underside of a
bird's wings and abdomen.*

IN A ROOM MADE OF CINDER BLOCK THAT SERVED AS THE town's police station, the officer pulled out a blank incident report from a top drawer and laid it on the desk between us. I spoke enough Spanish to tell him where it happened: *en la jungla, cerca de la cascada.* But I didn't know the Spanish words for "guns," "masks," or "fatigues." The silence of my missing vocabulary lingered between us until my arm reached across the desk and picked up his pen, raised it in the air. The officer turned the incident report over to its blank side and pushed it toward me. I drew a stick figure with long, blue, ballpoint hair: me. I drew the switchbacks in the Guatemalan jungle between the Siete Altares waterfall and the Amatique Bay that leads into the Gulf of Honduras. I drew my stick figure traversing the switchbacks—two men tucked into the bushes on her path— holding a rifle and machete each. My stick figure with the blue-ballpoint hair stopped in her path. She saw the two men as they rose from their hiding spot. She saw the long glint of black metal. My stick figure put her hands in the air. The stick men got close, they nudged stick guns toward my stick figure's pants. Toward her flanks. I didn't know how to draw a stick figure choking on fright. If she had a thought bubble it would have read: *Remember what they are wearing. Blue pants. Green shirt. Rape. Straight hair. Machete in his belt. Rape. Black boots.* I drew my stick figure emptying her pockets of cash. I drew her turning her back as instructed. The men with guns told her to run. My stick figure ran and didn't look back. She fell, bled from her knees, got up, and kept running. As I drew these crude pictures, I could not help but chuckle. More officers wandered in from other rooms of the station, catching the spell of laughter. Soon the room was full of belly-clutching blue uniforms. I laughed. The more I laughed, the more they laughed. The more they laughed, the more I laughed. I laughed so hard I cried.

Lore

The tender area between the eye and beak of a seagull.

(HERE IS THE PLACE WHERE I WROTE OF ASSAULTS THAT WERE not mine. True stories that shaped how I navigate blind corners, back seats, dark rooms, and thin doors. I deleted the details because they were not mine to share. But this white space is not quiet. It is choked in fear. It is frozen. It was dragged behind a bush. Pulled behind a neighbor's door. Pushed into an office. It entered her room at night without knocking. It blacked out her memory. It punched her in the face. It held her down while she cried. It made her date her rapist. It held a gun to her head and it pulled the trigger. This space screams with the hushed stories of the grade school friend, the high school friend, the college friend, the best friend, the other best friend, the other best friend, and the cousin, aunt, and grandmother. It is the terrible body of knowledge, passed tenderly, from one woman to another, as their eyes search the sky. Pages of silence that could fill chapters, books, shelves, auditoriums. This paragraph is gone. But it is not quiet.)

Mantle

The area between the bird's shoulders
and tail, along the spine.

THE RETIRED CHURCH WITH SUPERMAN-BLUE WALLS WHERE
the kids and I worked through math problems, made papier-
mâché pigs, and kicked a soccer ball in the fenced yard was just
around the bend. Johanna and Guillermo took my hands. *No
podemos caminar por ahí, hoy*, they told me. They pulled me
like a leashed puppy across the gravel street. I looked around.
The vultures churned overhead, same as every day. I asked why
we couldn't walk on the other side of the street. Johanna was
maybe nine. She said, *Una mujer fue encontrada*. Guillermo
was around twelve years old. He nodded and I followed the
tilt of his head toward the unfinished cinder block structure
across the street where a woman's corpse had been found that
morning. The structure had no door. Its windows gaped. *Se
prendió fuego al cuerpo*, Guillermo said. I saw black walls and
the flame-licked paint around the window. Guillermo's words
echoed through me: *They set her body on fire*. Johanna and
Guillermo were born in the *basurero*—forty acres of landfill
constituting Guatemala's city dump. Their mothers were out
under the churning vultures, waiting for dump trucks, picking
tin and glass and aluminum to trade for the quetzales needed to
buy beans and rice. By the looks of Guillermo's collared shirt
and Johanna's shiny plaited hair, no one would have guessed
they lived in the municipal dump. What marked these kids as
different was that they didn't cry. I'd learned this working at
the school for seven months: that when a child fell in the yard,
or cut a finger, or took an errant fist in the cheek, his or her face
would draw blank. It was that blank sternness on Johanna's and
Guillermo's faces—as they pulled me past the gaping window.
I wanted to slow down. To comprehend what the charred cinder block meant. But the kids who tugged on my arms knew I

couldn't. They knew I was just the brownish girl speaking white Spanish who came in the morning and left before dark. Looking over my shoulder at the blackened bricks, the chill I felt down my spine, it was not foreign. But it did grow. To reverberate with the bodies of women disappeared in gaping rooms the globe over. Mantles crushed in flashes of unspeakable violence. Evidenced only in charred echo down another's spine.

Digestive System

Gulls swallow food whole. Indigestible waste that can't pass through the intestines is regurgitated.

"MOM, HAVE YOU MET A SEX-U-AL PRED-A-TOR?" MY SEVEN-year-old asked as she tested the terrible new words in her mouth. I had no choice. I had to teach her the words. Being seven should protect her from sexual assault, but it doesn't. It makes her more vulnerable. So I squinted, then slowly recalled an incident from when I was her age. A man in a secondhand store, on the opposite side of a clothing rack from me, pushed the hangers aside between his body and mine. He had pulled down his pants and underwear and was yanking on himself. Overhearing this conversation on the couch, my husband in the kitchen looked up. The water from the faucet ran. Later that night he said, "You never told me that happened to you." And it was true. I barely remembered it myself. "It was a small thing," I replied. But was it? Was it a small thing? Or just one more swallowed whole, undigestible thing.

Sinews

Tough fibrous tissues that bind bird parts together.

LAST SUMMER, I CURLED AROUND MY SLEEPING CHILD IN A tent, eyes wide open with the escalating voices of men drinking down the dirt road. Last summer, I pulled over in the Nevada desert to help my son with his seat belt. Bending into the car, I heard wheels spinning on the gravel behind me. I stiffened and told my son to "look away" as a man leaned out the window of a gray van and hissed, "Hey Mama. You got a pop for me?" Last summer, a pickup tipped its headlights down the dirt road I was hiking with two girlfriends. One of the women flinched. I touched her shoulder. She froze. My eyes welled. The fragmented anatomy of assaults against the bodies of women, I first saw in the reflection of my daughter's distrust. Then in the sinewy membrane between the lives of mothers, daughters, sisters, and friends. But the crimes stacked up, crawled up my skin, lit up not just the closet but all the rooms of my life. Muriel Rukeyser in the 1960s, asked in a poem: "What would happen if one woman told the truth about her life?" Rukeyser answered her own question: "The world would split open." Except, women do tell the truth. Lives of women split open, over and over, in uncatalogued, undocumented, unreported incidents that fragment their bodies and futures. Women splay truth. For any who look or listen. And in the midst of it all, my daughter's downy body floats in the bathtub. The water holds my daughter as I once held her in my womb, in this only-place where she is able to relax her girl body. This soft place where she can close her eyes and rise above it by the air of her own lungs. Did you know a buoyant body has no weight? That underwater, a three-hundred-thousand-pound Blue Whale soars like a bird through air? It only requires a shift in perspective. Old stories adapted. Flight barriers surpassed beyond those even of Jonathan Livingston Seagull and "his brothers." New horizons we need to split open, to see.

Feather Dust

A powder that keeps the feathers of a bird
silken, also known as wing dust.

ONE DAY I COME HOME AND SEE IT CENTERED IN THE BIG window in the kitchen: the ghostly silhouette of a large bird's full wingspan outlined in feather dust on the glass—like the chalk of a crime scene. I run outside and scour the yard, but there is no evidence. Just as there is no red tape around my unremembering body in the hammock. No chalk outline of the girls' broken bodies left in the bushes at the lake. No map of the yellowed hairline of a wife's scalp or the charred edges of flame-licked paint. These are the images I consider as I trace the feather dust on the window with my finger. As I sit down and stare out the glass, my daughter crawls into my lap. "How did the bird leave its shape?" she asks as she follows my eyes to the ghost print on the window. I explain, "It hit our window and the dust from its wings left the print." She pushed, "But why? Why did it hit the window?" I answered, "Because she saw a reflection and thought it was sky."

PHANTOM BRAKING

MY FRIEND'S VOICE PROJECTED FROM THE CAR SPEAKER, "You're driving? Wait, are you leaning forward like a grandma, gripping the wheel for your sweet life?" She cackled her old-man laugh and I wasn't hurt because of our shared teenage years in which we were so terrible to each other, no offense was left to be taken. She'd been poking fun at my driving posture for decades, but I had no idea my anxieties had official suffixes—until one day I discovered their proper names.

Vehophobia is the fear of driving.

Amaxophobia is the fear of riding in a vehicle.

I've taken men skydiving for dates, night-dived the Great Barrier Reef in search of sharks, jumped between men brewing bar fights, and labored two babies into the world without pain medication. Was it possible now—after forty birthdays—I needed to add to my self-concept not just one, but *two* phobias?

The secret of my car fears was baton-ed from my high school to college friends, who took turns in the driver's seat of my maroon hatchback when we stuffed the trunk with beach duffels. While my girlfriends fought over shotgun, a newcomer would ask, "Doesn't Christina want it?" Someone would repeat my rationale, "No. She prefers the back. She hates to see where she's going."

After college, I enjoyed a ten-year vacation from my veho-phobia for the decade I didn't own a car. But I'm not sure if avoidance counted as reprieve. In fact, I'm certain it didn't because the "treatment" for these phobias is a behavioral therapy called *systematic desensitization*—which sounds, to me, like the opposite of avoidance.

Since my move into the mountains, I've surrendered to the societal and systemic pressures of needing a car. So I've now acquired an exceptional amount of unofficial "exposure therapy" via the infamous I-70 highway running through my mountain town. Under white-knuckled grip, I've encountered jack-knifed semis, skate-rink streets, break-away boulders, disoriented drivers with blood dripping from foreheads, ninety-mile-per-hour wind gusts, avalanche runouts, and meandering herds of bighorn sheep. Which should all qualify as progress in a therapy that *gradually exposes a person to fear and panic in order to reduce anxiety and stress.*

My car also hosts an arsenal of calming munitions: lavender oil, "chill out" drops laced with homeopathics, CBD lotion and CBD droppers and overpriced CBD-infused cans of sparkling water. I have a playlist of affirmations also at the ready. In silken disclaimers, they remind me to not fall asleep while driving—which seems the least of my likelihoods.

Just a few weeks ago, when I thought I was sufficiently numb to harrowing highway scenarios, I received an alert on my phone. I called my husband, "What the fuck is a squall?" He explained, "When you can't see beyond your bumper. That's a snow squall. Pull over."

Though my road vocabulary has increased since my move to the mountains, nothing quiets the voice that turns over with the key in the ignition. A voice that chimes, "Look at what you're leaving. At what you might never see again. Look at everything on the precipice!" I hush the voice. I reach for the small sacred heart that dangles from red string wrapped around my rear-view mirror. I rub the metal charm and say the kind of prayer non-praying people say. And then, looking into my eyes in the mirror, I reverse out the driveway.

I THINK IT STARTED BEFORE MY DRIVER'S PERMIT—WHEN watchfulness became my problem. It was in seventh grade when I began migrating toward the desks on the perimeter of the classroom. From the classroom's outskirts, I could watch the quiet boy doodling feathers in the margins of his textbook; could feel the hesitation of the girl who wanted to raise her hand but bit her lip; could read the backstory of the teacher in the sequence of photos on her desk.

Likewise, there is so much of I-70 to read. There's the width of space between the cars in front of me, politely distanced or disjointed by a bumper-riding rebel. There are the hillsides rimmed with animal fencing and the dark road stains of those who jumped it. There's the baby boomer fumbling with her smartphone to my right and the teenager trapped in the small world of his head to the left. There's the Ford—a mile back— with his high beams pushing people from the passing into the slow lane. There's also the cop who sometimes sits around this bend. And then there is night falling. Dimming all these stories. But not turning them off. They're still there. I just can't see them.

There's another unseen story on the road. Researchers have been investigating the mystery of a recent mass die-off of salmon in the Pacific Northwest. In a University of Washington news video clip, the body of a Coho Salmon shimmers green and gold with black speckles, her belly blushed pink hinting of her intended spawn season. But this Coho is horizontal in the shallow water of a stream. Her mouth gasps, her fins twitch, her black eye dims. She's dying.

She was born in this same stream, hiding among roots and rocks as she gained size and strength for her migration to the sea. As she moved from her river toward the Pacific Ocean, her gills and kidneys, in a bewildering feat, physiologically switched gears from processing fresh to saltwater. Three years later, she followed instinct from the ocean back to the river of her birth. She is one of the 0.1 percent who survived the journey home. Her intent was to lay 1,500–3,000 eggs in a gravel nest in the freshwater stream of her birth. But that won't happen. Rain fell on the roads overhead. It mixed with chemicals that poured into her stream and the toxic cocktail infiltrated her body, leaving her blushing body twitching on rocks.

This was the story revealed in 2020 by researchers looking into the urban runoff mortality syndrome (URMS) killing 40 to 90 percent of salmon before they could spawn. Research concluded a preservative added to car tires reacted with ozone to frankenstein into a chemical that makes Coho Salmon turn belly up. The chemical (6PPD) meant to "preserve" tires is massacring ancestral chains of salmon who've lived in the Pacific Northwest over four million years. Edward Kolodziej, an environmental engineer on the research team, said of the toxic chemical, "It's probably found on every single busy road in the world." He added the personal note, "I can't walk along a street without staring at all the skid marks . . ."

I, too, over-notice the skid marks. My poor husband is now the exclusive pin cushion of my road angst. The kids occupy the back seat, so I can't hide there anymore. It's from the passenger seat that my fingernails find their way into his forearm as my left foot presses an invisible brake pedal. There's a medical diagnosis for this too: *Phantom Brake Syndrome*. We are up to two phobias and one syndrome for anyone counting.

From the passenger seat, I watch my husband *not* see the skid marks. I see the black rubber footprints of car ghosts as they careen into cement barriers, barrel through meridian grasses, or end in the outline of a car's hood bent into a pole. I listen to my husband's small talk as he adjusts the volume to pop music—as if the dead-end stories aren't all around us.

He would call me crazy if I confessed to all the hidden outcomes in my head. The *Diagnostic and Statistical Manual of*

Mental Disorders (*DSM*) would probably also define me as crazy, but they'd call it something more polite: a disorder, a phobia, something wispy—like *vehophobia*.

AMERICANS HAVE 1.83 VEHICLES PER HOME, BURN 489 GALlons of gasoline per year, and drive thirty-two miles per day. In Senegal, there are only thirty-two cars per 1,000 people. Residents of the Netherlands average 4.4 bicycle trips per week. Hongkongers walk an average of 6,880 steps a day. These perspective shifts make me wonder if my car phobias are of a modern American make and model.

There are more stories I've witnessed in the world, but try to keep in my blurry periphery. Stories from a bare-chested centenarian in a thatched Senegalese hut: of her encounters with lions that are today critically endangered in West Africa. Stories from the monk to whom I taught English, his palm open between us to show how he held the handful of rice he ate dry as he fled over Himalayan mountains as a refugee of Tibet. Stories of the world's most endangered freshwater mammal—the Ganges River Dolphin—the last pod of which I sighted on a foggy horizon from Varanasi's ghats: pink-tinged backs undulating through the second most polluted river on the planet. Back in America, my hands—white-knuckled—stay the wheel; my eyes train to the yellow line on asphalt; my tires leach into my own rivers.

My phobias make the most sense when my children are in the back seat. When I have to numb the immense value of their small-framed lives to strap them into the car. Is there a phobia for fearing the extinction of biodiversity on earth? A phobia for fearing for the lives of my descendants and the collective generations to come? Is there a phobia for the fear of poisonous water? Polluted air? Forest fires? Droughts? Oceans without fish? Is there a phobia for sensing and seeing and empathizing and feeling too fucking much to function?

Traumatic incidents often precede phobias and, yes, I've witnessed the aftermath of brutal car accidents, rolled in cars myself. But I would posit these are not the traumas that formed my phobias. Instead, I propose that maybe I am one (of maybe millions) wrongly classified in the *DSM* who are barely surviving a culture of violent desensitization. One who intuits her downriver position in the web of interconnections, who feels the poisoning of her own blushing body from unchecked modern society. Linda Hogan, a descendant of Chickasaw storytellers, said of Western systems, "We have been deceived by what we thought was knowledge and by the many systems that have been born of this inadequate knowledge." Would I even recognize the clear stream of my ancestors if I could reach it?

Maybe desensitization is less the treatment than the problem. Maybe those of us "over-sensitized" do not suffer irrational fear, but the deficient numbing of alcohol and movies and sports and overtime and babies and stock markets and laundry loads and love affairs and the over-scheduled schedules that keep us obsessed with anything other than the precipice of life and death. Rachel Carson warned us of this route: "The road we have long been traveling is deceptively easy, a smooth superhighway on which we progress with great speed, but at its end lies disaster."

Maybe we are struggling to hear something under the mechanical mantras of "look ahead," "stick to your lane," and "don't look at the people driving parallel or perpendicular to you"—droning and individualistic commands that push the OK-ness of a blur-of-life in passing. Maybe the phantom *is* our desensitization. Because I've since done the math. My chance of dying in a car crash is one in ninety-three. My chance of dying from cancer is one in seven. Of dying by suicide: one in eighty-seven. By shark attack: one in 4,332,817. My chance of dying is one in one.

THE LATIN "VEHO" OF *VEHOPHOBIA* MEANS NOT ONLY TO ride—but also to bear. Fear of what-we-bear might not only be a good thing, but the anchor that roots us. My tin-heart-rubbing and foot-phantom-pressing are, after all, reaches of the same instinct: to grasp all that's tender and fleeting. At what point do we stop normalizing our increasing exposure to stressors and question instead the daily gears of modern living that traumatize us? That leach into our own beings?

My friends in college were half right. I don't hate to see where I'm going. I just don't like what I see coming. From the back and passenger seats, I've been watching. I see the littered interstates of forgotten ancestry and dead-end descendancy we pummel from and toward at seventy-five miles per hour. I don't need a check engine light to point to the brokenness I feel vibrating in my bones.

It was never my nature to barrel down asphalt. It was always my nature to be watery. Astrida Neimanis, a cultural theorist working at the intersection of feminism and environmental change, positions water as the fluid body interconnecting all beings and histories in a "corporeally connected aqueous community." She calls this theory *hydrofeminist* and offers me, finally, a suffix I want attached to my name. Importantly, she makes sense of what I feel when I tip my chin up to the rain, the ocean, the river, the salty tears that rivet my cheeks watching the Coho's eyes dim: "As watery, we experience ourselves less as isolated entities, and more as oceanic eddies: *I am a singular, dynamic whorl dissolving in a complex fluid circulation.*" Neimanis names what I've been trying to shape my tongue around for decades. Water is the connecting thread of kinship between human bodies and water bodies and animal bodies. It's not only the great equalizer, but the great integrator. The earth's oceans are my oceans. The earth's body, mine. What runs through the rivers runs through my veins. My urine, my tears, my blood are tomorrow's lakes, creeks, and fog.

My inclination for wateriness, my feeling too connected, my over-watchfulness, they only feel in check when I am immersed in a grander ecosystem. Sitting on a Pacific Ocean cliff, bobbing in the Caribbean Sea, following a valley creek to a body of water that will remind me of my own. Places my interior wilderness is free to merge with something unpaved and unchoreographed. Elizabeth Woody, the American Navajo Warm Springs Wasco Yakama author, said, "The song around salmon is the river's voice and the way the fish fight to live is our fight as well." Squalls of speed, cement, and numbed nature may be my—and the Coho's—inheritance. But to live is to blush and keep fighting, upstream.

HIDDEN GEOGRAPHIES

IT WAS MY SECRET WISH THAT CORONAVIRUS WOULD DESTROY Halloween, or at least the individually wrapped parts of it. I hate getting stuck in the grocery aisle in October, trying to decide whether I should buy organic bags of plastic-wrapped crap or traditional bags of plastic-wrapped crap. Regardless of which I choose, my kids will come home from school with ziplock bags full of plastic spider rings and plush ghost stickers and bite-size candies in synthetic wraps, distributed by well-meaning teachers and schoolmates. The holiday's plastic torments me and my polymer-guilt chases me all day, usually toppling me just an inch before REM sleep.

One night, the clenched jaw of my insomnia wandered to that infamous "island of trash" floating in the ocean of which we've all heard rumors. I wasn't even sure, exactly, where the trash island was located. Which made me sit up in bed. I was familiar with the geography of Earth's oceans—how did I not know this? I reached for my phone and the answer made it clear. Because there isn't only one trash island. There are five. Maybe more. And they are not islands at all, but gyres. The two largest vortexes of trash swirl to the west of Hawai'i and east of Japan. Two drowning eyes of the ocean that—together—make up what is called the Great Pacific Garbage Patch. Captain Charles Moore, when he discovered the GPGP in 1997, recounted the sight from his boat's deck: "In the week it took to cross the sub-tropical high, no matter what time of day I looked, plastic debris was floating everywhere: bottles, bottle caps, wrappers, fragments . . . I was confronted, as far as the eye could see, with the sight of plastic."

I had thought the length of the "patch" could be measured, that I could break the distance into miles and calculate the number of days it would take for me to walk across it. But it's more complicated than that. Because the trash in these swirling gyres is not only at the surface, nor is it plainly visible. Seventy percent of the trash sinks. Another portion hovers in between.

I remember that in-between place from scuba diving. Thirty feet down, I'd look up and see the Great Barracuda's steely eyes, his gills flexing and teeth glimmering, just a few feet under the water's top. And beside the Barracuda, a hovering milk jug or green plastic bag, bobbing to the song of the same ocean current. But this layer is invisible to the eyes of drones or humans overhead. Even more frightening of this trash layer between sea surface and floor are the "ghost nets" that tumble through it. Abandoned fishing nets and gear, often cut loose, or left in the ocean when snagged or forgotten, account for more than 10 percent of ocean plastics. But they don't always sink. Often, they keep drifting in the open ocean, entangling, starving, and suffocating sea life to no means or end. In 2012, a ghost net ensnared a Gray Whale off the coast of California. When rescuers pulled up the net, they found in the whale's tow a dead sea lion and three shark corpses, along with decomposing fish, rays, and crabs. That juvenile Gray Whale was freed from the ghost net, and the rescuers that night cheered. But four days later, a juvenile Gray Whale of matching description was found in nearby Long Beach Harbor, floating upside down.

As for the trash that does float on top of the trash gyres, many of those plastics have broken into the small bits from which they were once born in plumes of toxic factory smoke. These reborn pellets floating in the ocean are sun-faded, having leached their colorants and chemicals into the water, in a process known as photodegradation. The plastic bits look like fish eggs, crustaceans, squid, and little fish—at least to the albatross who feeds on tiny things that float on the surface of the sea. There is a photo of an albatross—an image that once surfaced from the currents of viral internet—that I recall with startling clarity. The photo was of the albatross's decomposing corpse. Her plumage of silver, gray, and white feathers were matted to the earth. A nest of bones—perfect interlocking vertebrae and hollow legs with still-webbed feet—was centered around a stomach opened to reveal white soda bottle caps, turquoise plastic shards, a generic black-capped vial, and the muted reds and blues of other ocean-tumbled human waste the albatross had ingested before her death. It looked not unlike the bags of candy my kids spread across the floor every Halloween. But my day-to-day mom life pinned down my subconscious, refusing to see the connection.

Last spring I retrieved Nash from an after-school program called Lego Club, where he dragged me by my sleeve to his table and demonstrated the wheels and wings and other rolling and soaring mechanics of the vehicle he'd invented. He was so proud, so consumed with thrill, that the aftercare teacher winked at me. "You might need to invest."

I gave in. I bought my son a set. I didn't feel good about it. I didn't feel good about ordering the Legos from the behemoth online retailer that eats small, local stores for breakfast. I didn't feel good about the price marked up double for the brand imprinted on each brick. I didn't feel good about the box it was packaged in, or the wages of the workers who packed the set, or the fuel that burned in transit of the box to my house, or the UPS guy who had to navigate the ice on my driveway to drop the package on my stoop. All those systems interlocked so smoothly to facilitate my participation in a plastic-indulgent society.

But I did feel good when my son picked up the box, shook its contents, and heard the rattle of 1,070 pieces of a ninja playset boasting a monastery and tea room with "hidden knife and chicken traps." I felt good when a squeal on the verge of insanity escaped his mouth and his body quaked with anticipation. There's little that delights a mother more than seeing her child beside himself in joy. And I suppose someone on a marketing team somewhere has made this calculation.

We cleaned a space on the big living room table and I felt the not-good coming back as each section of the set was captured in its own single-use plastic bag. And even if the bags were recyclable, I'd still feel bad because, though I recycle religiously, I know recycling is a sham religion. A system of faith born of ingenious plastic marketing teams who knew they only needed to downshift our guilt enough for us to look the other way. I know most of my "recyclables" will end up at the dump. That other of my "recyclables" might be shipped to another country that doesn't know the true cost of being the US's dump, or can't afford to say no. That recycling plastic involves burning and the inevitable emissions of pollutants almost certainly inhaled by communities and ecosystems lacking the privilege to complain or have their complaint heard. That even if I recycle myself, I am a tiny cog in an industry where 9 percent of plastic is recycled and 91 percent stuffed into shallow graves on the planet. So that moment holding the plastic bag over the bins was terrible. I made the same face as when I open a package of raw chicken and dribble the slime into the sink. But I pushed my shame down with the plastic into the trash bin. I returned as fast as I could to my son's lit eyes because he'd already found what he called the "construction manual." Observing his steel concentration helped further trash-compact my guilt.

It took my son seven days to complete the ninja monastery set. When he finished, he wanted to sleep with it in his bed. He wanted the sprawling Lego metropolis to have its own pillow. I conceded to the nightstand. For show-and-tell, we packed it up in a box with handles, and it came home from school missing some nunchucks and capes. When I told Nash he couldn't bring the Lego set camping for the weekend, he fell onto the ground and cried. But by the end of the next month, the ninja Legoland had been relocated to my son's bookcase. Another month later, dust collected on the monastery. The time was coming to return the set to pieces.

My conscience was also catching up. Yes, it was my plan to donate the Legos to the aftercare program where other kids might construct smaller designs from the pieces of the original set. But still, I bought the Lego set. I bought it new and I sent a message to those marketing teams at Lego that I was willing to compromise my values for their petroleum-based product. I made it clear I was willing to look away from the one thousand years that each of the 1,070 plastic pieces would live beyond my own life. All in exchange for a few sparkles of joy in my son's eyes.

What I had not fully considered was that the set had been systematically designed to be built once.

WHEN I RESEARCH "ALBATROSS PLASTIC," THE FIRST IMAGE that comes up is that haunting photo I remembered with the nest of silver plumage and bones around a stomach-bowl of sun-faded plastic shards. The image came from a film called *Albatross* that debuted independently as a free public artwork in 2018.

"Do you want to watch a movie with me, about albatrosses? It might be sad . . ."

My kids jumped up and down in excitement, if only for the promised popcorn. Popcorn popped, we settled into the living room. When Nash commented on the beauty of the imagery, I taught him the word *cinematography*. Together the kids cooed at the tiny puff of baby Fairy Tern waiting for his mother to return with a fresh minnow in her black beak. Together the kids bounced in their seats watching the albatross run in slow motion toward the camera as it took off in flight. Riva was sitting on my lap at the start of a six-minute segment of the albatross mating dance set to a piano piece called *Confidencias*. With the first notes of the music, Riva rose from my lap. She lifted her arms into the air, then tucked them in like albatross wings. She undulated her neck in sync with the slow motions of the dancing birds on the screen. As the camera panned to the ground where an albatross lifted to the tips of its webbed feet, Riva, too, rose onto her tippy toes. As the birds—chests arched—rolled their necks in smooth motions like prima ballerinas, so did my daughter.

Both children crawled into my lap when the albatross mother regurgitated a stream of seafood mixed with plastic trash into the mouth of her infant. Nash put his hands over his eyes and Riva covered her mouth when the biologist used scissors to cut open the belly of a dead chick, when the gloved hands pulled out the plastic shards, one by one.

At the end of the film, the kids were quiet. Nash asked me to define "documentary" again, and he repeated the word a few times as he picked up his mini-football and threw it against the wall. I waited until later, when we were seated around the dinner table, before I asked for their thoughts.

"Other movies end happy. That one didn't," Nash said.

"Should it have a happy ending?"

He paused. "No. Because then nothing would change."

I asked if they could guess which country makes the most plastic waste in the world. They knew the question was loaded and answered correctly: "The United States of America." Nash looked up at the ceiling. I saw the little invisible hands of his mind working around this novel problem.

The kids both agreed on the same scene as the most beautiful. They got on their knees in their dinner chairs, raised their arms, flapping their wings against invisible winds. They were reenacting the scene of the adolescent albatrosses building muscle for flights of seemingly impossible distances. Nash shouted, "Papa! When they fly off the island and over the ocean for the first time, they don't touch land again for three to five years!"

Riva added, ". . . but Nash, you forgot the most important part. The albatrosses have to throw up all the plastic in their bellies first—to be able to fly."

THE EASTERN GARBAGE PATCH (EGP) IS THE GYRE OF SWIRL-ing ocean currents that pass by the coastlines where I grew up and seems the most likely vortex of my own lost litter. *National Geographic* shows me a map of the currents and offers a photo of trash pulled from this vortex: a yellow Bic lighter, a crumpled white jug, a black toy gun, a piece of rainbow flotsam, a child's toothbrush with a teddy bear on the handle, a green cowboy with one hand in his pocket and a revolver in the other, a Batman mask, a blue plastic telephone, and a knot of old fishing net. The photographer chose children's toys as five of the nine items in the photo for a reason of easy reach. Childhood is innocent. Yet sparklers burn swiftly. What's left after the bright light dies is charred wire and a waft of sulfur. The photograph makes me think of the buckets of toys I carried to the Oregon beach as a child. Of the plastic shovels I fought over with my brother. The castles I built. The tides that overtook our work when we weren't looking.

It's a catch-22. Survival without participation in our society. When I was twenty-three, I went to Cuba. I didn't plan to go to Cuba. I was on my way to a remote Mexican island and had to go through Cancún to get there. In Cancún's streets, I was disoriented by the iconography of American fast-food chains branding entire blocks. Lost in the white sun hats on white legs on white lawn chairs on white beaches. Confused by the throngs of American college boys in tan cargo shorts stumbling out of bars. The familiar cultural traits tugged erratically on my compass, left me dizzy. I passed a sign that read, "CUBA FLIGHTS CHEAP," pushed into the air-conditioned room, and collapsed into a chair. The travel agent behind the desk smiled.

It wasn't until the heavy metal buckle was locked across my lap on the small plane that I realized I knew nothing of how to navigate the island. So I was unaware of Cuba's eclectic currency rules until I walked from ATM to ATM in Old Havana, watching each machine spit out my US bank cards with disgust. The bank agents, too, rejected my traveler's checks because they were "printed on US paper." Not even my long and straight Spanish learned in Guatemala translated to the clipped and musical version spoken on the island. As I walked along the boardwalk fingering the last few dollars in my pocket, a man approached me. He held out a baby sea turtle in a plastic bag and asked if I would buy it to set it free. I looked at the tiny, still-soft-shelled turtle scratching at invisible walls and cried.

IN 1997, A SHIP CALLED THE *TOKIO EXPRESS* PASSING NEAR Cornwall, England, was hit by a rogue wave. Sixty-two containers fell overboard, one holding 4.8 million Lego toy parts, most of a nautical theme. Lego flippers, Lego spear guns, Lego seagrass, Lego scuba tanks, Lego life preservers, and black Lego octopuses washed up on coasts thousands of miles from each other. The US oceanographer Curtis Ebbesmeyer confirmed one Lego octopus found on a beach of Texas "could be from the *Tokio Express*. It matches the drift pattern across the Atlantic."

The black plastic Lego octopuses are not endangered. Less is known about the Blue-Ringed, Smoothskin, Dumbo, Atlantic Pygmy, and Giant Pacific Octopuses. Octopuses are elusive creatures, most often listed as "data deficient" in terms of their endangered status. But Endangered Species International conducted surveys at twelve marine sites in Southeast Asia between 2013 and 2018, and they discovered sharp population declines or absences of octopuses. Those black plastic Lego octopuses fallen off the *Tokio Express*, however, might wash up on beaches for decades to come.

So now what keeps me up at night is not only the swirling trash-eye gyres of great garbage patches, but the decomposing albatross, the everlasting black octopus, the mini-candy wrappers, and the impending calendar of plasticized holidays in which we will "invest" in single-use pleasures and then sweep the evidence into green plastic bins of stupid optimism.

My kids don't yet roll their eyes, but I fear they soon will. The number of times I've picked up a small toy from the ground and called their attention, "Do you know how long this will last on this planet so that you could enjoy it for a little bit?" But they don't know. My son still mixes up Wednesday and Monday. My daughter counts thirty-eight, thirty-nine, forty, ninety-one, ninety-two. How can they possibly conceive a thousand years? And wasn't it me who sought their momentary joy in a lazy decision? Yet so much of the future has already been stolen from my children, must I take Halloween and birthday goodie bags too?

I *think* the culprit is me. That's why I lose sleep. When I get out of bed, I feel my guilt greasily glide over my fingertips as I touch the shampoo bottle, the neoprene sleeve around my coffee mug, the kids' lunch boxes, the cat's litter box, and as I put away the thin paintbrushes in the watercolor case my daughter uses to paint families of rainbow Narwhals. Can the true weight of my plastic guilt be measured? Can I calculate how many days it would take for me to walk from my values to the world I want to live in?

Except the culprit isn't candy wrappers.

My favorite course in college was economics. My teacher was renowned as brilliant, his door crowded with students from the wait list. One day he declared to the class, "Today I am going to show you the actual dollar value of a human life." He used statistics of how "high-risk" jobs (street construction work) pay higher salaries in direct relation to the value of risk of death. Two hours later, with a whirl of chalk dust wafting in the air, he arrived at the exact USD unit value of a human life. Thirty twenty-year-olds dropped their jaws. Another day, he declared to the class, "Today, I'm going to show you that the best thing we could do to save the whales is give them to the poachers." Again, in a flurry of swift statistics and sloping curves, he produced the ingenious answer: "Privatization of the whaling industry!" Economics is the study of scarcity and how people, businesses, and governments use resources and make "rational" decisions in regard to value. Had I looked deeper at this definition before I walked through that classroom door, I might have suspected some layers to the operative words *use, resource, scarcity,* and *value*. A few years after graduation, I cashed out my stock options at the start-up I worked for, sold everything in my apartment, and moved to Guatemala for a year. In a hammock strung between palms on a coastline, I read a book I had pulled from my hostel's free library. In *The Hitchhiker's Guide to the Galaxy,* a class of extraterrestrial humans land on planet Earth and need a currency to run their new society. They decide on leaves. They stuff their pockets with the leaves of trees. But there is a "small inflation problem," for there are too many leaves. One alien visitor sums it up, "The current going rate has something like three deciduous forests buying one ship's peanut." So this society begins to set the trees on fire. Their goal: to create scarcity. Their answer to increasing the value of leaves is to smolder the planet. And here we are now acting out the final scene of this dystopian, apocalyptic story of absurdist fiction written in 1979. A story in which there is nothing a "cultured" society won't destroy—in the name of "value."

MY INSOMNIA IS A SIGN OF MY MIND AND HEART FIGHTING for alignment. But I inherited this plastic culture as a child myself. I was taught broken definitions of "value" as a student, and "investment" as a parent. I was offered the false gods of plastic recycling and high-tech innovation for "climate inspiration." Meanwhile, fifteen million tons of plastic enter the oceans each year, plastic production is on track to triple by 2040, and the World Economic Forum estimates there will be more plastic in the oceans than fish by 2050. Oil companies push the "individual footprint" narratives because they need to distract us from the smoking gun of their Pacific-sized corporate roles in the mess. They point the sneaky finger of personal shame to distract us from the sheer power of our collective action. Because this is far bigger than my two bad Halloween choices in the supermarket aisle. This *is* the supermarket. It's *all* the pieces in the monastery Lego set and the "constructions" that were only ever designed for single use. The Lego factory is fully automated and operates twenty-four hours a day. It builds 1.7 million bricks an hour. There is one machine at the factory alone that makes 15,000 little yellow Lego heads—with varying arcs of eyes and eyebrows and lips—every sixty minutes. This is the cultural machinery we're up against—the future marching at us.

Unless we collectively get in its way.

A political scientist at Harvard named Erica Chenoweth studied political campaigns around the world and estimates it takes only 3.5 percent of a population to initiate real change through civil disobedience. Could "real change through civil disobedience" be similarly applied to culture? Might it be a matter of not doing more, but less? Of embracing something as simple as the collective *refusal to comply?*

Not letting any plastic pass through our fingertips feels impossible as an individual. But what happens when we collectively refuse plastic bags at the checkout counter? When we collectively ask the school to create guidelines for non-packaged snacks? When we collectively decide that "shopping our closets" is not only a trend? What if 3.5 percent of us stopped buying Legos, refused plastic forks, demanded biodegradable fishing nets, and co-invented plastic-free holidays? What if it's less about "doing something" than collectively not doing many things?

The activist and author Arundhati Roy once said, "Wars will be stopped only when soldiers refuse to fight, when workers refuse to load weapons onto ships and aircraft, when people boycott the economic outposts of Empire that are strung across the globe." This refusal to participate in exploitative systems is called nonviolent resistance. It's not an oxymoron. It's also not our cultural norm. But it could be. Just three people needed, of every hundred. Could I find three people?

For Riva's birthday, I texted some parents an invitation to picnic benches with cupcakes on a sunny afternoon. I chewed on my cuticles as I wrote and rewrote the postscript: "Please, no gifts." Would they think I'm cheap? Too hippie? Too idealistic? I hit send. My postscript lit up in little pink hearts. Many hearts. More than three. I sighed. Maybe we all sighed. It was a little thing. A very little, ordinary, thing, but as Bill McKibben has reminded us of the seeds of systematic change: "It's a quiet revolution begun by ordinary people with the stuff of our daily lives."

Coronavirus did not destroy Halloween. But it did show us how fast we can halt old habits and create new traditions. The first year COVID-19 swept the world, air pollution and greenhouse gas emissions decreased drastically within just a few weeks, giving scientists an "unprecedented view of results that would take regulations years to achieve." The global pandemic left us with no choice, but it did show us our capacity for a world of swift and sweeping systematic changes.

I'm no hero in this story, because we don't need heroes. We need critical mass metamorphosis. Do caterpillars know their capacity for wings? Did whales know they could evolve their legs into flukes? How does the albatross know when she's ready for a flight of seemingly impossible distance? I don't know, but they give me images to hold.

In the meantime, I will continue to plan camping trips so they overlap with events that celebrate with single-use plastics. At Nash's last "camping birthday bash," we pulled out our bins of pre-owned costumes, which included a black-and-white panda, rainbow unicorn, tarantula with eight legs, two dinosaurs, and an eagle with yellow-socked feet. The kids like to mix costume pieces into mythical creatures of their own invention. From the campfire, I spied my son in my periphery on his mountain bike, flying over a jump of desert dirt with his helmet tucked under the panda head, eight spider legs and two eagle wings catching the air behind him—soaring in joy.

This inventive leap, it's not beyond us.

SCREENING FORM

PATIENT AGE (USE DROP DOWN TO SELECT A NUMBER):
I'm forty-four, slightly younger than the age at which the
American Cancer Society recommends mammograms, but my
sister-in-law is a nurse and, post-pandemic, she suffers new
hurricanes of anxiety. She told me I'm "due" and, not checking
my own horizons first, the thunderclouds of the front caught
me unsuspecting.

IS THIS YOUR FIRST MAMMOGRAM? YES OR NO: My
obstetrician did recommend a mammogram a few years ago,
but she was working with the old guidelines. The guidelines
keep shifting after studies. That's where I have a problem.
Because it says right on the Mayo Clinic's website that some
of these studies have: ". . . suggested some women with early
breast cancer were diagnosed with cancer that may never
have affected their health." So will you just clarify? There
are women DIAGNOSED WITH CANCER that MAY NEVER HAVE
AFFECTED THEIR HEALTH? I'm shouting because it feels under-
shouted. Do you know what it means for a woman to have
her life diagnosed with cancer? Because I have a friend, with
two children under age five, who was diagnosed with breast
cancer a few months ago. I've been taking her meals. She hates
coconut. So I always make sure my meals don't have coconut

flakes or oils or essences. She's halfway through her chemo and her sister sent an update this week: *No need to adhere to earlier dietary preferences as she isn't really eating, so bring whatever you want for dad and the kids.* And I'm thinking about my friend who doesn't like coconut and wondering if she WAS or WASN'T one of the women diagnosed with cancer that "may never have affected her health." I texted my nurse-sister-in-law my questions about those studies and she sent me back a shrug emoji. But she also has a neighbor who has two little boys who play with her two little boys in the yard between their homes, and this neighbor was also just diagnosed with breast cancer. Hurricanes are often born of tropical waves in low pressure areas rolling through moisture-rich tropics. When we see spiraling high winds in a neighbor's yard, how are we to hear anything else but screaming storm warnings?

DO YOU HAVE A HISTORY OF HORMONAL CONTRACEPTION USE? YES OR NO? Of course I do. You know this because for the last three decades, you have pushed hormonal contraception on me while brushing a hand in the air assuring me of its safety. You pushed it with some good reason. Because three out of every four women I know, including all those good girls who religiously took their pills at the same time every morning, had an unwanted pregnancy and a frightening but needed abortion. It took me a while to figure this out. Many of those women didn't tell me until they were forty. We all kept our abortion secrets, like good girls. But for having been such a good shameful girl, I now feel fucking swindled. What I'm wondering is why you are asking me that question about hormonal birth control with side eye? Is it because there's a link between hormonal contraception and breast cancer? Because I've read that. I've read that these correlations are part of the math in breast cancer's increase of 242 percent between 1970 and 2014. And I'm giving YOU side eye because

I'm wondering why the same industry that recommended hormonal contraception to me is, today, doing diagnostics to test if I have a cancer that is statistically correlated to what you prescribed? And why the burden of hormonal contraception was designed for women in the first place?

FAMILY HISTORY OF BREAST AND CERVICAL CANCER: No history with my mother or sister, but my father's mother died in a hospital when he was four years old. He was the youngest of his mother's nine children. On my grandmother's death certificate, the wobbly typewriter letters float in the form's boxes: "CAUSE OF DEATH: Cardiovascular Collapse. DUE TO: Surgery (Hysterectomy) DUE TO: Carcinoma of Cervix." A psychic told me that what's written on this death certificate is not true. The psychic told me that my grandmother died from blood poisoning from the dirty tools used in the botched abortion of her tenth pregnancy. The psychic said the secretary typed in "Hysterectomy" and "Carcinoma of Cervix" because there was enough damage to my grandmother's female parts that it required explanation. Because abortion, in 1943, was illegal. And a legal explanation was needed. I don't know if the psychic is right and we won't ever know (see postscript) because the stories of botched abortions are all buried in shame and illegalities and inaccurate death certificates. My grandmother died when she was thirty-eight years old. And you know what I'm wondering about this story? I'm wondering how it might have ended if the medical industry had given her the safe abortion she might have needed. Would my father not have lost his mother at age four? Would I have once sat on my grandmother's lap? Would she have told me a story of her own mother or grandmother (names lost to me in broken lineage)? Can you tell me? YES or NO?

ARE YOU HAVING ANY TROUBLE WITH YOUR BREASTS? Yes. Ever since my friend who doesn't like coconut stopped eating,

I've been waking in the dark and palpating the armpit under my right breast. I don't feel anything with my fingers. But in my stomach, I feel that low pressure system around which hurricanes build. Yesterday, I pasted that quote from the Mayo Clinic into a text thread I share with my best girlfriends. One friend, whose mother died from breast cancer, texted back: "My sister was diagnosed with breast cancer and it resolved in six months! Completely gone on its own . . ." This friend has to get mammograms all the time. She lives in the hurricane's eye, a calm at the axis of rotation where blue sky, even stars, are sometimes seen. But which is surrounded by the "eye wall," an area of deep convection and the highest surface winds. Another friend on the thread, a nurse, said: "Chemo, drugs, trials, etc. Bankrupting people all over the country. It's a very fear-inducing system." The other thing I'm having trouble with is that I noticed you offer a can of spray deodorant from a brand popular in the 1980s in your mammogram dressing room. I turned that can around and saw the ingredients feature heavy metals and parabens. Then I sat down on that nice little plush chair of yours, with the soft robe you handed me in my lap, and thought: "Well how the fuck am I supposed to trust a breast cancer center that offers a deodorant with cancer-inducing chemicals and spray-on heavy metals in its own dressing room?" And since I'm practicing speaking up, I put this question (more gently) to the nurse and she turned her back to me and walked away as she said, "We used to put out chocolates and people said those caused cancer too . . ." And this made me feel bad. This made me feel shame. For putting a tired nurse on the defense. But now I'm wondering why you put her between me and you. Because this problem goes up higher. I don't have a problem with my nurse-sister-in-law swept up in the high winds, or my nurse-friend with her insider suspicions, and not even with the tired nurse on the defense about the chocolates in the waiting room. My problem is with you, Medical Industry. You, white-smocked,

white-haired, deep arrogant voice pushing medicine upon
my female body for millennia without adequate research or
clinical trials or warnings and then gaslighting my suspicions
when I voice them. You who look the other way from the
links between environmental toxins and breast cancer in favor
of pink ribbons and pink hats and pink shirts and pink walks
to fundraise for a "cure" you can market. You of whom a
Forbes article in 2020 headlined, "Profitability in the Health
Care Market Has Never Been Better." You, in whose higher
echelon, women of color are "missing almost altogether." The
problem is you've lost my trust. You've lost my trust and it's
going to take more than drop-down boxes to fix what you've
categorically destroyed.

**WOULD YOU LIKE 2D OR 3D IMAGING (PLEASE NOTE THAT
CALLBACKS ARE COMMON BUT LESS COMMON WITH 3D
IMAGING WHICH COST $100 MORE AND IS NOT ALWAYS
COVERED BY INSURANCE):** So I can pay one hundred dollars
for less anxiety? This smacks of smart marketing for a Medical
Industry in transactional relationship with an Insurance
Industry with the shared goal of profit. Yes. I'll pay you the
one hundred dollars. Because I want to sleep tonight. But I
will still get the callback. And in a calm voice that you have
spent decades perfecting, you'll offer me a choice of Monday
or Tuesday for a second appointment because you, "just
want to look a little closer at something." You will not use
the word, but I will find it on my uploaded medical record:
"SCREENING COMPLETED. COMMENTS: ABNORMAL"
and I will text my husband: "I feel like puking." That night,
my husband will lean against the wall and say, "Don't worry.
The chances are so small," and I will tell him that the friend
who doesn't like coconut posted on Facebook that breast
cancer affects one in eight women. That the National Center
for Biotechnology Information calls it a "modern epidemic."
I will tell him that I'm not as afraid of cancer as I am afraid of

anxiety. Because I think cancer eats anxiety for breakfast and the Industries of Medicine eat the profits of cancer for dinner. I will tell him that my appointment on Tuesday will probably be the first of many in which you will "just want to look a little closer at something" and I will be right. And my husband will get quiet and I will lie down in bed and try to sleep. It will take me a long time. I will toss and turn. But I will finally nod off, feeling knocked off my feet and swept—up and up—into the eye of your industrialized cyclone.

POSTSCRIPT: *Three years after the psychic told me this, in the process of copyediting and fact-checking this book, I reviewed my paternal grandmother's death certificate and noticed, for the first time, that under the smaller form question: "Other Conditions: (Include Pregnancy within three months of death)," the document is annotated in light cursive handwriting with, "93d."*

EMPTY THE TANKS

(Content warning for sexual violence and animal abuse.)

I'VE BEEN TO SEAWORLD. MY MEMORIES ARE MURKY. OF BLUE walls and hot metal benches and shrimp-smelling water evaporating on asphalt. I'm sure there's a photo somewhere in which I'm leaning against the turquoise tank, my little-girl arm pointing to the smooth black-and-white mass in constant turn of the pool's walls. I wonder if I flinched when I first saw the size of the Killer Whale in comparison to my own—over two hundred times my weight. Did I wave and beckon the starlet of the marine park closer?

I know I whispered to the whale because that was my nature. My house in Oregon—the center of my young girl world— was surrounded by horse pastures, and on my way home from every trip to the grocery store or library or school, I sat in the back of our tomato-red Suburban, scrunching my eyes under thick black bangs in deep wish. Because it was my theory that every human had a telepathic link to an animal and it was only a matter of trial and error to find the breed of beast with whom you shared a secret language.

To my great disappointment, the horses did not gallop behind our Suburban upon my mental command. They didn't even meander to the fence line or shuffle their manes in response to my manic whispers. But I was a determined little thing, and so I'm sure I scrunched my nose in wishful telepathy at the "Shamu" I saw at the marine park. Except "Shamu" was only a stage name, worn by a series of different Killer Whales in shows with titles like "Shamu the Yankee Doodle Whale" (1975–77), "Shamu, Take a Bow" (1982–84), and "The Shamu Adventure" (1998–2006). The Orcas jumped when told. They "waved" when told. They "smiled" when told. The performance was convincing.

It would not be until four decades later, while driving over Independence Pass in Colorado, that I learned the full story of one of those "Shamu" whales. I had downloaded the book *Beyond Words*, in which Carl Safina narrated the story of an Orca who was only four years old and barely finished nursing when she was hunted off the coast of British Columbia in 1969. Her family was encircled and chased to the docks where she was separated from her mother. Safina's telling of the sequence of abduction, isolation, and incarceration forced upon that small whale, named Corky by her captors, was unbearable. But it was one incident—the story of one glass-shattering cry—that made me pull over to the side of the road and weep. Emotions leaked, also, from some unnamed reservoir of my own body.

That night, I pulled extra pillows over my head and into my stomach, trying to muffle the thought of Corky's cry in my head. Unsuccessful, I grabbed my phone from the side table and moved from the bed to the collapsed corner of my living room couch. Sitting in the dark, I learned that sound is energy in acoustic form. It travels in undulating shapes and vibrates at a frequency measured in waves per second—or hertz. A bass guitar's natural frequency is 40 to 150 hertz, a woman's scream ranges from 30 to 150, and—according to the San Diego Opera—wineglass-shattering waves pass at 556 hertz. Orca vocals can reach 40,000 hertz, and the tank's glass that Corky shattered was an inch thick.

I opened a YouTube video to play a sound clip of a 40,000 hertz frequency tone. I tapped the volume down, anticipating the sound to be excruciating. But mid-video, unable to hear, I tapped the volume all the way up. My dog lifted her head from her bed. I watched her for a minute, returned my attention to my phone, and a Google search confirmed my suspicion: cats, rabbits, sea lions, opossums, and dogs can hear 40,000 hertz. Humans can't.

But that didn't muffle the vibration of Corky's story under my skin.

Carl Safina's book was published in 2015. The average age of death for a female Orca living at SeaWorld is twelve years old. In the morning, when I searched online for an update on Corky today, the chant of such volume in my head that I might have said it aloud was: *Let her be dead. Let her be dead. Let her suffering have stopped.*

To my horror, under the hashtag #emptythetanks is a recent photo of Corky, age fifty-eight. Her 8,000 pounds of wild muscle are perched on the edge of a cement tank, flukes poised in the air, back arched, chin up, frozen in pose for a stadium seating 5,500 humans with fingers and cameras pointing at Corky's forced "smile" of broken and missing teeth. Corky's teeth are gone or fractured from chewing the gates and concrete walls that enclose her. Her dental damage is significant as Corky is the single Orca who has lived longer than any Killer Whale in captivity. The "amusement" park where Corky works is open 365 days a year. Corky remains, today, a jewel of SeaWorld.

I slapped down my laptop. Didn't want to know more, and also needed to return to my own amusement park of modern motherhood: the merry-go-round of laundry, the roller coaster of screams from sibling strikes, the emotional drop tower of a wet-footed slip downstairs and a near-miss concussion. But not long after I collapsed into bed, I shuddered awake as Corky's scream boomeranged from my subconscious and hit me again. It wasn't a sound per se. But I remembered how my babies' low whimpers of night fever, on the other side of the house, could still startle me upright. They shared resonance. Except I could reach for my babies. Pick them up, nuzzle, and quiet them in my arms. While Corky lived a thousand miles away, under constant monitor of high-security cameras, circling a cement tank not twice as deep as her body long.

Needing more detail as to why Corky had once shattered a glass wall of her own tank, I dug deeper into her story. In 1980, Corky was eleven months pregnant. She was not new to pregnancy. She had already carried a calf to full term in 1977. When that calf was born, Corky tried to teach him how to swim in the circles the tank demanded. But the babe slammed into the walls, opening a wound on his tiny jaw. Corky buffered the babe from hitting the walls, but in doing so kept nudging the baby into a position where the calf could not sort where to suckle from his mother's mammary glands full of waiting milk. Unable to nurse, the calf withered. Humans removed the baby, winched in a sling by crane, from the pool to a place where they could force-feed him. A young scientist named Alexandra Morton, who was studying the communications of Killer Whales, was present that day. Morton described Corky's response after the babe was removed from her tank: "She flung her body again and again against the spot where humans stood to command her to perform jumps, wave her fin, give them a ride. Then, each time, she sank to the bottom and made the same call over and over for days, stopping only to grab a breath at the surface and then return to the bottom of the tank, where she lay on the drain."

I searched the newspapers in California that year. They used vague language like: "The first killer whale born in captivity . . . died soon after its birth" and "The calf, which weighed 300 pounds at birth, began losing weight" and "There was concern about the calf bumping into walls of the tank." But that baby never nursed. He died because he starved. Because he was born in a tank in which he could not learn to swim circles.

Six more of Corky's babies died in cement pools after the first. Not one calf lived longer than forty-six days. Alexandra Morton (who would later become famous for her thirty-year study of wild Killer Whales) dropped hydrophones into some of those tanks. She described her recordings of ". . . wispy newborn voices growing raspy and desperate as the babies slowly starved over a week to ten days."

Orcas are pregnant for about seventeen months. Corky today is no longer ovulating. But over the course of her time in captivity, she was pregnant more than 137 months. That's 11.42 years. I did the math three times: once to break the number into allotments of time that felt relatable; once to overcome my denial of the math; once to decide that 11.42 years of failed pregnancy is unfathomable—even, or maybe especially, as a woman who has experienced seven months of failed pregnancy herself. I don't like to remember those months. Sometimes I wonder if I've even lost memories. Memories that sat on the surface of life, while I lay upon the drain.

Alexandra Morton does not have a recording of the sound Corky made that broke glass. But she will never forget the day. According to the account in her book, she arrived at work and saw water pouring out of the park. She ran to the whale tank and found Corky "with a deep crease on the point of her face." Corky was more than halfway into another pregnancy. Morton had noticed that Corky liked to linger near the window of her tank that had a view of a gift shop where hundreds of miniature stuffed Orcas were stacked on display. This was the glass Corky shattered. The significance was not lost on Morton. She dropped to the floor amid the wet mini Orcas and broken glass—and cried.

A few weeks later, the baby Corky had in her womb was born dead.

ANOTHER MAMMAL SURPRISED BY A CROWD OF FOLLOWERS was Su Min. Su Min is a grandmother and retiree from Henan Province who, at fifty-six years old, became an "accidental feminist icon" with more than 1.3 million online followers. In the videos she posts to YouTube, her hair is pulled into a tight bun and a curt smile belies her age. She often can be found wearing a pink hoodie or gray tracksuit.

This unassuming grandma became an internet sensation because in the fall of 2020—after decades of adherence to the proper codes of conduct in China in her roles as wife, mother, and grandmother—Su Min installed a rooftop tent on her white Volkswagen Polo, waved goodbye to her abusive husband, and drove away.

Add me to the millions of fans following Su Min under #runawaywife. But who is Su Min to me? To American audiences? And where is the American version of Su Min? Because the "emergency" alert that recently arrived on my phone to the blare of a foghorn read something like this (I've changed names and ages):

> AMBER ALERT: Brandy Miller 1y, Damien Miller 7y, and Nolan Miller 5y. Last seen with Jessica Miller, who is 26y, 5'2" and has two bruised eyes. She's wearing leggings with a flower print.

The AMBER Alert system was created in 1996 in response to the murder of nine-year-old Amber Hagerman who was kidnapped while riding her bicycle in Texas. The system was meant to funnel moral panic into action. But it was built upon the misconception that strangers are the danger, when in fact the US Department of Justice in 2005 reported that fewer than 4 percent of murder victims under age thirteen were killed by non-family. These are the alerts that should be shaking every smartphone in America every day:

> REALITY ALERT: Men represent nearly 90 percent of homicide offenders.

> REALITY ALERT: More than twenty thousand phone calls are placed to domestic violence hotlines nationwide every day.

REALITY ALERT: More than one in three women in the United States has experienced rape, physical violence, and/or stalking by an intimate partner.

REALITY ALERT: 94 percent of the victims of murder-suicides are female.

Su Min escaped from a life of emotional and physical violence she characterized as "truly too upsetting." She shot to the surface of a selfhood disappearing down the drain. She left her husband, but not the cultural cage at large. Su Min hasn't yet said that she won't go back to her husband. She didn't even leave her husband until her children moved out of her house. Su Min has a daughter. And though her daughter is an adult, Su Min worries her daughter will feel obliged to care for Su Min's own husband in the absence of a wife. These tethers of children and inheritances of cycles of abuse point to urgent problems not fixed by our alert systems. Point a finger to the root problem that deserves our *moral panic funneled into action.*

Su Min's runaway "adventure" was only ever a positive spin on a symptom of global disease. Except Su Min has 1.3 million followers who cheered when they watched her shatter her own glass. And I don't think they watched only for entertainment. Later into her fame, Su Min reflected, "Before, I thought I was the only person in the world who wasn't happy."

I WILL CALL HER JANE BLANK BECAUSE SHE IS UNNAMED IN the news reports. I am unable to describe her other than the dead of her eyes that I know, because one in three women is sexually assaulted by a man, and we have all either been, or known, one of these women.

Jane's eyes might have been sparkling, curious, sharp, soft, or smart before they dimmed in October 2021. We will probably never know because Jane Blank is not known for who she was. She is known for being raped, repeatedly, on the El train in Philadelphia as it was traveling westbound. According to video footage, ten or more witnesses shuffled in and out of the train car as the man assaulted Jane Blank through more than two dozen train stops. No one stopped the rape. Doors opened. Doors closed. Doors opened. Doors closed. Jane's eyes went flat. Alexis Piquero, a criminologist commenting on the case of Jane Blank, said, "The onus is really on us as a collective . . . we need a world where people are doing the right thing when you see someone assaulted." The onus is also on men to stop raping people, but it's the shadows of Jane Blank's witnesses that stand, unmoving, for me as a reminder of our hardened arteries. Would I have stepped forward to stop Jane Blank's rape? I hope so, but who's to know which would have won: my spark of indignation and right action, or my trauma response of paralysis built by a lifetime of force-fed violence against my gender? In a span of fifty years, Corky suffered 137 months of forced and failed pregnancy. In 2023, the Supreme Court sentenced countless bodies to the unwanted captivity and imprisonment of forced reproduction. Did I fight when Roe was overturned? No. I sunk to the bottom of my tank and I cried. How many cried with me? And how many didn't cry, didn't feel the consequences themselves, but witnessed and did nothing?

When I was in high school, Trevor Gilmer told his friends, who told all the school, that the bloody white sock in the back of his black Jeep was the trophy of taking my virginity. When I found Trevor Gilmer at a house party that Friday night, I pushed him with two hands against a wall. I yelled, "Take it back. Tell the truth, you fucking liar." And with the eyes of the entire party on him, Trevor Gilmer looked around and then he looked at me. He looked me right in the eye and said, "It happened." This is how I learned that crowds believe men and men believe themselves. And that nothing has changed between a '90s high school keg party and the 2018 Senate Judiciary Committee.

Nothing has changed.

Except the pitch of my scream.

Those analyzing the case of Jane Blank have referenced the *bystander effect*, the phenomenon in which the more witnesses there are to a crime, the less likely any individual is to feel the responsibility to step in. We look around, see no reaction, assume it's "normal," and stay passive. Which makes sense of Corky's stadium seating 5,500 people. Which makes sense of the 330 million bystanders living in the United States who neglect the screaming fact that the tank into which women—and all marginalized people in America—are born is violent.

DECEMBER 11, 2023, MARKS CORKY'S FIFTY-FOURTH YEAR IN captivity. If SeaWorld would permit it, the Double Bay Sanctuary Foundation has plans for a sea-pen "retirement home" for her. In a section of ocean her family, the A5 Pod, still frequents, Corky could live and still receive the care captivity has made her survival dependent on. Remember, her teeth are worn or missing from fifty years of captivity. She's forgotten how to hunt food. She's now reliant on the systems that built her dependency. Su Min eventually returned home to her husband. She didn't own her own house, or the white Volkswagen. She didn't have savings. One anonymous writer posted in an update on Su Min, "The greatest pain in life is not that there is no hope or dream, but that after waking up, you are still desperate and can only wander in the same place."

In 2018, communications director David Koontz, speaking of the Orcas at SeaWorld, told CBC Radio Canada, "To take them out of this environment would be inhumane and irresponsible, and we will never take such a risk." Because it was *not* a risk to hunt Corky, separate her from her mother, and transfer her by flatbed truck and plane to California? Because it was *not* irresponsible to impregnate her repeatedly? Because it was *not* inhumane to isolate her from her family and hold her in a chlorinated cement chamber for more than fifty years? Yes, I have opinions on who gets to define what a risk is: the captor or captive. On what's a risk to a life versus a risk to a bottom line versus a risk to the foundation of a hierarchy that serves captors.

Patriarchy is not just a few "men in charge." It's an inundating network of social institutions and relationships that value the lives of straight, cisgender, male humans (ranked by wealth and whiteness) and confers to them power, privilege, and domination not only over women but over all other people and species. Dozens of male Orcas have been subjected to torturous lives of abduction, isolation, and captivity. Women passengers, undoubtedly, stepped in and out of Jane's train. Su Min can wave goodbye to her husband, but the international stadiums of witnesses that acculturate violence against women still surrounded her wherever she drove and set up her tent. Audiences, whether they accept it or not, are accountable. Terry Tempest Williams once said, "To bear witness is not a passive act."

I reached out to Howard Garrett, cofounder of the Orca Network, for an opinion on Corky's ability to safely travel to, and retire in, a sanctuary in the ocean. He said, "If William Shatner can be an astronaut at age ninety, Corky could theoretically be transported to her home waters and be cared for in every way she is now, but in a natural setting with more room to move and dive. Transport is not as stressful or risky as many make it out to be, with proper care and companionship." Corky's return to the ocean would also be symbolic: "A sanctuary is not just a place to live," Dr. Lori Marino, founder and president of the Whale Sanctuary Project, explains. "A sanctuary changes the cultural conversation from objectifying animals to respecting them . . ."

In 1993, ABC's *Nightline* did a segment on Corky. In it, the journalist Judy Muller, in a yellow jacket with feathered blond hair and chunky gold earrings, holds a black boombox in front of Corky's tank. She plays a recording of the sounds of the A5 Orca Pod (Corky's family) talking to each other in the wild. Orcas' vocalizations are not native but learned from family members and no two pods speak the same dialect. Scientists were curious as to whether Corky would recognize the voices of the family from which she was stolen. SeaWorld had previously denied the request to play the recording for Corky. But Judy Muller, with the cameras surrounding her, puts the staff on the spot. They relent. From the boombox, excited calls and chirps and whistles fill the stadium. At least four of the SeaWorld Orcas gather around Muller holding the boombox. They bob their bodies above the water. It's the first time Corky has heard the sounds of her family in twenty-four years. The camera zooms in on her as her body goes flat—horizontal—and begins to convulse. As tremors run the course of her flesh, the segment concludes, "But it's impossible to know if she's reacting to what she hears . . ."

THÍCH NHẤT HẠNH'S WORDS HAVE BEEN SWIRLING IN MY head with Su Min's destinationless car, and Jane Blank's relentless subway, and Corky in her tank. The famous Buddhist monk and peace activist was asked, "What's the most important thing we need to do in the face of the current ecological crisis?"

"What we most need to do," he replied, "is to hear within us the sound of the earth crying."

Does Corky feel the inheritance of the oceans she was denied in her whale bones? Does she long for the language by which six million years of her ancestry have evolved and shaped her great tongue? I don't know. But Corky's plight pierced my sleep. Her voice woke me and shook forth the scream that *is* my own. A scream that demands my daughter's rescue from her likelihood of violence by men. A scream at the reality that I am forced to teach her to swim in the circles of misogyny our culture normalizes. Misogyny normalized by Supreme Court justices, by elected presidents, by communication directors, and by the crowds who buy magazines with the slick bodies of women splashed across covers. Hierarchies by which everything wombed is seen as a target for extraction, reproduction, amusement, and exploitation. But of course, my objectivity of patriarchy is also murky; it's the only tank I've ever swum in. The scream haunting my nights, sourced in my womb and unmuffled by pillows, still tremors through my body. Circling, trying to find its way out. It speaks in a tongue that makes me tremble in grief for a loss I can barely name.

I'm sure my parents were pleased, all those years ago, when they treated their four children to a family vacation in California. They packed up the red Suburban with checkered sleeping bags, a blue cooler, tents, and cans of chili, and drove us a thousand miles south to San Diego. To SeaWorld, a thinly sliced piece of frosted American dream. They didn't know better. The dream of the amusement park was fed to them like the dead fish fed to Corky. The same flaccid story fed to me.

I called my mother. To bring forth more details of my foggy blue memories from that childhood trip. Could she remember exactly how old I was? "Oh yes, we actually went twice. The first time you were just a baby. I remember nursing you on the bleachers." That would put me in the stands, suckling at my mother's breast in 1977—the same spring Corky's first baby starved to death. My mother continued, "The second time we went, your little brother was in a stroller . . . so that means you must have been three years old? We were so excited because we found an empty bleacher that was close to the tank. We thought we'd found the best seats in the house— until the whale pushed water on us . . ." That was in 1980 and the spring of Corky's glass-shattering scream. I was only three, and my recollection—of the blue wall and shock of stinky tank water—is foggy because it's one of my first memories.

As of 2024, Corky is fifty-eight years old. Fifty-four of those years lived captive and performative and she is only one of the more than 3,500 whales, dolphins, and porpoises held captive around the world today. But once upon a time, Corky shattered glass. To shatter glass, the vibration of sound must match the resonation of what it shatters. What can our shared resonance with Corky's story tell us about shattering our own cages?

John Crowe was a professional diver who assisted with the capture of Corky's family off the coast of British Columbia. In the 2013 documentary *Blackfish*, he sits in a darkened living room. His burly beard and long gray hair mirror the image centered on his red T-shirt: Neptune, god of the sea, thrusting a three-pronged spear in a battle-ready pose. Crowe folds his heavily tattooed arms as he recounts of that day, ". . . they were trying to get the young Orca in the stretcher and the whole fam-damn-ly is out there, twenty-five yards away maybe, in a big line, and they're communicating back and forth." Crowe's big shoulders slump. He looks down at the floor. "Well, you understand then, what you're doing." He glances up at the camera under his tinted glasses, looks down again, shakes his head and exhales. "I lost it. I mean, I just started crying. I didn't stop working, but I just couldn't handle it." He lifts his hands to touch the creases at his forehead, covering his face, and continues, "Just like kidnapping a little kid away from their mother."

At the end of his account, Crowe shakes his head again and crosses his arms. "I've seen some things that it's hard to believe. But the worst thing that I've ever done is hunt that whale."

I'm not the only one haunted.

John Crowe heard it.

When Thích Nhất Hạnh said we need to hear the earth crying, I understood that sound as *a vibration of waves* we could reach for. Like when I furrowed my six-year-old brow in the back of the red Suburban.

I did not think it could reach back.

For those listening.

MY OCEANS

SHAKING THE ICE AT THE BOTTOM OF AN OLD FASHIONED, I
had let the confession surface with a shrug while forking kale
on my plate. But my friend across the table wouldn't have it.
She put down her silverware and placed both palms on the
table. "How is it possible I don't know this?"

"Not a sexy pirate," I defended myself, still stabbing at my
plate. "Not like some lone feral pirate . . ." I looked up and
over my friend's shoulder for the Blue Whale of my dream
job breaching a rainbow on the horizon, "I want to be a Sea
Shepherd eco-pirate!"

My friend put her white napkin to her lips. "Back up. Why
does this sound so much like a real thing?"

My dream vocation of battling ocean poachers was not something I had disclosed to even my husband or mother. For reasons
unknown, I had reserved the vision, indulged it only upon the
white wall of the laundry room while I folded toddler polka dot
leggings. But I'd been following Sea Shepherd for years. The
rebel group of sailors, researchers, and activists first became
infamous for chasing down Japanese whaling ships. Japan called
them pirates. But Sea Shepherd ran that title with a black flag
straight up their ship's mast.

After recounting these savory details to my friend, I continued, "Their leader, Captain Paul Watson, looks like a grade A

asshole: all wiry beard and jagged idealism and not a pinkie of diplomacy. Because the oceans are dying and he does not have time for this shit." I moved food around my plate. "I was looking at their job advertisement last week: *No pay. Long hours. Hard work. Dangerous conditions. Extreme weather. Wimps and whiners need not apply.*" I held my fork upright in the air like a trident: "More than anything in the world, I want to ram whaling ships!"

My friend blinked. "Christina, when did this begin?"

FROM MY SIX-YEAR-OLD UP-TIPPED CHIN, IT LOOKED HIGHER than the Sears Tower, and by all 1980s treehouse standards, it was not just outstanding, but authentically dangerous. The first level alone, cornered by four seventy-year-old Oregon pines, was a leg-breaking distance from the ground. The second floor required assistance of knotted rope. Yet my big brother did not stop building there. Still another seven feet up—and a stumble away from childhood death—was the lookout: a one-child-sized platform from which one could monitor forest paths for intruders.

I spent all the summer months in the forest behind our house, amassing pine cones and ordering a motley crew of neighborhood kids to amass more. When the kid in the lookout spotted a rustle in the bushes, we'd sound alarms and aim pine cones with a bike tube stretched between branches. We rigged pulley systems and zip lines. I ordered a strict rotation on the tire swing. We ran a thousand attack and evacuation drills. We called it a treehouse, but it was a tree-ship.

I didn't know what I was training for.

MY FATHER WAS NOT SO DIFFERENT FROM CAPTAIN PAUL Watson—either in wiry white beard or what my mom called a disorder of *oppositional defiance.* But out in his silver dinghy in the open Pacific Ocean, we didn't doubt Dad. Dad didn't doubt Dad. I think that's what makes a captain a captain. We just followed his lead, dropping crab traps and then salmon lines that we held with white fingers between shaking thighs. Eventually, Dad would have a hunch of crab-trap luck and his brown arms would flex as they pulled up our loot. Our job was to grasp the Dungeness Crabs between our diffident thumbs and forefingers; turning each over to reveal the sex, tossing females overboard and saving only the biggest males to boil alive. On the way to shore, we ran into sand bars, out of gas, or into more weather. They were the longest days of my life. I didn't whine. I didn't complain. I wasn't paid. And I learned something from my weathered dad: about loving the sea, and about conviction.

IN MY EARLY TWENTIES, I HOVERED UNDERWATER LIKE A samurai, legs folded, hands clasped behind my back to remind the student divers that scuba diving does not involve touching. I'd rap my metal air tank to produce a muffled *clank, clank.* When I captured the attention of wide eyes under masks, I kept one hand behind my back and unfolded the other in the direction of the steely-eyed Great Barracuda overhead, or the Cowfish fluttering through Fire Coral, or the fluorescent glow of a perched nudibranch. Always, I scanned overhead, looking for my ocean hero—the Spotted Eagle Ray—whose iridescent spots flashed in wavy sunlight as she soared through underwater skies in a slow-motion version of her bird-of-prey namesake.

My PADI divemaster ID number is 178842. I took up professional diving because I love the ocean and I'm a bad swimmer. Good divers know diving has nothing to do with swimming. Diving has everything to do with witnessing. My favorite dives weren't the wall dives, or shipwreck dives, or even the cave dives. My favorites were the *muck dives,* where it takes patience to spot a sputter of life camouflaged in tan sand: the waving grass of Garden Eels retreating under my shadow, a Slender Seahorse hooked like a pendant on a sprig of Sea Fan, or the flowing gown of an iridescent octopus in retreat. It was a new world revealed to me, except that 71 percent of Earth's surface is ocean and the oceans came first, which makes me the newcomer. All that time held buoyant in the womb of the world? It sank Rachel Carson's words in *The Sea Around Us* like an anchor in me: "As life itself began in the sea, so each of us begins his individual life in a miniature ocean within his mother's womb." Of the planet's blue belly, Captain Paul Watson's repeated admonishment also moored in my guts: "If the oceans die, we die."

ON THE QUEENSLAND COAST OF AUSTRALIA IN 2002, A YOUNG ship captain waved me away from the group, to the back of the boat. It was half-dare, half-flirt. "Do you want to do a night dive with sharks?"

Into thicker wetsuits we slipped.

Bobbing on top of black ocean, the young captain instructed, "Turn off your light. We'll wait in the dark and then I'll turn on my flashlight. Sharks swim toward light, so they'll swim at us. As you know, there's nothing to be afraid of."

I'm sure his ploy ensured all the pretty divemasters on his boat grasped his bicep and pulled closer. Despite my pride, the trick worked. I could not tally the black-eyed metal bodies that snaked toward us that night.

In the last fifty years, sharks off the Queensland coast have declined by as much as 92 percent. *National Geographic* tells me baby coral in Australia's Great Barrier Reef diminished 89 percent in 2018 from mass bleaching in 2016 and 2017.

The thing about witnessing is the expanded scope of concern. The things that swam past my mask, they didn't disappear into the coral and extinguish from my mind. They stayed. They swam into my expanded worldview. A world in which I'm wondering what, today, is left of those landscapes I visited only nineteen years ago? Ghost towns of bony coral? An exoskeleton of dead sea?

Today, if you drop sixty feet into that night ocean and shine a light, will anything—anything at all—swim toward it?

TWO MEN TOOK OFF ON FOOT. I FOLLOWED.

"What is it? Will it live?" I asked.

The answer tipped the circle of chins down. "A porpoise. Not for long."

One man restrained the animal's tail to protect it from the jagged rocks reaching up through Costa Rica's iconic tan sand.

I had been sleeping that week under the blue tarps of a conservation group, helping patrol a Pacific beach in rotating night shifts to stop poachers from stealing eggs from nesting sea turtles. Before sunset that evening, news of a beached animal reached our team.

When I caught up to the men who had run down the beach, they were huddled in crashing waves around a black thrashing mass.

I waded deeper into the water.

The porpoise stopped thrashing. Its black eye focused skyward.

I reached out, placed my palm above the porpoise's pectoral fin, and was grasped in the chest—*shaken* as if touched by live wire.

Whatever it was that moved through me, it pushed me onto my knees.

My head dropped. The bowels of the porpoise broke. And the water around me turned black with waste and blood.

I couldn't name it that night.

But what I found in the black water was something I could live, fight, and die for.

BEFORE I WANTED TO BE AN ECO-PIRATE, I WANTED TO WORK at the Charles Darwin Research Station (CDRS) on the Galápagos Islands. I flew to Quito and submitted my *Ficha de Aplicación* in Spanish along with three letters of recommendation. I listed my availability as *inmediatamente* and my "duration of volunteering period" as, *un año por lo menos*. No response time from the CDRS was promised so I took a ten-hour bus ride to the Ecuadorian coastline nearest in longitude to the Galápagos Islands. There, I checked my email daily from an internet café in Bahía de Caráquez.

While I waited, I joined the team of a reforestation project and passed my days watering and repotting juvenile *guachapelí*, guayacan, Fernán Sánchez, and ceiba trees. When not planting, I read. The volunteer coordinator, a tattooed gardener from New York City, left *The Monkey Wrench Gang* (Edward Abbey's most famous work of fiction) on my bed. In it I read: "The wilderness once offered men a plausible way of life. Now it functions as a psychiatric refuge. Soon there will be no wilderness. Soon there will be no place to go. Then the madness becomes universal. And the universe goes mad."

After five months of checking my email, I was out of money and accepted a job guiding college students through India. Soon after I got on my plane, I received an email from Patricia Zárate B., a marine biologist representing the Sea Turtles and Shark Conservation projects at the Charles Darwin Research Station. She inquired as to my availability.

Me and my Galápagos dream passed like ships in the night.

But that tattooed New Yorker? Her stories of seed-bombing vacant lots in the city stuck with me. Along with Edward Abbey's billboard-burning Doc Sarvis and his refrain: *When the situation is hopeless, there's nothing to worry about.*

These characters, they erected something in me that refused to sit back down.

I'VE ALWAYS DESCRIBED THE MAN I MARRIED AS A COWBOY. A guy who can slip under the hood of any car, computer, or sink and wrangle a fix. A man who always has a black smudge on his brow, cuts on his hands, dirt under his nails. I used the term *cowboy* because I couldn't find the right description. But a question sailed into my mind one night and I texted my mother in the morning.

"Mom, why do I know every word of *The Pirates of Penzance* musical?" I suddenly couldn't shake the songs from the comic opera out of my head.

She typed back: "Ha! You had such a funny relationship with that VHS tape. You watched that film on repeat for years."

But sitting up in bed, I knew why.

Because, that night, it was Kevin Kline who sailed into my dream on the bow of a ship under a snapping black flag. If my mother had thought her youngest daughter was suffering a first crush for the blond, rose-lipped, fickle young pirate-in-training, Frederick, she was mistaken. My eyes were squarely trained on the cuffed leather thigh boots, purple headband, and exposed chest of black curls on the "too-tenderhearted" Pirate King.

Waking up to this realization and staring at the ever-black beard of my husband wrapped in billows of white bedsheets next to me, I texted my mother back.

She confirmed, "Yes. You married the Pirate King!"

BETWEEN THE AGES OF THIRTY-FOUR AND THIRTY-EIGHT, I was pregnant four times. Four tides of blood nurtured four aquatic beings. Four globes of body and sea swelled in my belly. Four heartbeats I first heard by sonography.

Killer Whales, Narwhals, and dolphins hear ultrasound. They can decipher the sounds of two hearts beating in the belly of a pregnant woman just as well as a doctor with a Doppler. Porpoises have the highest known upper hearing limit of all animals. *When I fell onto my knees in the Pacific Ocean of Costa Rica, was it me feeling her pulse? Or her hearing mine?*

Two of the four heartbeats I nurtured in my womb stopped early. Those two missing heartbeats drowned me in an ocean of tears. But the tide came back, and I brought two babies into this world. And when my children's bodies no longer fed off mine, I visited the osteopathic physician with complaints of brain fog, rashes, and recurring nightmares. After months of testing, the toxicity reports trembled in my hands as the doctor explained her conclusion: my body was overburdened with industrial chemicals and heavy metals. Fumbling for comprehension, I asked if the toxins had anything to do with my pregnancy losses. And what about my children? I nursed them each for a year! Melting my body fat into milk. But the doctor had just explained that fat is where toxins lodge, and that the biggest toxin offload in a woman's life is when she nurses her first child.

In response to my questions, the doctor looked down.

Breast milk laced with gasoline additives, plastic manufacturing chemicals, heavy metals, and pesticides!

My body.

My children.

My milk.

My oceans.

THERE IS ANOTHER CHARACTER I WATCHED CLOSELY, AS A little girl, in *The Pirates of Penzance*. Angela Lansbury plays the nursery maid who tends to the domestic care of the boy Frederick on the pirate ship of hooligans. In the opening scene of the film based on the Broadway play, Lansbury hangs the boy's laundry on a ship sail. She wears a frilled apron over a baby blue smock and a white bonnet over her hair, which is rolled down either side of a center part. But this Lansbury is not the one who impressed her memory upon me. The Lansbury I remember is the one who returns mid-film and jumps out of the bushes in a red and gold-tasseled suit over a popped white collar. She has a cocked feathered hat over a sleek wave of bangs, and *this* Lansbury brandishes a single-edged saber.

She's, of course, not the main character. Her transformation, from nursemaid to pirate, happens offstage. But she does drop an important hint: She mentions her "accumulated" forty-seven years. And that gets me thinking: about my forties and the potential for my own offstage transition—from apron to black boots. It would, of course, be rosy to ignore the criminality of a pirate's nature. Their behavior is notoriously bad. But there is also something in which the commoner—or the woman caged by domesticity—thrills: It's the desire to give up unsustainable comforts, the instinct to desert laws built to repress her, the impulse to break free from corseting gender, cultural, and sexual roles. To leave behind the rules of colonized lands, and to seek laws of spirit that supersede those merely man-made.

MY DAD USED TO SCOWL WHEN I, AS A CHILD, TORE OPEN and ate packet after packet of white saltines, letting the hot crabs and clams on the picnic bench go cold. I have always hated seafood. This, at first, concerned me, because what kind of pirate doesn't eat fish?

You know what kind of pirate doesn't eat fish? An eco-pirate. The entire fleet of Sea Shepherd ships is vegan. Sea Shepherd Captain Oona Isabelle Layolle confirmed this fact when I met her over Skype after she answered the letter I sent her under the title, "A Too-Long Email."

I had heard about Captain Oona Isabelle Layolle in banter with a marine biologist at an environmental writers' workshop. We were exchanging shared ocean stories: hearing dolphins under the hum of a boat deck, jumping into the fireworks of phosphorescence, and the universal crankiness of boat captains, when I asked, "Do you know Sea Shepherd? I've been obsessed with them for years." The marine biologist said, "Funny, I might actually know a woman who's captain of a Sea Shepherd ship . . ."

A woman Sea Shepherd captain?! All along I'd been watching Sea Shepherd documentaries that featured men or Paul Watson himself. Captain Watson, of course, I admired for his uncompromising vision and intolerance for bullshit. But I had co-captained with enough male visionaries in my life to be intimately familiar with the unmentionable qualities that fringe them. I was also beginning to suspect a connection between the domination of women and denigration of oceans. Between ecofeminism and ecopiracy.

But there existed a woman Sea Shepherd captain?
My heart breached.

ONE EVENING, I USED BUTTERED POPCORN TO BAIT MY CHIL-dren into watching *My Octopus Teacher*. Their wiggly bodies nestled close to mine under a blanket. I desperately wanted to give my unbroken attention to the slow-building relation-ship between Foster and the wild octopus, but the kids filled the quiet of those buoyant scenes with one million questions: "How does he stay down there?" "Is it cold?" "What's he wait-ing for?" "Why's it called a Pajama Shark? They should call it a Jail Shark!" "Is the octopus going to die?"

Nash threw the blanket over his head at every appearance of the shark and Riva shuddered with tears over the octopus's decomposing body. I wiped tears from cheeks and rubbed backs, wondering if it had been a poor decision to include the kids. But Nash, after the credits, looked me in the eye and said with per-fect conviction, "When I grow up, I want to do that." But will my son have time to grow into it? Or any of his dreams of pro-tecting wild things?

Because already in 2022, solar-powered nudibranches are "too rare to research." In 2024, the Spotted Eagle Ray is classified as "Near Threatened with Extinction." And in the year of Nash's seventh birthday, a Chinese-flagged ship was apprehended near the Galápagos Islands with 300 tons of dead endangered species, including 6,600 sharks.

I recently took my daughter to the Pacific tidepools of my youth. We found a hermit crab and she squealed as it unfolded in the palm of her hand, but I noticed the sheen of sunscreen chemicals in the rocky pools behind her. A scientist in Colorado, last year, was looking for fragments of metals and coal in rain samples and what he found was microplastics. It's raining plas-tic. Raining plastic on the carrot seeds we scatter in our garden. Raining plastic on my kids' heads as they walk out the door to school. Raining plastic into the creek over our berm where fox, elk, and bear drink. Raining toxins on the soil that quenches the body of the lands we call home.

At night, as my daughter tucks her pink bear, brown mouse, and blue Narwhal under the covers of her bed, I'm thinking of *her* oceans. And I'm thinking of the oceans that pink bear, brown mouse, and blue Narwhal represent. In my daughter's favorite book, a Narwhal looks for alphabet letters. Meanwhile, in the Arctic, Narwhals are navigating depleting sea ice, shipping routes, marine construction, and military noise pollution. The fables I read and the realities of my children's future *clank, clank* in my head like metal on a scuba tank.

The threats are at the top of the stairs to my home.

They bang at my door.

THE DAY AFTER MY WHISKEY-INDUCED PIRATE CONFESSIONS to my friend, I reopen the Sea Shepherd Volunteer Job Description, which is bookmarked in my browser for easy reference. There is a Q&A section in which Captain Paul Watson is asked, "Some of your former crew has complained that they were put into unsafe situations. Is that true?"

The captain responds, "Of course it's true."

As I stare out my window onto the canvas of the cul-de-sac, I picture myself standing on the deck of the *Steve Irwin*, Sea Shepherd's 194-foot flagship. I imagine myself as one of the tiny human shadows hidden in the jagged black, gray, and blue camo of the ship's full-body war paint. On the deck of this vision, I'm minuscule next to Sea Shepherd's whale-sized logo painted on the bridge: a blazing-white skull crossed with Neptune's trident and the shepherd's staff. This ship was "laid up for disposal" *before* she was purchased by Sea Shepherd. She has since ground through ice floes, smashed through storm belts in the Southern Ocean, chased Chinese poachers to port, and ripped a three-foot gash at her stern when she "roughly kissed" a Japanese harpoon vessel.

To "monkey wrench" a system is to throw a tool into machinery that brings the machine to a halt. But do women even need a tool? Are we not already the predominant managers of birth and education and care and community? Are we not the machinery itself? Motherhood was not the end, but the beginning. Of recognizing the "unsafe situation" we are already in. Of having nothing to lose, and everything left, to fight for. The pirate in me, she is my protective rage manifest. A sacred rage that flares in defense of everything precious and dying. My domestic years—I see now—put an end to as much as they began. We need only the impulse to shake our sense of risk. For as Captain Paul Watson says, "Sometimes, the good guys wear black."

IN MY PREP FOR OUR VIDEO CHAT, I STALKED CAPTAIN OONA Isabelle Layolle's Instagram account. The majority of her posts were given to the ecosystems she loves: long stretches of beaches she's cleaned with burlap sacks, blazing red balls of falling sun shot from the summits of mountains she's climbed, the forest of her French Alps turning all shades of autumn fire. Also featured were a number of wild characters: a 180-year-old tortoise, two swimming stingrays, a black crow, the tiniest hermit crab in the palm of her sandy hand, an assortment of street dogs that Layolle hugged and scruffed by the neck, and the outline of the last pod of Vaquita Porpoises tattooed swimming over her shoulder blade. In one photo, Layolle was photographed at the helm of a ship. Her body was sheathed in white and yellow weatherproof neoprene with silver reflective patches on the shoulders and a black harness wrapped around her waist. Her brown hair blew across her face as her blue eyes scanned a distant sea horizon.

"Wait. She's hot, isn't she?" My husband interrupted my description of Layolle, turning from the skillet on the range and holding up the dirty spatula in his hand. After my interview with Layolle, I had finally confessed to my husband all my secret pirate dreams. It was a necessary progression: the exploration of my obsession with a best friend, my mother, myself, and then partner. Marking the occasion, I sipped whiskey on the rocks.

"Of course she's hot. Like rugged, sea pirate hot," I confirmed. On the day Captain Oona Isabelle Layolle appeared on my Skype video, she was wearing a light blue sweater and her hair was calm and shiny, unwindblown. We smiled. The conversation was easy. After I covered my twenty-one questions, I asked if there was anything we missed.

She replied, "We haven't addressed your last question . . ."

I blushed.

The last question in the list I'd emailed her was: *Is there a place for a middle-aged, writer-mom aboard any vessel you'll be captaining? (I'm half-joking.)*

Looking down and shuffling my notes, a shy laugh escaped. "You know. I've held this Sea Shepherd fantasy for so long, it was getting a little cagey . . ."

She broke through my ramble, "You can come on the next vessel I captain. But I'm done taking orders from others. I'm working for myself from now on. So I don't know when it will be . . ."

"Deal," I cut in.

I am charmed by this ongoing pirate plot and its merger with my real life path. Enchanted by the possibilities of a second life of rough kisses. The famous French intellectual and feminist Hélène Cixous once wrote, "Women must write through their bodies, they must invent the impregnable language that will wreck partitions, classes, and rhetorics, regulations and codes, they must submerge, cut through, get beyond . . ."—and that's a ship I can get on right now. I don't have to be a pirate to stand on the deck of my life, wind lashing my hair, with my protective feminine rage at the helm of my body.

POSTSCRIPT: *In the summer of 2022, Captain Paul Watson, amid irreconcilable organizational disagreements, cut all ties with the Sea Shepherd Conservation Society. He now oversees the Captain Paul Watson Foundation at www.paulwatsonfoundation.org. To learn more about Sea Shepherd's projects to protect marine life, visit www.seashepherd.org.*

OBITUARY

PATRIARCHY, BORN IN 3100 B.C.E., DIED AND WENT TO BE with his Lord after a long and global rein in human culture. Patriarchy, whose name in Greek translates to "father of a race," was raised by Religion and Tradition and upheld by thousands of years of books, social codes, curricula, taboos, and laws penned by men. Also known as Male Supremacy (to his brothers White Supremacy and Class Supremacy), Patriarchy worked, without tire, to build persistent and global structures of male control over all women—being extra careful to leave no other marginalized genders behind. Patriarchy's notable successes include outstanding rates of domestic violence, global femicide, rape culture, genital mutilation, governmental controls over women's bodies, and the US election of a pussy-grabbing president. Patriarchy's bond with Mother Earth was famous, leaving a near-perfect legacy of unchecked assault. Though Patriarchy rarely receives credit (the evidence "lost" in ancient human history), his most lasting influence was likely that of changing God's pronouns from *she/they* to *he*. Patriarchy enjoyed a quiet last century under the perception of progress toward gender equality: standing strong against women's attempts to "lean in," and fully endorsing the dream that women can "have it all"—so long as they stay on top of the laundry and under male "mentorship." Patriarchy's recent tributes include #metoo hashtags, gun-toting incels, catcalls, political witch hunts, the reverse victimization of "political witch hunts," and, of course, the insistent narrative that vulnerability is weak. Patriarchy is survived by a long lineage of women captive from the day their mothers put pink booties on their feet; women who dutifully remind their daughters not to be "too angry" and that "boys will be boys" in a societal case of Stockholm syndrome. Patriarchy's survivors include all the men who "abhor male supremacy" so long as none of their existing advantages or immunities are renegotiated, and all the husbands who have never set up a child's dentist appointment, submitted a summer camp form, or who struggle to see the tidy loads of invisible labor from which they benefit. Patriarchy brilliantly comprehended the value of this level of pervasiveness, knowing there is nothing more threatening to any institution than a collection of waking women. Ever the charmer, Patriarchy winks at us from heaven with each wrong identification of the perpetrator in "mom rage" and the prolific use of toxic positivity encouraging women to combat millennia of institutional repression with a high gloss "Smile!" It is really so tragic that Patriarchy died from fatal wounds when cut off at the one-minute mark of his last speech. Those whose lives were touched without consent by Patriarchy in the home, workplace, and streets are invited to an open casket viewing of his final shriveling. Colonialism and Bigotry sent regards but didn't want to get canceled. Guests are also invited to the cremation. In lieu of flowers, please send kindling. For anyone unable to attend, but not OK with the wrinkled hands still groping under the table of her country and culture, a memorial collection basket with blank cards will sit on Patriarchy's headstone. Upon the card, she may grab a Sharpie and surrender to her gripping compulsion to write it dead.

ACT III

FATHOMS

We are being asked to dream, or more accurately,
to become receptive to the dreaming earth.

—Francis Weller

QUIESEEDS

AT AGE FORTY, I TOOK AN INTELLIGENCE TEST. NOT THE STANdardized IQ, but a newer assessment created by Harvard doctor Howard Gardner. Dr. Gardner suspected intelligence couldn't be boxed by one overarching mechanism and might be better represented by the many dimensions in which different people process information. After filling in the little boxes of Gardner's survey and tallying my results, I was shocked by the conclusion.

I shot an email, in jest, to my boss for whom I had already worked over fifteen years, "So, my intelligence type is something called 'naturalistic.' How does that apply to what I do?"

My boss didn't laugh. It had not been his idea for me to take the survey. And he was a smart man. That I had completed the assessment on my own initiative pointed to a leak in my loyalty to my senior administrative position at the company he'd founded. I was unaware of the leak myself and had only thought the results curious. Dr. Gardner's test concluded my primary strength—as one high in "Naturalistic Intelligence"—was finding patterns and relationships to nature. How exactly did that align with the spreadsheets, surveys, staffing interviews, and statistical reports that consumed my fifty hours a week managing the deployment of international student education programs?

I laughed too because "Naturalist" was not even included in Dr. Gardner's famous book, *Multiple Intelligences: New Horizons in Theory and Practice*, when it was first published in 1993. Dr. Gardner only added the eighth "green branch of intelligence" to his model years later—around the time I was in high school. Dr. Gardner characterized the naturalist's intelligence as having an innate inclination for observation, a curiosity for seeing how things work, and an instinctual connection with nonhuman species. That description felt familiar, yet distant. It also plucked at the nerve of one of my greatest insecurities. My boss was famous for picking résumés from stacks organized by the prestige of Ivy Leagues. At company gatherings, he introduced staff with orations of their academic achievements. I didn't have that list, so he always described me as "the only person I hired based solely on a cover letter." I blushed because his deflection pointed a finger at my fear that I was not smart enough to fit in with the PhD types with whom I shared a mission statement. Except maybe it was I who had a different mission statement, yet unwritten?

I didn't have to struggle long with the question as a pandemic would effectively toss me from the company and drown me in stay-at-home orders, homeschooling, and quarantines from "the village it takes" for a modern mother to attend also to a career. But the enclosing walls of my house pressurized my creativity, and in the dawn hours, lit by a driftwood-scented candle, I churned a year of handwritten journal pages into the meditations in this book. My paragraphs finally shed their cover-letter clothing and became the essays they always wanted to be. The pandemic spat me out a writer, often with "nature" or "environmental" added to my introductions and bios. I found a new and sparkling sense of fitting-in-ness within the circles of poets and artists, who were easily distracted by the constellations in night skies outside nature-themed writing workshops. And indeed nothing makes me happier than chewing on the end of my pen over a blank page on which I lyrically doodle about the wingspans of manta rays, the mothering of Sperm Whales, and the life cycles of plankton. Yet I still doggy paddle in impostor syndrome. For I am not a biologist or cetologist, nor an ocean-ographer. I am just a woman with a pen, a profound love for water, and an eye for noticing patterns in the currents, eddies, and swirls of living.

There's a word for seeing relations in the world as flowing. *Atmorelational* is defined as "looking at the space or relation-ship between things as the primary point of focus." If you don't remember learning this word, that's because it's not in Webster's dictionary. You'll find this neologism only in the online dictionary created by the Bureau of Linguistical Reality. On the Bureau's website is where I learned how the term *atmorelational* was influenced by the work of the Caribbean poet and philosopher Édouard Glissant, and then offered to the Bureau of Linguistical Reality by Léopold Lambert and a group of Field Study 010 par-ticipants during the Paris Climate Conference of 2015. The word is new to the world because the dictionary created by the Bureau of Linguistical Reality is about the same age as my daughter. Heidi Quante and Alicia Escott, when they devised and launched the project in 2014, described it as a "participatory artwork" informed by the public for the purpose of "collecting, translating, and creating a new vocabulary for the Anthropocene."

Though this Anthropocene dictionary is online and exists in no paper, printed, or otherwise material form, I was so strangely thrilled that I created one for myself. I printed out each word onto a notecard and stacked them on my desk. Their physical existence brings me joy, this naming of things I have felt for a lifetime, but which had no official recognition. Words like:

Neopangea, neo-pan-jee–uh: *A hypothetical way of thinking the world is no longer geographically separated.*

Kincara, kin-car-uh: *A person of any gender who plays a loving, maternal role in raising children they have not physically birthed.*

Shadowtime, shad-ow-time: *The notion of a timescale in which the near future will be drastically different from the present.*

Epoquetude, epo-qu-e-tude: *The reassuring awareness that while humanity might succeed in destroying itself, the Earth will survive us.*

Surbrace, sur-brās: *Conviction to do the right thing after one has already let go of the outcome.*

I love these words. They name so many of my secret, but otherwise unhoused, sentiments. Which was exactly the goal of the project. Quante and Escott created the dictionary because they felt at a loss for words to describe the emotions, ideas, and situations relevant to the current reality of our climate crisis.

I feel a recognition of what's missing in the stack of cards on my desk. They give me permission to think outside the box of Webster's dictionary. To name things in my own life that hold audience in my heart but lack proper name. Words like . . .

The verb for missing the blue of a Colorado sky underneath a dangerous AQI of smoke.

An adjective for the ache in my bones for the absence of migratory birds in the sky.

The adverb describing my heart's retraction in contemplation of the loneliness of the last Vaquita Porpoise on the planet.

THOUGH THEY (PROBABLY) HAVE NO WORD FOR IT, WHALES know the atmorelational. Rebecca Giggs in her book *Fathoms* explains, "Because cetaceans evolved their communicative abilities in the absence of hands, facial expressions, head-on eye contact, and within an underwater environment unfurnished by graspable objects, they evolved a 'language' centered exclusively on their interrelationships." I love this notion: that in vast seas and the absence of cues, the space *between* whales became the point of focus. The whale's evolution gives me hope in the face of the growing isolation of humans on Earth. Maybe a shift of perspective awaits in the vastness? A revolution that holds the space *in between* things in focus?

A study in 2013 at the University of Pennsylvania analyzed nearly a thousand MRIs and concluded that while male brains have more connections within each hemisphere, women's brains are more interconnected with fiber pathways that zigzag *between* hemispheres that "facilitate communication between analytical and intuitive processing modes." When I read this, I sat up in bed, called my husband, and pointed a finger at the research on my laptop. "Babe! This is why I can't tune the kids' voices out when we are trying to talk, and you don't even hear them! My left and right brain sides do more talking to each other!" He leaned into the bedroom from the hall, cocked his head, then disappeared without comment back into the noise of the football game in the living room.

The right and left brain functions have sometimes been oversimplified (or incorrectly reduced to the idea of individuals "favoring" one side or the other), but what remains true is that the two sides work differently. While the left hemisphere might process the sounds that form a sentence, the right hemisphere might spin abstractions off the language. In general, the right brain is less logical, nonverbal, and recognizes images, integrates feelings, appreciates aesthetics, and can synthesize multiple dimensions at once. Leonard Shlain, in his book *The Alphabet Versus the Goddess*, further delves into the powers of the right brain: "When people find it necessary to express in words an inner experience such as a dream, an emotion, or a complex feeling-state, they resort to a special form of speech called metaphor that is the right brain's unique contribution to the left brain's language capacity. The word metaphor combines two Greek words—*meta*, which means 'over and above,' and *pherein*, 'to bear across.'"

To *bear across* from *over and above* sounds a lot like the *atmorelational*. Could the language of the atmorelational *live* in the right brain? A mode of intuitive processing often repressed in human society alongside the oppression of women and the arts and the queer and all the cognitively non-normative?

This question brings me back to Gardner's "naturalistic" category into which I had no idea I slipped footing until that fateful survey day. Except maybe I did not slip footing as much as I found a little ground. Like the nook under the rhododendrons where I crawled when I was five. Like the tunnel I dug through the blackberry bushes when I was eight. Like the hidden bay near the river where I'd cry when the dramas of high school punched too hard. Like the Cenote caves of the Yucatan into which I scuba dived over a hundred feet, where the nitrogen narcosis wove tree roots into a vision of my suspension in the basket of an Oriole's nest. Seems I've always been looking for nooks in nature where I could find home. And that my impostor syndrome was less a task of fitting in, than finding an identity in which I could burrow.

WHALE SONGS MIGHT NOT ONLY TRAVERSE THE HEMISPHERES of the planet, but also their brains. In a 2017 study, accelerometers were attached to Blue Whales to record their precise movements. Researchers discovered the whales demonstrated a preference for left-turned movements in shallow waters. These "lefty" whale movements likely correlated with right-brained thinking. Cetaceans also use echolocation to bounce sound off underwater landscapes to "see" the size, distance, speed, and density of objects in returning sound waves. Bioacousticians consider this holosonic picture language a multidimensional form of communication. When Leonard Shlain wrote, "A medium of communication is not merely a passive conduit for the transmission of information but rather an active force in creating new social patterns and new perceptual realities," he was not talking about whales. But I am. Humpback songs once nearly went silent when they were hunted to only 450 individuals in the 1950s. It wasn't only the mass murder of a species, but also the near-genocide of a unique picture language. Which makes me wonder how the biodiversity of human language and consciousness has likewise been harpooned?

Quante and Escott similarly point to the immense cultural power of the *absence* of words in language. They note the word "genocide" was only invented in the 1940s when lawyer Raphael Lemkin combined the Greek word *genos* "race, people" with the Latin *cīdere* "to kill" and used the new word to describe "the destruction of a nation or ethnic group." But it was only after the word was created and used that humans could fully conjure and hold the tragic human phenomena of *genocide* in mind. What other realities have we disappeared by lack of a proper noun? And what other possibilities—after we break constraints to a book founded in 1806 by a racist man named Noah Webster—can we freely begin to fathom?

HUMPBACK SONGS ARE TYPICALLY MADE OF REPEATING PATterns that can travel ahead and behind paths of migration. When one whale hears another's song, the pattern can evolve into a more complex version of the same song. But once every three years, Humpback songs change in structure entirely! A team at the University of Queensland explained in Gigg's book, "When their songs cannot become more ornate and still be remembered . . . then the degree of complexity crashes. A whale singing a less demanding song stands out against those attempting poorly learned, but more complicated tunes." During these cultural shifts, new whale songs sweep the seas in simpler compositions. Scientists call them "revolutionary songs."

As for my own vocabulary revolution? The stack of new words on my desk has moved to a new home in my heart. *Neopangea* has recollected the continents into a shared shape, bringing my host families in Senegal and India and Colombia as close as they have always felt in my memories. *Kincara* is the flushed face of my childless-by-choice best friend after driving through a snowstorm to sit on the couch and teach my daughter her first chords on the guitar. *Shadowtime*—that alternate reality right over my shoulder—aligns my gratitude in equal step with my grief. I find *epoquetude* when I sit in the gnarled-root arms of a three-thousand-year-old Bristlecone Pine tree and surrender to its densely storied resiliency. And *surbrace* is my daily practice of letting go of my fear, to focus on loving this life one good day at a time.

This integration of novel words into my new worldview, "affecting perception, cognition, and decisions," is called linguistic relativity. A theory built on the idea that language is the expression of the spirit of a nation. Which gets me thinking of how new language—a new melody—could, in turn, influence the spirit of my country. And of what new verses have the potential to sweep our culture in undulating revolutions of new, uncomplicated meaning? Ursula K. Le Guin spoke to this power of the art of words in her National Book Foundation acceptance speech: "We live in capitalism, its power seems inescapable—but then, so did the divine right of kings. Any human power can be resisted and changed by human beings. Resistance and change often begin in art. Very often in our art, the art of words."

In 1970, *Songs of the Humpback Whale*—an album recorded by a top-secret US Navy hydrophone listening for Russian submarines—went multi-platinum. Soon after, the Marine Mammal Protection Act was debated by the US House and Senate. Christine Stevens, the famous animal welfare activist and originator of the Save the Whales campaign, participated in the debates. She rested her case by playing Humpback songs before Congress.

The Marine Mammal Protection Act was subsequently signed into law.

In 1977, Humpback Whale songs were put on two phonographic "Golden Records" and sent to space aboard the Voyager shuttle for the ears of extraterrestrial life. Carl Sagan curated the record and titled it "A Love Song." The probe is still adrift and transmitting today. And what a body to bob in! In 2023, NANOGrav (the North American Nanohertz Observatory for Gravitational Waves) reported a "major discovery" recognized by an international team of scientists. They found compelling evidence for the physical existence of space-time "waves." The report confirmed time isn't straight, nor space smooth. Rather, space-time churns and ripples. And among these waves, the Earth itself bobs. The astrophysicist Michael Lam described their conclusion: "The picture that emerges is a universe that looks like a choppy sea."

I love that bobbing in the black sea of our universe is our astrophysical nature. That whale song, despite our inability to translate it, fosters such awe we've brought it into our homes, echoed it off the cold marble walls of the US Capitol, and set it adrift in the choppy sea of space. The universe's oceans. Earth's oceans. My oceans. When I feel myself disintegrating on top of a cliff surrounded by sea, it's a homecoming I feel.

Quieseed, kwee-sēd: *A seed that stays dormant due to an intuition not to seed until it finds a fertile environment.*

I once planted myself for half a year on an Ecuadorian coastline where I dragged around burlap sacks, machetes, empty jugs, and shovels as my work on a reforestation team. My favorite of the little trees in the plant nursery was the ceiba. Under the plastic tarp of the greenhouse, the ceiba sapling grew to the same height as the other saplings swaddled in cups of soil. You could not have guessed that the little ceiba tree would grow to more than 230 feet in height. Yet there was already stature in her trunk, and in her sparse leaves of strong sloping lines. As the ceiba sapling grew into a juvenile, her trunk became thorny. Every time I found a teenaged ceiba in the forest, I stopped to touch the shield of her spines around her trunk with my gloved palm. I admired the ceiba for how she put a hand to the world in order to protect what was dormant inside her.

Looking back upon the non-funny revelation I shared with my non-laughing boss, I see now the tension of the dormant quieseed within me. My buried love for atmorelational ways of knowing that didn't fit into traditional academic or IQ boxes. And also a hint of my future, where the jumping of linked metaphors in a long letter was more vital than the bullet points of a résumé. Of lyricism, Rachel Carson once said, "If there is poetry in my book about the sea, it is not because I deliberately put it there, but because no one could write truthfully about the sea and leave out the poetry." Poetry, too, lights up the right brain. Tills the liminal. Prepares the land for holosonic visions that might collapse the complexities that no longer serve. Leaving space for something new to sweep through.

By the time a ceiba tree sheds her thorns, the forest has already learned to allow space for her trunk that can span ten feet in diameter and undulates like a vertical wave bridging earth and sky. Ceiba trees, in maturity, send their branches over the top of the forest, bursting thousands of brown pods every spring into white silk fibers that are so soft I once collected them to stuff my pillow. The ceiba tree embodies what every woman knows of what she's birthed from her body, be it babies or poems or art: that she can grow beyond limits, that she can be pulled into liminal places, that her toes can curl in cold earth underworlds while her fingers twist manes of clouds.

That she can blow seeds of a new future in a breath of wind.

BABY JESUS THE GIRL

MY DAUGHTER MAKES ALTARS. I PULL OUT THE CHAIR AT MY writing desk and there's a semicircle of foam hearts push-pinned into rainbow towers. On the shelf above her bed, where she sometimes plays "for just a little bit" in the dark after I put her to bed, there are jagged pieces of lapis, amazonite, opal, pyrite, turquoise, and rose quartz—stolen from her brother's rock collection—arranged into a midnight Stonehenge. On the bottom stone step of the stairs that lead to the garden, she's collected retired white snail shells, wilting dandelions, and an iridescent blue Magpie tail feather. In the middle of this assembly she used a forbidden and fat-tipped permanent marker to draw her stick-figured self. She won't be blaming this one on her brother as she's even autographed the work, "RIVA."

But I will never point out the markings on the cement step to my husband, who would be unhappy—if he were to notice. And I will not make Riva return the crystals to her brother, who has not registered their absence. And I will not take apart the rainbow towers even when I need the push pins. Because I am so delighted each time I discover one of her altars featuring the objects she has deemed special enough for sacred arrangement. But there is more. More I have not examined about her inclination or my delight—until I'm called to defend it.

It was the night of an impromptu double date. My husband and I were returning home after dinner, and his parents happened to be at the restaurant across the street. So we wandered over to share a nightcap. The mood was already well warmed by a second bottle of Pinot Noir. It was the kind of mood, of course, that can flip like a coin. I felt that coin, balanced on a thumb, when my mother-in-law threw out the disclaimer, "I'm not sure I should bring this up, but . . ."

Before I finish her sentence, I want the world to know that I asked my mother-in-law to be in my labor room for the births of my two children. And between those two children, my mother-in-law was the only person I called to my house to sit outside my door as I tore up my bedroom in the pain and grief and blood of a pummeling miscarriage. She was the only woman to whom I showed the tiny fetus disintegrating in my palm at the end of that labor. This is the woman who choked on her tears with me, who held me—a powerful and benevolent matriarch who raised a son who confidently respects his fiercely independent wife. So when my mother-in-law says what she says, I blame the bottle of wine and a lifetime of Catholic conditioning.

This is what she said.

"I think Riva should go to Sunday school."

Riva is our daughter.

We also have a son.

The anger that rose in my body shocked me, shook my wineglass until I put it down—held it down—by its base to the table. I felt my husband's hand on my thigh. Not the sexy-hand-on-thigh, but the leash-on-rabid-dog-hand-on-thigh. My husband does not usually speak for me. That he did at this moment was a sign of the deepest extension of trust between us.

"Mom. This isn't a good subject. We've got this."

My husband doesn't speak for me, and he also doesn't talk back to his mother. But warmed by the wine, she didn't notice, and continued, "Riva just seems so inclined toward the mystical . . ."

My jaw seized and my husband squeezed my stiff leg again.

He repeated with more emphasis on the period, "We've got this."

That time she heard it. The full stop at the end of his sentence. She put her wineglass down. Pushed it a little toward the center of the table.

I did not say anything because I could not say anything. Because I was drowning in anger. Choking on a lifetime of facts stacked up and toppling over. Falling down and also adding up, to something I could not, at the time, name.

A WEEK AFTER MY MOTHER-IN-LAW SAID SHE THOUGHT RIVA should go to Sunday school, I woke up with a note on my night table. It said: *Fuck the church. I'm looking for God.* The handwriting was falling off the margin of the page and barely legible—written in the dark by my own blind hand. I didn't remember writing it.

The cool air of approaching autumn that slipped through a crack in my bedroom window had snuffed the midnight-kindled fire. So I ignored the note I'd left for myself. I got out of bed, shuffled my stiff feet through the dark house and down the stairs, tickled my children awake, made pancakes, found matching socks, filled water bottles, and stuffed lunch boxes into backpacks. But when the front door closed and my husband's truck backed out, I walked past my nightstand where the note fluttered and pulled me closer again. I picked up the loose-leaf page. How had my subconscious decided to chew on this? And why, in the night, did this full moon of repressed anger arise?

Repressed anger, of course, seems the tattoo of Roman Catholicism. And indeed, I bear that scar, today old and hard as pews. My Catholic imprinting usually makes its strongest and most surprising showings at the gatherings that mark traditional rites of passage. I shock myself at baptisms, weddings, and funerals when the Our Father, Glory Be, Hail Mary, Holy Rosary, and Nicene Creed all fall from my mumbling lips in perfect intonation. Even my husband looks sideways at me from his bowed head, knowing nothing of the practicing Catholic girl I once was; knowing little of his own Christianity other than the right time to bow his head.

He doesn't comprehend the extent of my Catholic upbringing because I've never spoken of it. He doesn't know I learned how to speak publicly from behind the lectern at Mass. That I dipped my fingers into the font of holy water at the doors of church two, four, sometimes six or eight times a week. That I've read the Bible cover to cover. That I can smell a church—its dripping candles and frankincense and old-lady rose perfume and fresh-pressed clothing and new Sunday shoes, and the dust in the corners of arching glass—from three blocks away. That just as I can hear my first best friend's laughter echoing down the halls of my grade school memories, so do I know a river of rosary beads flowing between my thumb and forefingers.

When I do smell a church, I at once want to follow the scent, to find its source, to push back a heavy wooden door and peek in. To revisit my thousands of childhood memories housed in the eight years I played hopscotch after school in the alley between the church, rectory, and small Catholic school where my mother was principal.

Today, though, my conditioning pauses at the holy water font. Reaching for the fountain with my right hand remains a reflex as compelling as breathing and walking. So, I really have to stop—breathing and walking—to *not* stretch my fingertips for the font. The act of touching holy water to make the sign of the cross is meant to remind a Catholic of her baptism. But I do not want to be reminded. My baptism feels like a relinquished chapter of my life. But maybe that was never enough. To relinquish. To only "voluntarily cease" my status as a Christian. Which might have something to do with the note on my nightstand.

Curious, I googled. And then fell over my computer laughing. This laughter, this falling, just a touch too full-bodied to be free of implication. It was the biting-laughter, the defeat-laughter, the no-you-didn't laughter of being beat to the punchline. Because the headline read, "Want to leave the Catholic Church? Officially, you can't."

When I was done with my empty belly laugh, I lifted my head, dried my eyes, and read on: "Formal acts of defection were introduced in the 1983 Code of Canon Law to solve a regulatory issue in some Catholic marriages. Unintentionally, that allowed defection for any reason. Pope Benedict XVI closed the loophole in 2010."

In the year 2024 there exists no formal way to disaffiliate with the Catholic Church. I do not consider myself any kind of rabble-rouser. I'm married to a man who favors flannel and flip-flops. I have two children, highlight my hair, drive a 2006 Volkswagen, wear lip gloss, and hike an old black Lab every day in the mountains behind my house. But this news—this news that the Catholic Church has laid eternal claim on my soul from the day my parents dipped my crying head into holy water? Well, this news makes me want to scream until the white kitchen marble under my computer cracks in half.

So there might be some repressed anger.

Maybe I have walked a fine line. Maybe decades of childhood indoctrination made me package my Christianity as a sort of backstop for the .00001 percent chance that Christ beats climate disasters to the punch. Maybe I left "Christian," along with my college internships, on my résumé, *just in case* it became relevant. And maybe this repression of my rejection had something to do with the profanity on my night table.

This reminded me of a girl I once met on a cycling trip around the Big Island of Hawai'i. Pedaling by my side on a gravel road in a breeze scented by mango and guava trees, her thick blond hair trailing behind her, she whispered to me, "So, I just left the Mormon church. Want me to tell you all the top-secret things I was told never, ever, to tell anyone?"

Those secrets were fascinating. Many curiously having to do with the dimensions and details of undergarments. But that's her story. Mine is that I thought of her because I wondered: Well, what did *she* do—officially—to leave the Mormon church?

WikiHow had an answer: "Step 1: If you decide to leave the Mormon church, outline your reasons very clearly in your mind. If you're certain that you'll never want to rejoin the Church, write a letter to the bishop and request to have your name removed from church records."

That seemed diplomatic. So I asked WikiHow how to leave the Catholic Church and it offered the following list of telling instructions:

How to Become Catholic: 13 Steps (with Pictures)
How to Be Married in a Catholic Church
How to Visit a Catholic Mass (with Pictures)
How to Make a Good Confession in the Catholic Church

I didn't read any of those how-tos, but I did spend a few minutes with "How to Be Goth at Church," which was of apparent interest to more than me with 62,858 views. Those instructions did offer a tip that felt appropriate to my mood: "Avoid shirts with extremely noticeable skulls."

My mother-in-law had no idea she was poking her finger through the bars housing a basement beast—because I had no idea. My rage felt of a special breed, caged and left in a dark basement for a modern woman's lifetime.

Where and when, exactly, did my relationship with the Catholic Church crack? Was it in second grade on Patron Saint Day, when my teacher told me my first name, Christina, meant "messenger of Christ"? When I instead colored in my name tag with the saint associated with my middle name, Mother Teresa?

Or was it my senior year of high school when I signed up for a spring break mission trip in Los Angeles? I don't know why I signed up except that I was seventeen and into subconscious self-destruction. But on the final day of the mission, when a youth group leader rushed into the room, all hands-in-the-air with news of an "exciting opportunity" to hold up counter-signage on the corner of a street hosting a gay pride march, I took one step back from the crowd and said *no* with rare certainty. My friends shook their heads and left on the bus without me. I didn't talk to anyone on our flight home. Maybe that was the beginning of the end?

Or was it when my mother, in 1996, wrote letters to 256 active bishops in the United States making an argument for why women should be ordained as priests? Was it, exactly, those quiet minutes in the car when my mom, with her eyes on the road and the corners of her mouth turned down, said that only ten bishops responded to her letter and seven of those letters began, "Now dear . . ."?

Or did Christianity and I break up when I met my first love? An atheist boy I dated through four years at a Jesuit university. This boy I loved, he pulled me not to atheism, but away from the Sunday Masses my schoolmates attended. He pulled me toward the sciences. Away from guilt. Toward the corporeal. Away from spirituality. The last of which was the problem: the two sides—the Church and the Mystical, not the same or opponents. But he and his influence on me were things I could not differentiate. So, to my Catholic repressions, I added atheist challenges of anything beyond the physical. I put them all into that cage together, pushed it back on the shelf of my psyche's basement—unfed and unwatched.

Part of my problem was lack of an alternative. My mother had the instinct to find something different. She organized an annual gathering of her women friends, a group of ladies in their forties and fifties who gathered in a parched house among windswept dunes on the Pacific Coast. She called it her "Wings Retreat," but as soon as she rolled her maroon suitcase out the door, my father would begin his grumbles of "lesbian witches." He felt threatened; I see this now. But as a girl, I watched and learned what men called women who didn't need them. Women who dared walk out domestic doors. Women who found, among themselves, new license to laugh and fathom. Women who no longer feared trials for summoning their fire. But my mother could not, or would not, separate community and Christianity.

Out of old habit, I was still peeking into churches throughout my twenties, including along my five-hundred-mile walking pilgrimage across Northern Spain to Santiago de Compostela. The "Camino de Santiago" terminates in a chapel alleged to be the resting place of the body of one of the original twelve apostles, Saint James. I had walked for five weeks to get to Santiago. I walked slowly, carefully, quietly. When I finally stepped into the cathedral, my body chilled in the cold air escaping the mouth of arching stained glass. I froze. My body, for the first and final time, knew it didn't belong. I turned around and walked out.

The Camino de Santiago is considered "one of the oldest Christian pilgrimage routes in the world." Today, most pilgrims know the Camino actually existed a thousand years before Christ, when pagans followed a silky night sky illuminated by the Milky Way to the Atlantic Ocean. "Camino" translates as the "road," "path," and "way." There's still a route from Santiago to the sea. If you follow it for three days, you arrive in the seaside city of Finisterre. The name translates as the "land's end." Of course, the pilgrimage is still claimed as "Christian" with no way to object or defect—something the Camino and I have in common.

I HAD A DREAM WHILE WALKING THE CAMINO DE SANTIAGO that I would not have remembered had I not just found it written in an old journal. In the dream, a fire burns. People dance on the outskirts. Two children step closer to the fire. They stand side by side, one taller, her hair longer. The younger one is maybe seven. Both girls clutch ostrich-sized eggs. I, across the fire, look into their shifting eyes. The dancing stops and someone makes a quiet command. The older girl clenches her egg closer to her chest and hesitates with pleading eyes. But the silent command is repeated, and she steps toward the fire. Something leaps from inside me, reaching for the girl, but I'm held back. I watch the girl, her eyes now vacant, drop the egg into the fire. The girl turns into the darkness behind her and disappears. The younger girl watches her depart, then turns her body back to the fire, trembling. The fire rises up. This time, as loud as I can, I scream to the child. But she doesn't hear me. She looks in the direction of the command that is now directed at her. The fire drops and I am suddenly within sight line of the child. She looks across the fire and for the first time—sees me. When our eyes meet, I look down and find the egg in my own hands. The command comes again, louder. The girl across the fire, she looks at me and I can hear her. She wonders if I know what's been sacrificed already. She wants to know if I have what it takes.

ON THE LAST DAY OF MY PILGRIMAGE, I WALKED THIRTY-FIVE kilometers. I could hear the ocean louder and louder, but the heat of the hills created mirages of shimmering false summits, making the forty-five pounds on my back heavier with every step. When, at sunset, that narrow band of blue finally gleamed atop the hill, I collapsed and cried.

I descended into town, bought a bottle of wine, and followed a winding road up to Finisterre's famous lighthouse. At the top of the road, I heard a faint song in the wind, turned toward the direction of the voices, but found myself at a dead end. A beam from the lighthouse swooped into my view and illuminated a trodden path into the bushes. With a touch of adrenaline, I followed the path.

The voices escalated, their volume pulling me in. I pushed blindly through the dark until I came upon a group of women dancing around a raging fire, their cackling laughter echoing off ocean cliff walls. One of the dark figures jumped on a rock, dangled a pair of underwear and then dropped them into the fire. The group threw up their hands in jubilant hoots. I jumped onto a nearby rock, jabbed a pointed finger in their direction, and bellowed, "Witches!"

This accusation, it was an echo of my father's voice. But it was mock-accusation. It was—at once—my finger-pointing moment of self-accusation and self-acceptance.

Bewildered firelit silhouettes all turned to front their accuser, smiles spreading across their flickering faces. They knew me. Accepted my admission with a cheer, throwing up the shadows of their reaching arms on the rock walls as the fire flared.

MY MOTHER-IN-LAW IS RIGHT. MY DAUGHTER IS INCLINED toward the mystical. Riva speaks of sky gods and ghosts and afterlives and plant lives and wind spirits. She also refers to "baby Jesus" as a girl. She comes home from a sleepover at Grandma's house and says, "I like Jesus. She sounds nice." And I tilt my head and say, "Yes, baby Jesus is a nice girl." Because I like the sound of "girl" as a sacred thing.

My daughter will not go to any Sunday or Bible school. Because my daughter will not be taught that men are born under aligned stars, that men are the owners of miracles, that men sit at tables with more men, that men are the teachers, that a man died for her sins, and that men, only men, teach behind pulpits. She will not read a book written only by male authors, thrusting the stories of men upon hers. She will not have her altars stolen from her.

My daughter will not go to Bible school, nor will my son— not that anyone asked. He too makes a curious sense of death and afterlife. He too watches the sky. He too asks the Russian doll questions of how we came to be. But no one has asked him to go to Sunday school. No one thinks an indoctrination to patriarchy is needed of him. Because it's not. Because it's his water to swim in. Not hers. I don't know what comes next. But I am certain that for the something-new to come, the old hierarchies built upon white and male supremacy must first fall. As Audre Lorde famously stated, "The master's tools will never dismantle the master's house."

Now that I recall, my first touch of church doubt tapped me on the shoulder when I was twelve. It was a Sunday and I remember the exact pew. About seven back, centered in front of the pulpit. When the liturgy was over, all the people in their lingering scents of laundry detergent and aftershaves filed out. The altar boys were extinguishing the candles. My mother was chatting with a parishioner in the aisle. I was alone in my pew, standing, facing the center, when I felt a tap on my shoulder. I remember the distinct feeling of composing myself. Of feeling caught off guard in a private thought. Of realizing I was not alone when I thought I was. I shrugged it off, straightened my shoulders, and turned around. No one was there. So shocking was the absence that the memory still grasps my arms in goosebumps. But what I remember now is that the tap turned me away from the pulpit. Away from that altar that men, only men, were allowed to stand behind. The tap—it turned me to the back of the church—toward the doors.

A door to which I have found a new and official loophole! Yes, a Vatican-sanctified key to my instant excommunication, revised and codified in the very hot month of June in the year 2021. Here is the updated canon law, word for word, fresh off the Vatican's web pages:

> § 3. Both a person who attempts to confer a sacred order on a woman, and the woman who attempts to receive the sacred order, incur a latae sententiae excommunication reserved to the Apostolic See;

A Google search confirms that *latae sententiae* excommunication translates to an "automatic excommunication" wherein someone (in this case, per the Vatican's order, a "woman"—because how dare "she" take a sacred rite into "her" hands) in committing an act, incurs an excommunication penalty.

I texted this exciting news to my mother.

She texted back, "Oh dear."

She called my childhood priest, and they conferred while I shopped for "used cassocks and sashes" on eBay.

My mom, a week later, came around on my plan. "OK. You'll be excommunicated. Does it really matter? Do we care?"

I texted back, "Yes. It matters. I care."

Five minutes passed and then she texted back, "I care too."

My mother-in-law also treads now with extra care. After her unfortunate prompt unlocking the cage of my repressed anger, she sensed her indiscretion. At the end of a recent shared hike, she gently explored, "When I walk into an old church, I feel ages of prayers, and that feels beautiful to me. But what do you feel?" I smelled the candles and saw the glints of stained glass as she set that scene, but I swallowed hard and replied, "I feel persecution. The persecution of millennia of peoples forced to their knees." Her eyes looked sad as she scanned the horizon. But we can come from different places and still meet in a middle that holds life sacred. The way I called her to my home the day I held the tiny miscarried future in the palm of my hand.

UNDER THE BIG WINDOW IN MY WRITING ROOM TODAY IS A sill. On it: a metal frame of a Buddhist mani stone with an etched stupa I photographed hiking in the Himalayas; a brass Durga goddess from India with her eight arms carrying the weapons she uses to unleash divine wrath in liberation of the oppressed; a sharp rock with embedded white quartz I found on my walk in the woods last week; a tarot card of Temperance with her one foot on land and the other in water; and the little landscape of push-pinned rainbow towers Riva left on my seat last week. I push back my rolling office chair and swivel around. On one wall, a two-by-four-foot portrait of Our Lady of Guadalupe. On another wall, a blind contour of cattails painted by my best friend's hand. On another wall, a floor-to-ceiling "spider web" of push-pinned cards, each inscribed with my notes on the intersections of womanhood and nature.

It's not only my daughter's inclination. It's mine.

I make altars.

My daughter made an altar and she put it in a room of my altars.

And neither of us needed cassocks or sashes.

So I am done ignoring the notes I've left for myself. Now I see that all I ever wanted to do was look for godliness wherever it could be found. In temples on the outskirts of town, but also in the woods and in the creeks and at the summits of mountains. Feeling the tugs of my being pushed and pulled, but also interwoven, with the workings of something infinitely dimensional. Accepting the interdependencies of nature as my religious nature. Following, also, my instinct to just keep walking. To walk by the church and reach that place three days west of where everyone told me to stop. To perch on cliffs at the "end of land" with my hair lashed by wind, with all the old male voices drowned in the roar of that crashing sea. To reach that humbled place where I can drop to my knees in the sand and reach with my fingertips for that holiest of waters. My own sacred ordination. By my own girl hands.

And this I have to say to all the women I admire and love, the same women who uphold the imperialist and sexist religion that pushed me down: Take my daughter to the woods and name the birds and the berries you know. Take her up the mountain and tell her the dreams you remember. Walk with her along the ocean and tell her about your grief, your rage, your old lovers, your dead dreams, your lost babies, your remembered mothers. Tell her all the stories and offer respects to all the paths on this planet where one can tryst with the mystical. Maybe I did not choose. Maybe you did not choose. But let this be her inheritance: Choice.

To hold what she wants sacred.

RESUSCITATION

THERE WERE TWO BOATS THAT DAY. I DIDN'T FAULT THE PEO-
ple on the party ship; the pulse of music pumping from the
ship's speakers insisted they stay in their reality and apart from
ours on the little boat. And from the ship's top deck, six floors
above where our dive boat had emergency-docked, we probably looked—not like ants—but like figurines. Toy figures taking
turns pumping the naked chest of a limp body. A man's body
that might have looked only asleep had his arms and legs not
fallen in backward angles under the vertical rays of high noon.

The speakers rimming the deck of the party ship thumped a
playlist of chart-topping, sing-along songs. The volume discour-
aged discussion. Encouraged stiff refills of bottom-shelf alcohol
into plastic cups. It was the kind of music that would ensure
patrons went home with a specific blur of the immense-fun-had.

The party ship had docked in a pool of sparkling blue
Caribbean Sea along the coastline of Isla Mujeres, named by the
Spanish in the sixteenth century for its temples and images of
Ixchel, a Mayan goddess of gestation. The hosts of the party had
converged all the bikinis and boardshorts at the rooftop bar for
pre-lunch cocktails. So the patrons leaning casual elbows over
the rail and looking at the scene on the dock below were tipsy.
Tipsy enough with the alcohol tingling their empty bellies to
watch, and then swallow the dissonance down.

I didn't look over my shoulder when someone behind me made the call to stop. I knew the call was coming because I've taken enough first-responder courses to know. No one would feel guilty for not trying long enough to restart the heart that had ceased pumping blood. When the call was made—I felt it in the air. I felt the man whose turn it was to cup his lips over the dead man's mouth to deliver rescue breaths—as he sat back on his knees and didn't lean forward again. I felt the other man— his stacked, starfish-ed hands compressing the unmoving chest—as he too stopped, and wiped sweat from his forehead with the back of his arm.

The heart had stopped pumping blood before the body surfaced from the water. This I had seen in the wrong color of skin that bobbed in the ocean as our dive boat drove toward it. I was still dripping seawater from my own ascent when my husband and three men pulled the body in. Still dripping seawater when the boat crew stood pale and unmoving. When I instructed them to find the marine VHF radio I knew was onboard from my own divemaster training. The death was the fault of a hidden but preexisting condition, but we didn't know this. The rounds of CPR my husband commenced pushed enough air into the man's lungs to make his body blush only once and long enough for us to notice the absence of hope—twenty minutes later, when it was gone.

In diving, there is something called the safety stop. At the end of a dive you pause five meters below the surface. There, you wait at least three minutes. This stop off-gasses the excess nitrogen accumulated during a dive. In these five meters of water, rays of sun still streak wavy gold before they are swallowed by the depths below. In these five meters, the bubbles of the air you exhale flurry in rising white rings. In these five meters, the top of the ocean disorients you. When the three minutes are done, you raise one arm and reach for the sky on the other side. You don't need to kick. You need only inhale. The air in your lungs lifts you, till your fingers touch the roof of the ocean—where gravity and the turbulence of the waves reclaim you. This is the ascent I had made before I climbed the ladder to the freeboard of the dive boat, seawater dripping from my shoulders.

On the wooden dock jutting from the hip of Isla Mujeres, in the air between the men leaning back on their knees, the heaviness of our collective inability floated. It floated up and reached the people hovering over the rail of the party ship, people holding their plastic cups—but not drinking from them. People who might have been whispering to each other, "Did that man die?"—had anyone been able to hear anything over the droning music. So they whispered words not heard. The same thing we whispered to ourselves on the dock below. This minute was long and quiet. I think time tried to slow it down, to cushion it—our new comprehension of brevity.

And then the ambulance arrived. I knew this by the men in matching suits and matching composed faces trotting— not running—down the dock. I watched the composed men with the composed truth they carried with their med kits, over the shoulder of the woman whose two hands were in my two hands. The woman whose husband was in the back of the boat, encircled by listless men and the hush of inability. She was the only one who didn't know the call had been made. Who didn't know the CPR had stopped. She didn't know—didn't feel it in the air—because she didn't have a place for it in her body. The absence of her husband's heartbeat.

My newborn daughter was on the boat. I hesitate with this inclusion because I don't know what people will think of a mom who brings her ten-day-old infant aboard a dive boat. A mom who first talked with the captain in Spanish. A captain who brushed his hand toward the clouds as he talked of his many children, all once babies. *No te preocupes*, he said. A mom who was in fact not worried, because the baby slept twenty hours a day, and the baby was tucked under gauzy cotton and the snug embrace of her car seat under a bonnet of shade. The baby did sleep through the forty-minute dive, and the twenty minutes speeding to the dock, and the twenty-five minutes of CPR. The baby's sleepy new consciousness may even have brushed with the departing man's spirit. In a swirl or a wink or a wave. Or so her mother will wonder for months, years, at those times when she's thinking of the wife's hands in hers.

When I think of the wife's hands in mine, I remember that booze cruise towering over me on the wooden dock. I remember the onlookers with the numbness in their veins, with the ringing in their ears, and the music that refused to stop. I'm reminded of that party ship at the checkout line of the supermarket where the glossy paparazzi magazines corner me with what they think I should want, or hate, or lack. At the sports bar with high-definition screens flashing sacks and rushes and scrolling banners of upcoming coverage of climate disasters. Past the metal detectors in the hockey stadium where hawkers sell hot dogs and beer and team-colored pom-poms, with the rows of screaming fans between me and emergency exits. I remember it while chopping carrots while glancing at alerts on my phone while waiting for my children to be dropped off from carpool, and in all the places I struggle to stack the needed dissociations to march forward. Places where Mortality reaches her dancer's hand to my ear.

Mortality calls me back to the upside-down worlds between light and dark, the dreams into which we venture every night and neglect by light of day, the night sky in which we occupy a single planet of eight around a sun belonging to a solar system beyond which there might be—according to astronomers—"billions of worlds." I'm called to the undiscussed darkness of our impossible existence—and why it goes without daily consideration. Not that it isn't our first instinct to ask these questions. I field them every day from my children: "Mom, who had the very first baby?" Riva asks. "Mom, what happens when you die?" Nash wants to know. They inquire as they roll their forks in spaghetti on the kitchen island. These questions seem to me the most important in our one-of-billions world.

Except we are always in a rush. And I am just as guilty of pushing these questions aside. Because these questions require me to stop chopping carrots and stop feeding the dog and stop looking at my phone for texts from my husband. These questions require a blanket and a couch or maybe a hammock or a sleeping bag under a night sky. These questions require the extension, trust, and embrace of my full imagination. Which does not fit on my cutting board with the carrots that need to be chopped.

I had watched the man who died, on the boat before the dive. Under his scuba mask his eyes seemed too wide. But still, he centered his palm over his regulator, crossed his legs, and back-rolled into the ocean, allowing gravity to carry him underwater and into that waiting place under the waves. I had turned to his wife and asked, "Is your husband OK? He looks a little scared." And she had said, "Oh, he's done this a thousand times."

THERE WAS A SECOND DIVE SCHEDULED FOR THAT DAY. ONE we'd never make.

The divemaster had only described that site to me as El Museo. At the dive shop on the north end of the island, he'd outstretched his arm to the south. I was distracted by the baby—said yes without asking questions, knowing how easily a structure of coral could be nicknamed a "museum." So it would have truly been a wonder so unknowingly to descend upon the nearly five hundred life-sized statues at the southern tip of Isla Mujeres constituting the world's largest—literal—underwater museum.

In the section of the installation called *The Silent Evolution*, eco-artist Jason deCaires Taylor shaped ninety human figures from molds of people belonging to the local fishing village of Puerto Morelos. The sculptures were carved from over two tons of neutral-pH cement and sunk twenty-six feet into a stretch of barren Caribbean seabed. At the edge of the submerged crowd of bodies, a cement child clutches a purse, her chin tipped up, eyes closed, as if making a wish. Near her, a bare-chested mother encircles her full-moon belly with her arms, her brow furrowed, gaze upon the ground. In the middle, a teenage girl with hair swept into a bun, spine upright, and light on her forehead, looks up—for the sun in the lapis sky of the ocean. The collection is described as "a movement of people in defense of the sea."

I want to be among them. With my sleeping daughter sculpted to my chest—weighted by my wonder for this brief and shared submersion into wavering existence—cemented in tonnage for eternity. Except even cement decomposes. Most of the figures' facial details are today covered by crustaceans, algae, and coral, having evolved—in the years since installation—into the complex reef structures hosting biodiverse marine life that they were meant to become. Coral reefs are thick arms of the ecosystem, spreading across only two-tenths of a percent of the seafloor, yet supporting over 25 percent of marine species.

But the reefs are dying. The preexisting conditions of the ocean body may be overlooked (even gaslit), but are not hidden: feverish temps, disrupted flows, diseased tissues, and connective disorders. The Global Coral Reef Monitoring Network (GCRMN) reported in 2020 that up to 50 percent of the world's coral reefs may have died in the last thirty years.

Party above. Rupture below.

Yet this installation—artfully planted and intentionally unattended—has multiplied into a vast and biodiverse underwater garden. Nature's fey reclamation of the sculptures makes me squirm with metaphysical intrigue. The pocked surface of a pink Encrusting Sponge dips into the eye sockets of a face, brown-yellow Fan Leaf Alga streams upward from a nearby scalp, and a colony of Red Coralline Algae crawls from a neck down a cement chest. What else can we artfully sow and allow to decompose into something more beautiful?

Carl Jung wrote, "The afternoon of life is just as full of meaning as the morning . . ." I would argue the search for meaning is even more essential, more expedited in pressing need, in the face of the ecological death we are witnessing. Jung suggested also that we are meant for more. To do things in the last half of our lives not only for ourselves, but for society and for the sake of our souls.

That afternoon light feels collectively upon us.

When I think of the wife's hands in mine, I stop chopping on the cutting board and look up. Because I'm thinking of all her hope and story and life as she'd known it—with the new truth standing just behind her shoulder. I'm thinking of all that hovers and winks in the wavy five meters between the light and gravity of living. Of the other future into which we have the chance to descend. And I'm thinking of that quiet congregation at the bottom of the sea—the evolution that awaits—cement faces, chins up tipped, foreheads lit by a sun from another side.

HOW TO HOST A POD OF WOMEN IN WATER

1. Pick a date. Pick a date a year away so it will work for anyone who wants to join, but know there are those who don't want it to work, who won't feel called, who do not want to know what might catch up and shake them—if they stop treading.
2. Pick a place with water. An ocean, a river, a pool, a lake, a hot tub, a creek, a local hot spring, even a kiddy pool in the backyard might work. Water is essential. If this is not yet obvious, this is not a get-bikini-ready event. This is a "bring your stretch marks and reduced metabolism and cancer scars and leftover baby-weight and hot-flashing peri- or post-menopausal body" event. This is a gathering where the agenda is only water and getting in it.
3. Pick people. Start small. Dig through your life and find a pod of friends ripe for this experience. Which they all are. Pick friends who have seen you cry, or throw up, or get so angry you broke something, or made you laugh when you wanted to die. Those people. Ideally, you have also seen this friend cry, even if it was twenty years ago. It doesn't matter. Tears shatter time. These friends will not be perfect

and if they are, do not invite them, except *perfect* is a construct meant to be broken and water is great for holding the shattered. Pick friends with baggage. Friends who have, at times, been inappropriate, annoying, flaky, or exposed their deep flaws. Maybe she didn't answer the phone for months because she had a new lover. Maybe you were abroad and didn't call when her best old dog-friend died. Here is what you are looking for: People who will show up and get in the water with you. Because you remember a story. A story about Sperm Whales. Whales who were inclined to live in small pods, but when they faced near-extinction in the 1800s, did something different. The smaller pods—they collected. The matriarchs of the pods, they somehow communicated, maybe sang a need to merge. They boosted their size and alliance and defense by congregating into "extensive herds" of more than a hundred. But we're organizing humans. So let's start small. For this gathering, three to thirteen should suffice.

4. Other than the date, place, and people, don't plan. Because what women don't need is more shit-to-plan. Women in my circle who, no matter what kind of feminist we call ourselves, still do 70 percent of the laundry, make 85 percent of the dentist appointments, clean 90 percent of the toilets, and still in 2024 wrap our own holiday gifts. So do not plan activities, talks, outings, or dinners. Ask for one volunteer to organize food—emphasis on organizing, not cooking. Rotate this volunteer each year to someone with no new baby, no sick parent, no dying dog, no undiagnosed autoimmune disease, no raging perimenopause—variables that take their turns on women.

5. Before you get in the water, give each person space to talk. Ask each woman to name what she needs and what she brings. Let the woman who has a story migrate to the woman who needs to hear it. One woman will offer divorce advice. Another will need help with a defiant toddler. A few

will want to talk about sex or death. Others will need space to discuss the -isms they battle with their employees or boss. Three will cluster to figure out how to transition out of jobs they hate or away from lovers they fear. Someone will want a very quiet companion on a very long walk. One will need to get high. Others, a bottle of wine passed by its neck, back and forth, in the woods. One person will definitely want to burn something. Many will need to laugh until they cry or cry until they laugh. One woman, when she describes what *she needs*, will stomp her foot like a wild horse's hoof. When she does, all the women will feel it. Their feet will twitch.

6. Get in the water. But first watch the women on the cold cement, pulling up their shirts and tugging off their socks, their skin prickling in cold air, say, under the looming 12,966 feet of Mount Sopris in Colorado. Watch the women grasp their own bodies in a shiver. Observe as they point one foot into the natural hot spring, then another. See how they fall into the water's embrace, how eager they are for warmth, for relief, to be held. Watch how their chins tip up, their eyes close, their arms fall back and open, dragging in the water behind them. The women—in water—they will huddle.

7. The oceans of whales and women are both vast; the distances they must travel to connect—immense—so slow down in these first minutes of immersion. Feel your body slip between the bodies of the other women, your shoulders touching, gliding seamlessly with other girl bodies. Remember what you read about Sperm Whales: that they have little permanent in the sea except for each other; that they communicate in patterned sonar clicks, codas that can vibrate through thousands of miles of water; that when they share space, they touch each other a lot—they nuzzle. Knees will touch in the pools. Thighs will glide by each other. Hands will reach for shoulders. The women will twist

as they laugh until they are touching each other's faces like they touch their own in the mirror. Bodies will bead with sweat. Bodies will clasp, wave, breach in reunion. One woman will get too hot. She'll pull herself onto the ledge and roll her spine onto the cold stone. She'll bask with the sun on her steaming skin, eyes closed but listening. You'll know she's still listening when her chest and knees bend together as she laughs at the confession of another in the pool. The confession of a mother who served cereal for dinner. The confession of another who reads erotica before bed. The confession of one who let her son pee in the bushes of a church. This is why we migrate and collect. For the shared wet skin of confessions that strip us to likeness. For a place where women's bodies, in a seamless nuzzle, can say what needs to be felt. For the laughter that wakes what sleeps inside. Because there is no laughter like the laughter of a woman shaking off the sleep of laundry and carpools and interrupted dreams. A woman waking from domesticity.

8. Leave all the babies home. A location with unstable Wi-Fi and no cell service helps. Francis Weller said, "What we need in these times is attuned and attentive individuals who can sense the distress we are feeling and offer us assurance, soothing and safe touch to help us re-modulate our inner states. This holding environment is a form of ritual ground . . . initiation that occurs outside the familiar landscape of family and friends, the daily round of meals and work. It occurs in a time outside time." These are time-outside-time days. The few in the life of a modern woman in which her sentences and sentiments are free to roam, to run on, to flow into oceans of grief and fear and acceptance and disclosure, to meander, evaporate, fall back to earth, and cycle until they remember the oceans where they began. Know that babies are born of a mother's tides, but those tides are sourced and need to be resourced, pulled back out, reclaimed by the oceans that origin them—before

time, before babies, before bodies. The ancestors of whales once walked on legs on land. These "walking whales," *Ambulocetus*, moved closer and closer to the water. In the water, their legs merged into flukes. The modern whale has only a trace of her old pelvic bone. So stay. Stay in the water till your fingers prune. Till you grow so light and dizzy you think you feel webbing growing between your fingers, your toes. Stay so long in the water you want only to swim in deeper and deeper, till there is nothing left of you that belongs to the land but a trace of pelvic bone.

9. Before the gathering, do not attend to the invisible loads of labor left at home. Oh, I know this is tempting! I know how much you want to prep casseroles for Dad to pop into the oven. How easy it is to make sure your partner does not run out of the diapers and wipes next to the changing table. But do not leave a tidy list of doctor and dentist numbers on the fridge. Do not call your mother-in-law and ask her to cover the kids for a night. Do not pre-pay the babysitter to give Dad time to go on a bike ride. Yes, these are all very, very nice things to do. But if you stop doing these things, a curious thing will happen. Your partner will run out of diapers and go to the store. Dad will find the right phone number and take the child to the right doctor. Your husband will scramble eggs for dinner and the kids will clean their plates. Dad will descend into the boiler room of moms' hidden labor and when you come home and a child from downstairs cries up, it will be Dad who beats you to the instinctual response. Because instincts are born of habit. Habits of practice. Practice of opportunity. Opportunity of your absence. Dad did it because of your non-doing. And besides, aren't we all fucking sick of being very, very nice?

10. On the last day of the group gathering, in the hottest of the pools, feel the pebbles under your curled toes when you hear the story of your abortion fall—for the first time—from your mouth. Feel tears river down your cheeks. Feel

the dammed story break, wash through you. Feel resuscitated. And when you are done, look up. One of the women will turn her back to you. She will drag her body through the water toward the other side of the pool and look into the valley of foggy mountains and then she will begin to talk. She will tell the story she has never spoken of. And when she is done, when she turns around with her shoulders softened, her skin steaming—then another woman will begin. And she too will not stop until she is done. And after the silence, another woman will laugh. The kind of laugh that tips into another place. She will laugh and say she can't believe it and she will tell her story too. At which point every woman in the hot water will have shared an urgent telling never told. And when all the women with the pebbles under their feet, and the slippery shoulders of bodies on either side, are done, when they look up—they will learn that there are scars women don't talk about until they have sat for three days together in the water of timeless-time. Scar tissue of miscarriages, violent partners, abandoned art projects, hated phases of motherhood, the mothers and daughters we fight and make up with. They will learn how water holds. How stones of stories are upturned, tumbled, smoothed. Remember that women have been meeting at water for as long as women have been pulling water from rivers. Make eye contact with this remembrance across the pool. Let your laugh tip into another place.

11. Go home. Go home with your skin softened, your hair unruly, and a pebble from the pools in your pocket. Go home feeling still-held. Then, revel in the holler from your children when they run barefoot to meet you at your car. Sweep them into your arms and know this width of gratitude comes only from absence. Read countless books to them that night. Accept all the encores till the children make fists with their small hands to rub the sockets of their eyes. The last book you read—your daughter's choice—still

has your own mother's neat handwriting with your father's last name penned in black marker on the cover. The seams on *Stone Soup* are threadbare from the one thousand times you made your mother read this book to you as a little girl. It is the story of a hungry vagabond who convinces an old woman who answers the door to the house he knocks on, that "soup can be made from a stone." The little old lady, reluctant, but wanting to see the magic, lets the vagabond in and pulls out her biggest pot. Together, they drop the stone into the water. But as they wait for the water to boil, they decide to add salt, onion, spices, stock, and whatever they can pull from the garden. By the time the stone soup is ready, it's—of course—"fit for royalty." After retiring the book to its shelf and tucking the covers around the small bodies of your children whose eyes are already closed, walk upstairs with the story of water and stone in your mind. Knowing water as an ever-waiting-body. Needing only a pebble of calling. To manifest of existing ingredients, what was indeed ready to be made.

THE SHIFT

THE DAY I RECEIVED THE INVITATION I STOOD UP FROM MY chair, backed away from the computer, and put my hands over my mouth. Then I leaned down, daring to peek at the line on the screen again:

"The First Lady would like to meet you."

I wasn't allowed to tell anyone. Before my boss assigned me as the liaison between our organization and the White House, he'd sent me a boilerplate nondisclosure agreement he assumed we needed based on his conversation with the First Lady's chief of staff. So I passed the two months between receiving the invitation and my flight to Washington, DC, with only my metaphorical hands covering my jaw-dropped mouth.

My date with the White House fell at the end of the same week as my company's annual staff training, at which more than a hundred international educators set up tents under piñon trees in the Sierras south of Mammoth Lakes, California. The event hosted people representing more than nineteen countries who met daily for a rigorous outdoor classroom schedule of guide training covering themes of intercultural communication, curriculum, and risk management. If you took a walk around the camp, you might hear Mandarin in the kitchen, Nepali at the slackline, Quechua in the "tea house," Wolof at the meditation tent, or Mongolian at a picnic table in one of the four "classrooms" under fluttering tarps. My first year at this training, I was a participant—and so overwhelmed by the MAs and PhDs and the vast experience and sheer wisdom of the group that I had to take regular breaks in my tent to breathe through my impostor syndrome. But the collective mission was flint to my kindling. I joined the organization's admin team within six months and facilitated the training for the next thirteen years.

The summer of 2016 was the first and only time I got a manicure before strapping my sleeping bag to my backpack for the annual gathering at the campsite, from which I needed to fly directly to Washington, DC. I hoped the manicure would hold. I didn't want to show up at the White House with Sierran dirt under my fingernails.

The manicure, of course, didn't hold. As my plane departed California, I was still picking at my nails as I fretted about what the FBI might have learned about me before approving my day badge. Did they know I was pulled over twice the day I got my driver's license? Or that a Cuban immigration official once stamped a temporary page in my passport? Were they privy to the terrible secret I'd never confessed even to my husband: that I didn't get my absentee ballot in enough time to vote against Bush in 2004?

I landed in DC with my boss and a male colleague. Our company is based in Colorado—both administratively and culturally. On a typical day we wear flannel, denim, and down vests with ridgeline logos. When an event calls for "mountain formal," we might leave the denim home. In over a decade of working together, it was the first time I'd seen my coworkers in suits. Their clothing looked exaggerated, like something pulled from their dads' closets—neckties like lost shoes dangling over phone lines. My own goal was to look as nonchalant as I didn't feel. I wore a ribbed black pencil skirt, white silk blouse, and only a touch of flair in my shoes: white kitten heels blooming red and black carnations with petite caramel ankle straps. Despite our efforts to look corporate, we still couldn't hide the week of alpine desert sun exposure on our forearms and cheeks. All three of us were tan, chapped, and rosy—and this was the first thing Michelle Obama noticed as we filed into her office. "Well, you all are not from DC, that's clear!"

Michelle looked smart as always, in a dress of geometric patterns, with her hair sleek and shiny. "But those shoes"— Michelle raised her eyebrows as she glanced down at my feet. She made eye contact with me, flashing a wink, "Girl, welcome to my world."

This same candid warmth had already set the tone for our entrance. To get to the First Lady's office we walked down the East Wing's long hall of small offices and huge photographs. In the slow motion of tense time, I studied each of the hall photos: the six-foot-one Barack Obama hunched down to meet a child's eyes; the first couple slow dancing, heads tucked together under the inauguration gaze of 37.93 million; an empty podium awaiting the arrival of the forty-fourth president as captured through hundreds of smartphones raised in the air; the eyes of the President and First Lady as they met across a waiting room seconds before doors undoubtedly opened to a burst of flash photography. Between the framed photos, I peeked into the small offices. Heads were huddled over desks and screens and stacks and memos. Not just any heads. Women's heads. Brown heads. This I noticed.

In her office, the First Lady had to prompt me as I'd forgotten to tell her my name. She shook my hand and made eye contact. "Christina, it's nice to meet you." Michelle sat down and we followed her lead, as a team of people on cream-colored couches perched their BlackBerries on notebooks and knees.

In the room downstairs, where security had asked us to wait before our meeting, my boss had said: "OK. I think we should write down *everything* she says, got it?" I had been fine with the instruction at the time. Because that was always my job. To notice and take notes on what I noticed. I was very good at listening. I was very good at hearing underlying questions. And

I was an expert at preemptively answering unexpressed needs. For these reasons, my boss had picked me before to accompany him to important interviews and meetings.

As the meeting started, I felt my boss jostling for his pen and notebook on my left. But I did not rustle in my bag. I did not look for my own pen and notebook. Not the way I have always done in every other board and meeting room I've ever been in. Because something happened in that room I did not expect.

I looked around. Soft eyes and smiles met mine.

I sat back in my seat with relief.

And curiosity.

What was happening here? Why did I feel myself on the edge of an easy laugh? Why were the boys in their suits looking so stiff? Why was it so easy to sit back and make eye contact?

Then it hit me. From the chief of staff to the aides to the head of the Secret Service and all the others appointed to discuss our collective business—all the people in the room, aside from my male colleagues, were women. It was the first room I had ever walked into in my life where the leadership was tone-set by a predominance of women.

After Michelle briefed us on the exact task (which can remain private), my boss asked her if we should procure nondisclosure agreements for the additional people we needed to contract for the assignment.

"NDAs? We don't need those," said Michelle.

And then she said, "If there's one thing I've learned since walking through these doors, it's how to trust. Now it's your turn."

When Michelle said "trust," she said it like it was a sword she had pulled from a rock. This caught me off guard. I knew the verb personally, but I did not associate it with the government of the United States of America. The way she said it made me pause: Was trust built on shared experiences, or those diverse? Or did it meet in the middle?—in that place between what we know and what we risk in reliance on one another?

During the meeting, we discussed the number of Secret Service agents needed to support a private intercultural event in South America that we'd be organizing in a rural village. I asked if the Secret Service agents spoke any Indigenous languages. I asked how they might house and feed themselves in such a remote location. I asked if they had any local knowledge with which to navigate some pretty special, and unique, cultural landscapes.

The woman representing the Secret Service team cocked her head at me and waited.

I continued, "I think we might need to assign you one of our guides for your team of Secret Service agents. Someone who knows the languages and communities, to act as a liaison."

And the woman representing the Secret Service did not hesitate. "I think that's a very good idea."

Was this really happening? Was one of the highest offices in the United States of America actually accepting leadership support from our nongovernmental, albeit specially experienced and trained, team of civilians?

When our meeting at the White House was done, my coworkers and I walked across the lawn to a bar. We ordered pints and sat quietly, still shuttered up in awe.

Finally, I said to my male colleagues, "The winks!"

They both looked at me in confusion. "The whats?"

"The winks! So many winks!"

Laughs of relief tumbled from me.

The men looked at each other and furrowed their brows, conferred with their eyes, then agreed. "We didn't see any winks."

I was shocked. How did the First Lady and the other women in that office flicker those gestures of knowing and agreement to me in a way that so eluded the men?

IT WAS AN EXACT YEAR LATER WHEN I WAS PROMPTED TO fully comprehend what transpired in that room in the White House. I was back at my company's annual training in the

Sierras. All the educators were spread under the piñons like a rainbow of Patagonia-branded polka dots. I was standing in a small breakout group with Saw Min from Burma, Luis, who was born in the United States but lived most his life in Guatemala, and Mateo, a Bolivian-American based in the Bay Area. Mateo was facilitating a workshop titled "Diversity and Inclusion."

Mateo's first invitation was for us to share how we identified in terms of race, sexual identity, and socioeconomic variables. My eyes scanned the forest as I searched for my own answer: "I identify as a heterosexual woman. My father was orphaned as a child, so I'm unsure as to his ancestry, but his first language was Spanish. Regardless, I've always looked white enough to 'pass' which has allowed me to slide into a life of greater socioeconomic entitlements that still shock and confuse me."

When the murmur of associated identities quieted, Mateo jumped back onto the wooden picnic table. "I invite you to now answer this question with each other: When have you felt included in a diverse group of people?"

My little breakout circle kicked pine dust waiting for someone to go first. As I rummaged through my memories, many surfaced: the night I was hosted by a Sufi community in a midnight prayer circle on a coastline in rural Senegal; an evening in which I was served the kava bowl repeatedly in a farewell ceremony in Fiji; a dinner hosted by an Italian family in the Alps of France. But the image that shoved its way to the forefront of my mind—the moment that sat down in my head and would not leave—shocked me. It was that day in the East Wing of the White House.

I cleared my throat.

Saw Min, Luis, and Mateo looked at me.

I looked at my hands and told the story of the winks at the White House.

When I was done, no one said anything. They were practicing active listening. A 101-skill of experiential education that asks listeners to fully concentrate on, work to understand, and remember what is said. Where not the act of talking, but the act of listening, *is* the response. I concluded with the questions I'd stumbled upon myself: "Have white men in boardrooms and offices and clubs and all the other places behind closed doors always enjoyed such feelings of unquestionable inclusion? Has it been their assumed entitlement to sit back in their seats, relax, make eye contact—to feel always on the edge of an easy laugh? Is professional inclusion something I've actually been missing my entire life, knowing no better because I could not conceive of it before I experienced it?"

I looked up and met the eyes of Saw Min, Luis, and Mateo. No one kicked dust.

I HAD WRITTEN BOTH "SKIN-TO-SKIN" AND "BREAST CRAWL" into my birth plans—those infamous sheets of birthing instructions that often get shoved off the hospital tray in the more-common broken birth stories of un-ideal labor. But I was lucky. I had uncomplicated, natural births. And a doula who waved the sheet in front of busy nurses and doctors. So according to the instructions, my babies were placed low on my chest. There they heard the rush of blood in and out of my heart's ventricles, which probably sounded a lot like lapping waves. On my chest, my babies squirmed and rooted for the breast they could smell. They wiggled and reached until they found and latched, turning to my face with their upward eyes. This skin-to-skin contact, it flushed me with oxytocin, a hormone released from the brain that triggers the "let down" of milk and flushes a mother with feelings of relaxation, trust, bonding, and love.

Motherhood sharpened my senses. It was soon no longer just my children who perked my ears in the middle of the night with the slightest of squawks, coughs, and whimpers. My body was tuned, so over-tuned, that I often wandered into the dark cul-de-sac to break up cat brawls. I regularly opened the sliding glass door to call inside my gray-muzzled Labrador when the cackle of coyotes traveled over the berm. I stood on our deck under countless full moons, looking for the mother fox barking to her cubs. I yielded to all the calls from landscapes of innate wilderness I did not formerly know. I quickly learned the various cries from my babies, distinguishing a sucking "neh" of hunger from a slow "owh" of a needed nap. I watched, listened, and learned to read the blink of their eyes and the tension in their tiny fists. I learned these cues from intimacy. Relentless intimacy—sometimes dreamy, often forced.

But here's my question: In that room in the East Wing of the White House, did I not need my pen and notebook because there were other subtle flows of communication only seen by those trained to watch? Was there a different baseline of trust based on similarly gendered experiences of the world? In which ears have been tuned to specific variations of voice? Eyes trained on subtle clues of body language? I'm not sure, but I do know that women have been taught, out of necessity, how to read a room. Women (and all those marginalized) have learned how to glean the barely perceptible warnings and acknowledgments of the nonverbal language found between the lines and *in* the margins.

The famous French writer and literary critic Hélène Cixous knows my prior experience of speaking in rooms of men: "Every woman has known the torment of getting up to speak. Her heart racing, at times entirely lost for words, ground and language slipping away—that's how daring a feat, how great a transgression it is for a woman to speak—even just open her mouth—in public . . . her words fall almost always upon the deaf male ear, which hears in language only that which speaks in the masculine." But Cixous also gives texture to that mysterious element of women's voices when they flourish: "that element is song: first music from the first voice of love which is alive in every woman." Cixous also hinted of the world in which the music of women's voices flows unhindered, "The new history is coming; it's not a dream, though it does extend beyond men's imagination . . ."

Which takes me back to the room in which I birthed my daughter under the blood moon. I love my husband, but when my cervix dilated to seven centimeters, I hated his hands. I snarled when he tried to touch me. In the pause between contractions, I looked up at Emily. Emily was my doula, but she was first my roommate, my "house sister," a best friend. Emily and I had dropped countless tears into the couch cushion between us. So in those seconds between contractions, when I had no words, I didn't need words. Emily moved in. She moved my husband with her body away from mine. She placed her hands on my hips and squeezed the way a woman knows how to squeeze the birthing hips of a woman. My husband didn't even notice his displacement. Five years after that day he cocked his head while I was recounting the day and said, "Wait . . . there was an eclipse during Riva's birth?" He does not know I remember more of the moon's face than his that night. He remembered night. I remembered eclipse.

SINCE MY EXPERIENCE AT THE WHITE HOUSE, MY READ OF every table I've sat at has shifted. And so did the way I engaged with daily life. It began with my dentist. Then my physical therapist. Then my primary doctor. Then every writing instructor with whom I signed up for a class. I didn't discuss what I was doing with others. Maybe I worried it was sexist. I just slowly shifted every room in which I engaged with men—to teach me or heal me or touch my body—to rooms where women were doing the teaching and healing instead. It took me four years before the shift of my alliances was complete and I did not entirely notice my full transition until I slipped.

I enrolled in a class taught by a slightly famous, older, white male author. This man offended so deeply in his ignorant and uncareful handling of a Black woman participant's expression of anger for institutional racism that I slapped my laptop closed on his Zoom face. I pushed the computer away and fell onto my bed, throwing an arm over my eyes, exhaling the longest sigh of my life.

"You hate men, don't you?"

I hadn't noticed my husband enter the room. He was leaning a shoulder against the wall.

Not removing my arm from my eyes, I mumbled, "Patriarchy, babe. I don't hate *you*."

When he left, I sat back up and filled out the class feedback survey with some bitter paragraphs and then opened a new email addressed to a writing mentor. I wrote to her, "Why is emotion in writing such a bad thing? I'm being told this even by writers who are considered the most radical of feminists. But I'm livid! I can't *not* write through these emotions!" She reminded me that I knew better than to be momentarily swayed by the fame of an old, white, male author. She reminded me that if I had, as I'd told her, committed to classes and instruction from only women, BIPOC, and queer teachers that I should stick to it.

"Protect yourself," she advised.

And isn't that just it? My shift in alliances—it's safer. It's restorative. It's reconciliatory. It's a turn toward active listening and those who speak the language of knowing how to read a room. It's also a turn away from those who live in dangerous blind spots. A study in 2020 concluded Black newborns in the United States are three times more likely than white babies to die when looked after by white doctors. Male primary care physicians spend 15 percent less time with patients compared to women primary care physicians. Women are more concerned with climate change due to value systems more associated with altruism, compassion, fairness, and social justice, which means, also, that men are *less* concerned. That men have value systems *less* associated with altruism, compassion, fairness, and social justice.

Dangerous was my white male teacher in his mishandling of the Black woman's anger. Dangerous as life has always been for a Black man pulled over by a cop, for a brown person entering their own home in a white neighborhood, for every woman walking alone at night anywhere in the world, and for the health of our planet's body in the political grip of global patriarchy.

WHEN I INTERVIEWED SEA SHEPHERD CAPTAIN OONA Isabelle Layolle, she told me a story. She said she grew up on a sailing boat. She loved life on the sea and working on boats but she was always and only offered the job of hostess. She envied the deckhands—their work, freedom, and higher pay, so she thought, *I will have to become a deckhand*. Layolle became a deckhand, but the other deckhands—male deckhands—did not share the work with her. They did not explain the jobs and they pushed her away. She told me, "They didn't let me do anything, because I was a girl. It was so hard to always have to fight, just to learn." And so Layolle decided, *I will have to become a ship captain*. And that is what she did. She got her captain's license and then she pulled together her ship and crew. She ran their mission to protect the most endangered marine mammal, the Vaquita Porpoise, the way *she* wanted. She recounted, "What's really tough when you're a woman is that you don't have a reference. It's so hard to find the way you want to lead, because there is only one example—the men's way."

Hélène Cixous said mothers write in "white ink," and I think this is beautifully intuitive; that how I question, propose, relax, laugh, compose sentences, and walk in this world is colored by the degree to which what is summoned into my chest can "let down." Yet those safe places remain rare. Only in the prompted and active listening circle under the piñons did I reflect upon not only an entire career, but a lifetime in which all of the corporate tables I've sat at have reflected America's abysmal statistics of leadership diversity.

All except one table.

In that room in the East Wing, would that push-aside of hierarchy, would that insistence on trust, would that hush of active listening, would that humble and cooperative style—would it have happened in a room full of white men? What losses does American culture suffer in each passing day that we miss the opportunity to seismically shift? This shift, let me be clear, is not a shift to "girl boss" leadership of the same tired white supremacist, capitalist, and patriarchal systems that have led to this collapsing planet. I don't want inclusion into any supremacist boys' club. I'm talking about leadership in its feminine shape. In its nonbinary and gender-flow state. In its biodiverse expanse. I'm talking about the shapes of stewardship that could spread, when old powers cede; a shift from take-leadership to care-based leadership. From hierarchical patriarchy to a "mother culture" that is not restricted to people with wombs but inclusive of all bodies that "mother" art and water and animals and poems and soil and the ancestors that came before, and the generations of descendants to come.

I don't wear heels anymore, but I kept those shoes I wore to the White House. I save them for special occasions. Not holidays, but for the days I want my feet and the paths they have tread to feel specially recognized. For the days when I want to feel Michelle Obama's wink of inclusion and the hope of collapsed hierarchies in my stride.

Oona Isabelle Layolle decided, "I will have to become captain." To run the ship Layolle wanted—*her* ship, in a *different* way—Layolle could not just learn the rules that men had written. She had to become captain. And I would not be able to hold my own new hope for a new shape of leadership had I not experienced it in the executive heart of the United States of America.

On this long night into which we collectively labor, an eclipse hangs in the sky. A rare source of illumination watched by quiet species, oppressed peoples, and unvoiced ecosystems. A shift in perspective hangs within reach. As well as hope for *all* the realities we cannot conceive—until they wink at us.

GOOD GRIEF

THE REEK OF ROTTING CORPSE SHOULD HAVE STARTLED ME from my switchbacking thoughts, but I must have been on the other side of the breeze. Instead, it was the ground that brought my presence to my feet. Because the path was moving, but not the way the ground usually moves when I hike up the valley. When I noticed the ground moving—when I stopped—the ground kept moving. The path squirmed. And that's when what I heard *registered* with what I felt under my shoes. Which was the crackling of a blanket of wriggling maggots flattening under each step.

Death was the theme of the third of ten weeks comprising my "Good Grief" eco-anxiety group therapy program. Specifically, the capitalized prompt was: "HONOR MY MORTALITY & THE MORTALITY OF ALL."

Though I had not expected millions of maggots crunching underfoot in punctuation of the week's assignment, I did know their source. Two days earlier, I had found the fox's corpse alongside the trail, her body so fresh from life I had steadied my eyes on her belly looking for slow breaths. The collar of white at her neck had been matted with the foam of—I suspected—some unleashed, hunting-breed dog. It probably only took a good shake or two to snap whatever interlocked the fox's skull from her spine, to slacken her body and deaden those piercing eyes I so often saw squinting at me from the chokeberry bushes.

That day, I left the dead fox on the path. Walked faster so as not to let my sadness catch me. But with the new prompt to inspect impermanence, this time I tiptoed closer to examine the wriggling heart of decomposition in the fox's body. Did I know maggots could clean the flesh off bones in just a few days? Why would I know? I'd never watched a corpse decompose from flesh into tufts of matted hair before. It was never my inclination to watch. And it certainly isn't my culture to study death. It might even be my culture to look away. Yet, here it was—death underfoot.

I had not signed up for the eco-grief therapy program because I wanted to look closer at death. I signed up because the course promised a safe space to "lean into painful feelings about the state of the world." Painful feelings? Those I had plenty of. Stacked into wavering towers on the bedside table of my mind. Threatening to topple.

The Good Grief program featured, on its website, a colorful infographic with a tier of ten sequential steps to "Personal Resilience & Empowerment in a Chaotic Climate." It looked orderly. Approachable. Like a list I could checkmark my way through. The first assignment arrived in all caps by email with a Zoom link.

Step 1: Accept the Severity of the Predicament

IN OUR FIRST VIDEO MEETING, TEN FACES SLOW-BLINKED IN Zoom squares under which appeared their names, pronouns, the Indigenous land they occupied, and the ages of their children. The hands that belonged to the faces fiddled with pens and water glasses and errant strands of hair as the facilitators began the session with a briefing that mentioned "probable systems collapse."

I searched the eyes of the other participants. I was startled. I knew the collapsing ecological, economic, and cultural systems the facilitators were referencing. But "systems collapse" were still taboo words I kept locked in my chest by my ribs. And here they were? Pulled out, repeated, and pinned like laundry to lines! Taboo realities, just flapping in the wind for all the neighbors to see? Yet no one in the group of Zoom participants looked up. They looked down. One swiped her eyes. One petted her cat. Another turned off her camera. (There was only one man in the group.)

After the briefing, I was given three uninterrupted minutes to share my own feelings about *the severity of the predicament*. This is what tumbled from my quivering mouth:

Christina Rivera, she/her, stolen Ute land, children ages 7 and 10

Yesterday I was writing and crying, something I often do together. Sentences move me forward in a stuck world—tiptoeing, word-by-word, into a reality I can't otherwise approach. Because I don't know what to do with the images I saw yesterday on Instagram. They were of a cove in the Dutch Faroe Islands where the bloodied bodies of 1,400 White-Sided Dolphins were dragged onto the beach. The super pod of dolphins had gathered together, not knowing that men (men-men-always-men) would snatch upon the intergenerational gathering, surround and drive the terrified families with speedboats and Jet Skis onto land, where each dolphin—elders, matriarchs, pregnant mothers, and youth—was slashed in the head to death. The ocean was red with their spilled blood and I could only watch a few minutes of Sea Shepherd's video capturing the massacre before the jagged rock of grief pushed up my throat. Humans are terrible and I am human and my children are human and my husband is "man" and my son will be "man" and I can't reconcile this. So I scroll faster, lest the jagged thing catch up and projectile from my mouth and then I will pull out my hair and the neighbors will call the police and I will need straps or medication to keep my hands away from my head. Except I need my hair because I have to pick up my kids at 3:15. So just fuck humans for being so fucking terrible that I have to live in rage to keep my sanity. For making my grief such a razor-thin edge that a slip of footing would slice me in half.

I trembled through this "share" in my first allotted minute. The second minute I muffled my face with tissues. When the faces turned to another for her share, I turned off my video to let my monsoons of rage and grief take their turns moving through me. Climate emotions, I should have known, wouldn't be an orderly rainbow of steps. So though the prompts of the program were sequential, my path through them wasn't. Here they are in my own order.

Step 6: Practice Gratitude, Witness Beauty, & Create Connections

WHENEVER SOMEONE CLASPS THEIR HANDS AROUND MINE, looks me deep in the eye, and whispers, "In these times, it's more important than ever for us to feel grateful . . ." I shudder with the inner scream: "I AM FUCKING GRATEFUL. HOW ELSE WOULD I KNOW HOW FUCKING BAD IT ALL IS?"

Our march toward ecocide is excruciating and for all my odd raptures with death, I am equally committed to loving life. Not a day passes in which I haven't found awe in the felt of a flower petal, a rainbow of ambers on a wet leaf, the smell of approaching rain, or the lotus-flower footprints of a Red Fox depressed in caked mud. Life stops me in my tracks. Nature tips my chin. I am quite alive to the details that make life shimmer, so this American obsession with faith, optimism, passive hope, and steamrolling positivity feels—to me—in direct correlation to our collective case of climate crisis denial.

So when I looked for an eco-grief program, I sought descriptions with the fewest mentions of the g-word. In the Good Grief program, I liked that gratitude shared a sentence with the directives "witness beauty" and "create connections." Those I could summon without baring fangs. I also appreciated that the ten-stepped program had roots in Alcoholics Anonymous. AA is famous for its culture-breaking tenet, "Addiction is not a choice," and that fact reminded me that capitalism wasn't my choice either. Nor patriarchy. Nor a country and culture steeped in racism and misogyny. Alcoholism is a disease. A sickness of compulsive and out-of-control behaviors. Those traits feel familiar. But also point to greater illness—a cultural disease.

The climate futurist Alex Steffen says climate crisis made us lose our footing in time. He calls the bardo between our nostalgia for the past and our apocalyptic reality "transapocalyptic." He says we're living through a period of discontinuity, "when the experience and expertise you've built up over time cease to work." But just whose idea of nostalgia were we considering? So I have problems with Step 6. Maybe I'm not ready. Maybe I have to walk farther, to come back to it.

Step 8: Grieve the Harm I Have Caused

I DON'T KNOW WHERE MY DAUGHTER'S INSTINCT TO BECOME a mother comes from, because it was not mine as a child. But she repeatedly says that of all the things she hopes for her future, she wants "to be a mama." How and when will I tell her the earth is not stable and already overtasked by the number of humans on it?

I know she feels the peace shifting. She felt a tremor in the plumes of black smoke from wildfires she watched burn from the roof of our house last fall. She felt society shaking in the cancellation of her fifth birthday due to a global pandemic. And then there are the fears she feels through me. The shift of Colorado weather to "new normal" permanent drought. The tenuous future of the avocados and raspberries that she favors, threatened by hive collapses of wild bees that pollinate fruits. Her mother's tears for the songbirds that fell out of the sky in their migration south last fall. Yellow Warblers and Violet-Green Swallows and Flycatchers with bold wing bars that fell dead in starvation by the thousands. They fell in Arizona after their flight across Colorado skies. Songbirds live eight to twelve years, which means those birds were born, and died, under my watch on Earth.

So when I saw "grieve the harm I've caused" on the list, it made me tremble with long-corked and shaken pressure. Ready to drown myself in my long list of individual offenses, I was caught off guard when one of the facilitators introduced the module with, "Guilt can be a place where we get so comfortable wallowing, that we *allow* it to hold us back from moving *through* grief."

This stopped me. Could my guilt be a crutch? A bottomless well of self-inflicted abuse that conveniently stuns me into inaction?

More frightening: Could my eco-guilt be a tool of strategic gaslighting by behemoth environmental offenders? Had the corporations with easiest access to the levies of true systemic change consulted with behavior scientists to discover that spinning an individual in the emotions of guilt, fear, and regret was a great tactic to stagnate and confuse activist energies? Had they pointed at my own ecological footprint while, behind my back, rewriting their own stories in green ink in pretty pamphlets?

I will never be done grieving the harm I've caused. I will never *not* second-guess the need for my voice in the world. I will lament, forever, the disproportionate trash I have left on the planet in the wake of my privileged life: the fuel planes burned moving my body across continents, the polyester particles my dryer tumbles into the air, the styrofoam in which my husband brings home Chinese food on nights when I feel "tired." But moving my guilt from the altar of self-incrimination to the table of honest acknowledgment might be the better step forward.

Step 5: Develop Awareness of Biases & Perception

BY STEP FIVE OF THE PROGRAM, I HAVE SEEN EVERYONE IN the group cry, or rage, or ramble into stupefaction. We have each turned off our videos and turned them back on. And we have all held the space for others to leave and return.

It's a privilege—not just an honor but an unfair entitlement—to share this circle. To add oneself to the group roster undoubtedly required childcare and/or able-bodied partners, financial security, and leisure time. This fact does not escape the attention of the participants. Together we cry because we get to choose to "show up" emotionally, while so many people, so many marginalized bodies, acutely face the consuming realities of climate crisis daily—of poisoned water, toxic air, shifting rains, unchosen wars, ignored famine, and disregarded personhood.

I am prepared, in this session, to feel both sad and mad. The facilitators emailed us, in advance of the group meeting, a little infographic with clip art symbolizing the twenty different cognitive biases that "screw up" human decision-making. What looked like a video game controller represented "pro-innovation bias" and the tendency to overvalue the hope of technology in solving ecological problems. A thick-lashed bird head accompanied the description of the "ostrich effect" in which we ignore dangerous information by burying our heads in sand. There was even a bias to describe our lack of awareness of our biases: The "blind spot bias," it was dubiously called.

This exercise of inspecting all the ways humans are pre-programmed for failure put me in a more forgiving mood. Forgiving of myself, of my friends, of my country, of my species, because we are immature and faulty creatures, wired to pay attention to immediate threats, to have sex and survive, to over-focus on the present rather than the future or past.

Still, if we can put a human on the moon, it seems within our mental capabilities to bring "Hyperbolic Discounting" into our collective self-awareness, which is the egotistical perception that the life we are living now is more important than the lives of our descendants. Has it always been this way? Oren Lyons, Native American faithkeeper of the Turtle Clan and chief of the Onondaga Nation, wrote, ". . . one of the first mandates given us as chiefs, to make sure and to make every decision that we make relate to the welfare and well-being of the seventh generation to come." Which gets me wondering if some of these perception biases might be newer than we think—or as new as white settler colonialism.

But can I, personally, imagine seven generations forward? Can I picture a descendant who is a seven-layered extension of my body, my toxins, my traumas, my love, and my care of the Earth? It's hard, but I can start with the child in front of me. As it turned out, it wasn't so hard to talk to her about her future. I answered her questions. I didn't lie. I lamented the harm my generation has inflicted upon hers. I told her we'll move through our compromised future together. Maybe it was the tone of my voice, but she accepted the realities. When she joined me at a rally for reproductive rights, she spent two hours on her poster. First, she drew herself: blue shirt, envelope pocket, with a heart necklace under her round seven-year-old face. Behind her self-portrait was a great scribbled turquoise ocean that made the Earth's lime-green land masses look like the islands they are. Around the planet, she drew fifty-three stick people. In block letters arcing above the planet it said: "LET GIRLS DO WHAT THEY WANT. THEY MIGHT NOT WANT TO BE MOTHERS."

Step 2: Practice Being with Uncertainty

WHEN DID I LOSE MY FRIENDSHIP WITH UNCERTAINTY? Because we used to be so close: back when we hiked for a decade through Himalayan ranges, wandered megalopolises with limited foreign language skills, dropped into crevasses of coral reef with a small tank of air. It was my job back then. I was paid to take people to the edge of their vulnerability and handhold them into the ring of the concentric circles we called (in the field of experiential education) the "Challenge Zone"—a narrow path bordered outside by the "Comfort Zone" and inside by the "Panic Zone."

But how have my uncertainties shape-shifted in the face of climate crisis? Did my friendliness with the world of unknowns break with the addition of a child to my hip? Or singe with the smoke of wildfires stopped at my front door only by towels jammed into the crease? Or rise with the day's marker to the maroon top of our local Air Quality Index (AQI)? When did I make the smallest circle of the "Panic Zone" my official home of parenthood?

This winter, my son had hockey on Thursdays and Sundays, and the sport required a duffel bag so big he could grow six inches and still zip himself into it. One day, while trying to gather Nash's arm pads and knee pads and chest plate and jock cup and weird large-knit leg warmers and padded shorts and skates and skate covers and two different hockey sticks and the helmet with the dumb snaps that only an adult can close, I dropped the black bag on the floor and yelled at my husband, "Hockey is not a climate apocalypse skill!"

Because that's always in the back of my mind when I am at the cusp of my tolerance for things that don't make sense. My husband, the eternal optimist whom I need lest I'd never get out of bed, seemed unwilling to entertain human existentiality without hockey. He had no answer for me that day, and we were already late to the ice rink. But that moment, with the black body-sized bag at my feet and the tears in my eyes, was important. Because it meant my fear of climate crisis had tipped. My fear of climate crisis outweighed my fear of *denying* climate crisis. I had unconsciously stepped into the bull's-eye of panic. I needed help to step out.

When I told my husband that I would be taking ten Wednesday evenings off from parenting to meet with an eco-grief group, he didn't ask questions. His silence said all I needed to know about his opinion on my need for support. I didn't need to resolve my grief, conquer it, or push my way back into any mirage of "comfort zone." I needed a place to face my grief—a challenge zone—in which to wrestle, or dance, with my feelings, depending on the shifting realities. A place where I could practice holding uncertainty, again, by the hand.

Step 7: Take Breaks & Rest

AFTER EXERTION, A BODY NEEDS REST. I REMEMBERED THIS from my years dating a gym aficionado and the workout planning we did to ensure our muscles would heal and mend and—in that *act of rest*—grow stronger. Similarly, the mental and emotional muscles of grief and activism need the leaving-alone time that nurtures strength. It's only my capitalistic conditioning that calls me lazy and chastises my long walks, my day naps, and my multiple trips to fill the bird feeder. Hence, Audre Lorde's famous conclusion that caring for oneself is "an act of political warfare." So I'm going to log my early bedtime, my many cups of tea, and even my sink of dirty dishes and the after-school program for my kids, under the column: SELF-CARE WARFARE. Counting each investment in my "sustainable distress" as a picket sign for revolution.

Later in the week, I was hiking a gravel road surrounded by a family of aspens at peak gold, when my old dog picked up the scent of a path I'd not noticed before. We followed the trail up a drainage that carried spring overflows of snow melt. Up, up, me and my old dog climbed like young goats until we reached another level of land unobservable by even the binoculars of leaf peepers below. We slowed our pace, breathing in the grove exhaling oxygen upon our heads, taking in the swath of forest rarely watched, until the path was split in two by a boulder. At the split, I stopped, took three steps back and saw the boulder had two humps on either side of its shoulders. Instead of proceeding around it, I climbed up its mossy side, slid into the middle of its heart, my back curved, held by stone arms. There I rested. Letting go of everything I was holding. The rock held me. And this was self-care too, I decided.

Surrendering to being nothing but held.

Step 9: Show Up

IN 2020, I LEFT MY CAREER IN EXPERIENTIAL EDUCATION. AT my last company retreat, I stepped into the circle of my colleagues, heart racing, arms pleading, "But shouldn't everything we do be rising to the challenge of our climate emergency?" People looked down. No one answered my question, and it didn't matter because a global pandemic was about to furlough our circle into far-strung pieces. When my kids finally went back to school, I returned to the workforce as an environmental writer, which better aligned with my personal aims, but also lacked the vigor of chaining myself to old-growth trees.

"Show up" was the smallest program step in words, yet terrifying in scope. Especially for someone who spent most of her day sitting on a chair, at a desk, looking out a window. That didn't sound like showing up to me. That sounded like checking out. Like cozy-living in a daydream where I stood at the fantasy helm of an eco-pirate ship scanning horizons for whale poachers to chase. Except there's a scratch at the door behind me and the dog needs a potty walk and Riva can't find her other cowboy boot and Nash wants a snack.

My son told me the other day that the thing I'm the very BEST at is "being boring." I *had* recently told him that the secret to happiness was never being bored, so in his ten-year-old psychology, a compliment might have embedded in that superlative. But still, how does the most boring person in the world *show up* in the fight against climate crisis?

In 2023, I was hired to write a local government campaign for a carbon-free future. They hired me because they'd read my essays. They wanted me to "lunge for the emotional jugular." To drive people to action. After I watched intelligent presentations on their science-based and data-driven solutions, they asked how I thought we should approach the messaging. I responded, "We start with fear. We start with anger. We start with confusion and guilt and panic and cynicism and pain and grief. We start by acknowledging the full spectrum of valid feelings. Because that's the place where we all can meet." This full arc of sentiments I knew only and intimately from my own ten steps of immersion.

I now work in "climate communications," but so does my best friend, who paints giraffes with their spots falling off. And my sister-in-law who worked relentlessly as a nurse through an epidemic. And my bestie who professionally guides people through traumas with ketamine. And my esteemed old colleague who pushes corporate boards to align their integrity with their DEI initiatives. And my old friend running the midwifery center. And my friends working with sad teenagers, and recovering addicts, and people without homes. And definitely, definitely, my best high school friend whose body has been wrecked by decades of institutional and societal abuses; my friend with the physical flare-ups that leave her bedridden from where she writes poems like:

They say
*You have always
been angry*

I tell them
*I have always
been a woman*

These people fight by caring. They are fighting the climate of our crisis. Which is a cultural crisis. They are the healers and bridge-builders and frontline responders and disrupters and caregivers and visionaries who fight by doing what needs to get done and saying what needs to be said and feeling what needs to be felt. If we feel and are moved by our feelings, then we're doing the work. Because this is not an individual sport. It's a collective quest. I don't need to do it all if I'm one of many. And from a perfect storm of great caring arises the imperative to defend and protect our collective body. *Our* Earth. *Our* oceans. We may not live to see the outcome of this imperative, but I *can* live with the slow-stepping soul of knowing we cared. Per the wisdom of Dr. Clarissa Pinkola Estés Réyes, "Ours is not the task of fixing the entire world all at once, but of stretching out to mend the part of the world within our reach."

As for the most boring person in the world? Her writing might be a boat, transient and creaky in construction, but also able to ride winds across oceans with a helm from which she can fly her sentences of undying love under a snapping black flag.

Step 4: Do Inner Work

A YEAR AFTER COMPLETING MY GOOD GRIEF PROGRAM, during a checkup with my osteopath, she will scan my file, meet my eyes, and ask, "And the nightmares and insomnia? Do you still have those?"

It will take me a minute. I will look up at the ceiling and search my memories, and I'll recall the years I woke in cold sweats and listened for bomb sirens, or hurricane warnings, or looked out my window in certainty of what was reaching for me from the darkness. With a tilt of my head, I will say, "I guess I don't really have those midnight panic attacks anymore."

"That's wonderful. Can you name why?"

I will recount, "I joined this eco-grief support group last year and just naming my fears, and crying through my admissions of guilt and feelings of helplessness—I felt seen for the first time. After that, I began talking to my husband about my grief, and to my kids about my sadness, and openly with my coworkers and friends. And I finished writing a book about my personal feelings of loss from the extinction crisis. My sadness isn't gone. But the nightmares went away."

I will sign up for a second eco-grief course with a new set of faces and names and the swaths of stolen land they inhabit. And those people, too, will make me feel—at my most vulnerable— encircled, sane, and seen. But the Good Grief cohort will always be the first with whom I learned to weave shared mourning. Those who taught me: there is an equally great tenderness to great grief, when we let that weave hold us.

Step 10: Reinvest into Meaningful Efforts

ONE NIGHT AT THE END OF MY GOOD GRIEF COURSE, I WOKE from a feverish sleep, grabbed a pen from my night table, and wrote onto the blank page in the front of the nearest novel I could reach:

> I would have chosen this life. Knowing me and knowing the lives available in the history of humanity, I would have chosen this existence on the precipice. This last fight. I would have expected it to be painful and I still

would have chosen it. And maybe—maybe—my children chose this life with me, too.

My path up the creek was wriggling with decomposition, always moving just under my feet. It was only a matter of facing what I already felt. Of letting my sadness catch me.

I watched the fox decompose, saw flesh turn to dirt, return to earth, humbled in the way Latin's *humilis* ("low, lowly"), comes from *humus* ("ground"). To decompose is a *dissolution,* and a dissolution is "the closing down or dismissal of an assembly or body," and maybe there are deaths we shouldn't fear. Man's massacre of a superpod of sentient creatures is not a new story. It's an old story. An over and over and over-again story. Of man stealing bodies, land, voices, and lives of the marginalized. Of the structures, systems, and cultures man built to validate violence. But something rots. And this time I'm downwind. When a whale dies, her body falls to the ocean floor, sustaining a succession of marine communities from Great White Sharks to Sea Sponges to microscopic biota. Maybe decomposition does not lurk, as much as it waits.

Step 6 of the Good Grief program urged me to reflect on *beauty, awe, connections.* My children constantly wrangle me into the present moment in their absence of the clock they don't yet hear ticking. So the dog takes me on a walk—through tall grasses wet with last night's storm. And Nash chatters with me while grinding down a carrot—pointing to a Sandhill Crane stalking the berm out our kitchen window. And Riva stomps with cowgirl confidence out the door in her boots—and I follow her thinking there is no moment better than this. The G-word isn't so bad when my grief is counterbalanced by the weight of my attention to the little things I love. So I follow their lead. Down paths I wouldn't otherwise go, retrieving what I wouldn't otherwise find . . .

Last week, I was hiking behind Nash, following him as windingly as a young boy meanders down a mountain. I told him my story of the decomposing fox and mentioned I had later looked for the skull, but it had disappeared. At the end of our descent, Nash wanted to drop into a drainage, a place where mountain lions often roam in spring. Firm in my commitment to follow his path (including places I wouldn't otherwise go), I waved him forward. Ten minutes into the drainage, Nash bent down and popped up with the full-snouted, pointy-toothed skull.

"Mom! I found your fox!"

Nash's life, his stories, his unordered beginnings and endings—of loving and living and grieving and dying—they loop with mine. And those eyes that watched me from behind the chokeberry bushes—they sit now on the windowsill behind my desk. Piercing me in reminder of the twisty nature of wonder, and of this winding path we've embarked upon—at the very least—together.

FOG RESCUE

LAST WEEK, I DREAMT I UNFOLDED A MAP. I INSPECTED THE creases and braille-like topography connecting one section to another. I kept unfolding the map, to a long, river-meandering length. It was my job—I knew—to fold the map back up, into a shape I could pocket. The creases were there; I just needed to feel for the pleats of least resistance. Refolding an unfolding.

The dream was not lucid. I was not "aware I was dreaming." But the dream did wink at me from between the levels of consciousness I more often frequent—like the scummy sink of last night's dishes and the "dreamless" slumber of parenting exhaust. I use quotes because sleep is almost never dreamless. But the alarm clocks and crying babies and screaming needs of the logistics of everyday life are quite efficient at drowning the whispers of night's visions.

Lucid dreaming has been an interest of mine since the day my mother seeded the skill into my six-year-old subconscious. After a bout of recurring nightmares, she told me: "If you can *remember* you are dreaming, you can move everything in your dreams as you'd like." Her instruction, planted into such a young brain with no garden walls, was a sunflower seed that grew swift and thick. One night, instead of running from a truck-sized tarantula, I turned and faced the hairy-legged thing. I squeezed my eyes as hard as I could. It probably looked as you'd imagine of a six-year-old: long lashes, scrunchy face, cute nose wrinkles. The spider fizzled and fell off my dreamscape. I acutely remember, afterward, the zooming feeling of leaving the technicolor world of soft edges and wiggling my stiff fingers under cold bedsheets.

Soon, I was ending every dream—nightmare or adventure—with what I thought of as my "hard blink," and the more I practiced, the more I roamed free and powerful in lucid landscapes. Decades later, I distinctly remember a dream in which I was trying to teach a new best-dream-friend how to "come back" to the "real world." I instructed her on the mechanics of the hard blink and we held hands for the countdown. 5, 4, 3, 2, 1 . . . Zooooooom.

I can still feel the emptiness when I awoke without her hand in mine.

At some point, I lost my lucid dreaming skills. If I had to point at a year, it would be around my eighth. I suspect many women would point to eight as their year of stolen nerve. Because it's around that age when your big brother makes fun of you for the fairy footprints you found around the base of a tree. Or the boy you like on the playground laughs and points at your scuffed knees. Or you see your mother crying on the deck stairs, still holding the apple she picked up but did not throw at your father. In year eight, the borders of fancies and villains and realities leak and merge.

It's been forty years and my urge for lucid power is back. Probably because the terrors came back. Not the spiders of my childhood but the waking nightmares featuring tidal waves and flooding houses and crumbling cliffs and emaciated climate refugees and fevered children—all on the set of a shriveling and quaking planet. Dr. Báyò Akómoláfé, a philosopher and professor of psychology, observed of the Anthropocene, "we are all fugitives" and "we are being chased."

During the day, I feel chased mostly by time—impending soccer practices, overdue fraction worksheets, unscheduled dentist appointments, and my own impatience for early bedtime—but those are just distractions. In the night, there's no busyness to hide behind. My subconscious puts together the puzzle I don't have time to piece together during the day. The edge pieces align in a frame of smoky skies and littered ocean floor and burning old growth on either side.

With all these dire images in my head, it seems as fine a time as any to reclaim the ability to travel—without plane or mask—great distances in retrieval of elusive answers hidden in other levels of consciousness. Dr. Clarissa Pinkola Estés Réyes described this descent into the middle world in her description of the home of the selkie: "This midway point between the worlds of reason and image, between feeling and thinking, between matter and spirit—is the home of the medial woman. . . . The seal woman, soul-self, passes thoughts, ideas, feelings, and impulses up from the water to the medial self, which in turn lifts those things onto land and consciousness in the outer world."

Amid the too-real world of melting glaciers and boiling coastlines and shifting jet streams, I want to visit the cool buoyant home of this soul-self. I want to pull on my seal skin, dive in, descend, and maybe even retrieve a thing or two from the depths. But I have a feeling I'll need my six-year-old dream prowess to get there.

So I've been studying and practicing dream lucidity. With meager results.

To lucid dream, you have to learn how to *snap* your conscious mind into remembering it's dreaming, usually by noticing a detail that doesn't exist in the waking world. The dream world, you see, is lazy: it looks *like* the waking world, but if you push on its edges, the dreamscape can crinkle and clue you in to the fact you're dreaming.

For example, if you look into a mirror in a dream, your reflection might warp or morph into another face. Or if you open a book in a dream, the words might drip or jiggle off the page.

But dreams are snarky. I once spent an entire night in dream-land asking everyone I met, "Have you seen any mirrors?" The fuzzy people I encountered all looked me in the eye. "Nope. Haven't seen any mirrors around here . . ."

Maybe these apparitions all fell into fits of laughter after I walked past them. Or so I imagined when I woke and cursed my snickering subconscious. Just last night, after setting the intention for a lucid dream, I fell right into a nightmare where I was pursued by a psychopath. But something felt off, because I wasn't actually afraid. I wasn't panicking because I *knew* I had control. I kept stopping in the dream and rummaging through my backpack—certain I'd forgotten something critical! Like maybe my intention? Snarky, I tell you.

But it feels good to be dabbling again in my old obsession. Eight years ago, I was at a writing conference when the teacher—a renowned male author—broke his lengthy oration to ask the crowd, "What IS the importance of dreams to writing?" It was my first writing conference and I was petrified. I had not once—in three days—raised my hand or spoken above a measured whisper. But I was so excited my quiet obsession was being validated—by a famous author no less! My hand shot into the air. "Dreams can answer questions! Give us parallel worlds where we can problem-solve without hard consequences!"

He cut me off.

I was speaking of those messy projections of seemingly nonsensical night visions.

But he was speaking *metaphorically*—of the act of using one's *goals* to manifest manuscripts. He called on someone else, emphasizing his conventional answer by throwing a finger into the air with emphasis, "Exactly!"

I was deflated, woken in bed alone again with the emptiness in my hand.

I didn't raise my hand at a writing workshop for another two years. But I am an older woman and more mature writer now.

I have finished a book in which, in almost every essay, a sub-conscious voice has meandered from darkness to dawn and sat down in my pages. So in my new daydream, I'm raising my hand at the front of class again and this time, the famous male author is gone and I'm answering my own question: *Because dreams remind us that we are more than creatures of day and light. That the unconscious has mysteries of existence yet to unravel.*

CATABASIS WAS A NEW WORD TO ME. IT MEANS "GOING BACK down."

I learned the word in a podcast where Dr. Báyò Akómoláfé spoke about the need for a new weave of spirituality and the sacred to meet today's global climate challenges. He said of the Anthropocene, "We are not dealing with a want of methods or confidence. We are dealing with the corrosive incertitude and indeterminacy of collapse . . . and the fragility of our sense-making approaches." As a species we've entered a collective nightmare of our own making and Dr. Akómoláfé is pointing a finger at the inadequacy of our daytime rationales, and at the fallacy of our above-ground and conventional approaches.

I have worked with, befriended, interviewed, and circled up with a lot of phenomenal activists. Some of them ask me what else I "do"—you know, "besides write." As if the question hasn't already waterboarded me. But I do hope we are working different angles of the same problem. Because I want to get under skin. I want deep vulnerabilities explored. I want culture to shift. I want borders to recede. And then I want to dive deeper. Under the paradigms of our cultural currents. And the way I plunge into catabasis is with words—with sentences and questions and quests that challenge traditional sense-making.

This descent into the place that hovers between the physical and metaphysical recalls a story I first read in Carl Safina's book *Beyond Words*. In the retelling, Alexandra Morton—the same scientist who dropped the hydrophone into Corky's tank on the day her live calf was taken from her—was following a pod of Killer Whales in the Queen Charlotte Strait between the mainland of British Columbia and Vancouver Island. The A5 Pod was difficult to follow, and the last time Morton had seen them, they were traveling west toward the open sea. Morton's inflatable boat was soon enveloped by fog she described as thick as "a glass of milk." She couldn't see the sun, didn't have a compass, couldn't make sense of the wave patterns, and heard a cruise ship moving toward her but couldn't decipher its direction. Suddenly, five black fins popped up in the water around her boat. The A5 Orca Pod, Morton realized, had turned back. She picked up her oars and followed them until the outline of her home shoreline materialized in the breaking fog. Once she could see land, the pod turned around. Morton reflected of the encounter, "For more than twenty years, I have fought to keep the mythology of Orcas out of my work . . . Yet there are times when I am confronted with something beyond our ability to scientifically quantify."

Like Morton, I'm feeling a calling of the mythological I have too long dismissed. A call to travel beneath the surface and visit the unlikely places where black fins cross a milky barrier between what's possible and not, and lead me to land. That's why I'm trying to find that magic door to dream lucidity I once found without looking.

Francis Weller had words to describe the courtship with this "larger dreaming animal." He described the world as "riddled with spirit, ancestors, community, cosmos and the dreams of those yet to come" that requires an *initiation*. He said of this threshold crossing: "Something dies in the process. Something needs to die in the process. And something needs to come forward. Some new shape of identity wedded to the silt and slope of the land." This makes sense of the many times I've died in my dreams. Sometimes there is panic. Sometimes I shudder awake and jump out of bed like I would from a sinking ship. Other times, I take my last breath and let go. I sink. But never is there not another side. Some new shape my last breath moves toward.

Rainer Maria Rilke's poetic prophecy strikes a similar bell to Weller's: "Again and again, some people wake up. They have no ground in the crowd and they emerge according to broader laws. They carry strange customs with them, and demand room for bold gestures. The future speaks ruthlessly through them."

Going down to wake up.

Of course. Where else will we find new, bold, and ruthless futures?

It strikes me that I am having fewer original thoughts and that's probably an important transition. To step aside. To make room for voices that know more about oppression, more about resistance, more about fugitivity, more about the ancestral and native laws that guided interconnected life on this planet before the broken treaties and policies of white man. More space for the laws of spirit that supersede human laws and for the dreams *of those yet to come.*

The dreaming books remind me that lucidity is a process, a practice that can take months of looking into mirrors and opening books and "reality testing" the waking world. A *reality test* involves small tests during your day to figure out if you're truly awake—or if you're dreaming. Like pushing on a wall to see if it holds your weight, or checking your wrist for your pulse, or flipping a coin to see if it adheres to gravity. What the dream books don't tell you is that by cultivating dream consciousness, we cultivate speculation of our waking world too. By challenging the laws of gravity in dreams, we also inspect the forces *that attract a body to the center of earth.* Our planet, our collective unconscious, has inner workings in deep need of metaphysical examination. The constructs of our "realities" need testing.

I keep checking my pulse, but, sadly, I've had no lucid dreams. Or none I remember. Of course, that's the trick. Because if I can't remember my dreams, how can I remember if I've had a lucid dream? The true homework—as my map dream smirked—is remembering: *the refolding of an unfolding.*

Last night I left half a glass of water on my night table. It's another lucid dream trick: You fill the glass, get in bed, drink half the water, and leave the rest in hope the undrunk water will connect your sleeping body to your physical body in a sort of transcendental thirst. I woke in the morning with the dissipating memory of standing in the middle of a hall of lockers, trying to remember the code to slide open a long metal box. I looked down either side of the hall, waving my arms at passersby, trying to get their attention. Unseen and weary, I finally just followed my fingers and put in a code. The box opened. Maybe I do have what I need—in my own creases and folded stories?

Despite my lucid dream failures, I have had one reliable subconscious-exploring success. If I ask a question before I sleep, the answer often shows up on my nightstand by morning, written in my own sloppy midnight handwriting. And that makes sense: that this is less an experiment of wishing for answers, than asking good questions and meeting in the bardo between matter and spirit.

That Orca pod that shepherded Alexandra Morton back to land? The matriarch of that pod was A23, also known as Stripe. Stripe was Corky's mother. A fathom is a measure of ocean and six feet deep equals one fathom. I love this equation of depth and imagination as it feels the only measure where such a coincidence—Stripe rescuing a woman who had once shed tears at the edge of her stolen calf's tank—could exist.

We are lost at sea in a collective fog as a cruise ship pummels toward us and our sense of direction—our old paradigms—fail us. Maybe it's time to stop paddling. Time to reassess the rules by which we make sense. Time to tip our chins to the sky and close our eyes. As Francis Weller advised, "Slow down, uncenter and forget yourself for a moment, let the world find you . . ."

Can we open our eyes—after this uncentering—slowly? Reaching for the strings of kinship that rise from the water and tug us forth? The fog, the currents, the depths below, were only ever the same as those inside. And if we surrender to our tiny place in something bigger, swirling, who knows what might appear? Like the four-foot dorsal fin of a matriarch—and her eleven-million-year-old ancestry—showing us our way home.

This week, from Riva's backpack, I pulled a large rectangle of purple butcher paper with a photo at the top in which the shining white lip of a rippled lake met a dark wall of shoreline. Between the two contrasting tones, a cloudy mist blurred the distinction between land and water, and under the image, Riva had written in tall letters with a No. 2 pencil: "Fog. Looks smoky as a fire. I love how it is so mysterious. Mysterious as a dark cave and when the sun shines on it, it makes a very faint rainbow! Don't you think it's the best part of nature too?" If it's synchronicity, inheritance, or coincidence, I don't know, but I smiled and taped the purple paper to my window; loving that she is not afraid—indeed called—to the path through the misty in-between places.

The fog, the shore, the bardos between, and this descent from the surface of things summon her back: the Leatherback sea turtle who swam on our planet's oceans through the rise and fall of dinosaurs, through the rise and rise of man. The Leatherback who can dive four thousand feet on a single breath. The Leatherback and her pilgrimage from land, through seas of lost years, back to the shore of her birth. Finding her mother's phantomed path—on the same dark coast, under the same cool moon. North America, before it was baptized with colonizer names, was known to many Indigenous peoples as Turtle Island. The white-crested ridges on the top of the Leatherback run in slight curves, lengthwise, longitudinal. Joan Tavares Avant, Wampanoag Deer Clan mother, further paints the image, "One reason is the continent's shape. The North American area has the shape of the turtle's shell with a spiny ridge, the Rocky

Mountains . . . The continent also has thirteen regions that correspond to the thirteen plates on a turtle's shell." When I picture this Turtle Island, it's Linda Hogan's whisper I hear again: *there are names each thing has for itself.*

A turtle's heart is slow to die. Did you know this? I didn't. Turtles die as slowly as they live and a turtle's heart can beat for five days after death. Pulsing, pulsing, between lucid life and the quiet of what's next.

Under the thatched roof in Guatemala, I met the Leatherback hatchling in the palm of my hand. Her winged arms swam. The questions she inspired, of these inconceivable times, still paddle. But in her undying heart, I fathom.

We won't rest until we reach the sea.

ACKNOWLEDGMENTS

Thank you . . .

To all the researchers, artists, activists, scientists, and people named or cited in this book, for the work you do, via which I get to be the writer I am.

To the literary magazines and editors who took chances on a little-known writer and her experimental essays in their first published shapes: *Bat City Review* ("Four Circles"), *Orion Magazine* ("The Endling"), *Terrain.org* ("The 17th Day"), *The Kenyon Review* ("Two Breaths"), *River Teeth* ("Red Talisman"), *Catapult Magazine* ("Oncoming"), *Atticus Review* ("Hooded"), and *The Fourth River* ("The Smooth Sides of Darkness"). And to the Pushcart Press for honoring "Two Breaths" with a prize and "The 17th Day" with a special mention. That day, I cried.

To my core pods of women for the care and encouragement and love with which we lift each other up. Thank you especially to Caitlin, KT, Parke, Liz, Emily, and KB. Witchy cackles of gratitude to the Avalanche women, my Rocky Mountain valley women, and my Otter House women. Thank you for shaping my life and squeezing my hand through the highs and lows of incubating and birthing this book.

To BK Loren for every single comment left in the margins of my roughest drafts and for the brilliant authorly and life advice I will revisit over and over and forever. I wouldn't be here had you not been at that first trailhead waving me over and along every step of the way.

To my "literary fairy godmother" Kate Moses, for sharing so many cups of tea over Zoom and first drafts as we broke open ideas and dreams and shapes and laughed so, so, much together.

To my engaged, persistent, kind, and wonderful agent Julie Stevenson, the first person who said with professional confidence, "This is a book of essays. Let's let it be what it wants to be." Thank you for your vision, faith, and friendship. And thanks also to all those fine people moving all the gears (with care, professionalism, and ethical considerations) at MMQLIT.

To Marisa Siegel for her unhesitating confidence in this project, ever-swift and astute guidance, and profound editorial care of this book. To Anne Gendler for her eagle (copyediting) eyes, open mind, and kindness and diligence in answering my too-many questions, and to Natalie Roth for her astute proofreading. Gratitude also to Kristen Twardowski, Charlotte Keathley, Madeline Schultz, Nicola McCafferty, Dino Robinson, Christopher Bigelow, and the rest of the wonderful team at Northwestern University Press.

To Captain Oona Isabelle Layolle for her invaluable time and for living the hardworking activism I fantasize about.

To Elizabeth Sawyer for her J Pod stories, uplifting engagement with the world, and the gracious use of her gorgeous photography.

To all the brilliant teachers who shaped my DIY-MFA curriculum and the wonderful students and administrators who constitute the literary communities at Lighthouse Writers Workshop, Orion Magazine's Environmental Writers' Workshops, Corporeal

Writing, The GrubStreet Writing Center, Catapult (RIP), Elk River Writers Workshop, Hugo House, Writing by Writers, Writing Workshops, and The Shipman Agency. Thanks also to the #binders full of timely advice, shared experiences, and enthusiastic milestone support and to Amanda Montei and Oksana Marafioti and all the writers in my many offshoot workshop groups who traded tender pages and gently helped me to see between my lines.

To Millay Arts, Craigardan, and Wellstone in the Redwoods for offering me the delights of time and space in artist residency, which shaped this book at various critical stages.

To Where There Be Dragons for the seventeen years of meaningful work in the world that infused these pages with global experiences, for the magical international community and epic dance parties in the woods, and also for the professional development funds that pushed me along my literary path.

To my mothers and sisters: Mary Jean, Patti, Annalise, Stacey, and Parke; each matriarchs I admire and esteem.

To Catherine Herrmann for treasured guidance through all my bardos.

To Courtney Zenner for being my "writing work wife," calling me at every turn in the path (despite my aversion to phones) and for our endless text chain of literary revelations and exclamation marks. You are a faceted gem and I treasure you.

To the wonderful humans (especially Carrie, Nisha, and Mina) who helped mother my children while I was working, at "writing nights," or away from home on writing retreats.

To Pearl and Nyx, old and new black dogs who waited so patiently as I stopped every five minutes on our hikes to jot down "one more thing."

To all the fine marketing people at 970Design.com for patiently attending to my pesky ways with professional restraint and outstanding vision.

To my husband, Slade, for the laughter and joy and intellectual engagement and security in my life, and especially for that time you stood up to some (shall-go-unnamed) authorities for the (non-financial) value of my writing in the world. That was the best. Thanks also for once saying, "I knew when I married her, she'd disappear a couple weeks every year," and for accepting me as that person, and for being a competent parent in my absence who doesn't call with domestic questions when I'm away. I respect and adore you.

To Nash and Riva: for asking hard questions, insisting on truth, accepting my apologies, and for choosing this life and journey with me.

To my ancestors and guides who whispered to me through the night and woke me with notes to take to my pages. I'm listening.

NOTES

Act I. Submersion

Epigraph: From Linda Hogan, *Solar Storms*. Copyright 1995 by Linda Hogan. Reprinted with the permission of Scribner, a division of Simon & Schuster, LLC.

Blood Moon

5 **Leatherbacks travel as far as ten thousand miles a year.** "Species Directory: Leatherback Turtle," National Oceanic and Atmospheric Administration (NOAA), accessed November 14, 2023, https://www.fisheries.noaa.gov/species/leatherback -turtle.

6 **"Leatherback Turtles May Become Extinct within 20 Years."** "Leatherback Turtles May Become Extinct within 20 Years: Study," *Nature World News*, February 28, 2013, https://www .natureworldnews.com/articles/719/20130228/leatherback -turtles-become-extinct-within-20-years-study.htm.

Two Breaths

10 **A "mother culture" it's called by whale biologists.** Carl Safina, *Becoming Wild: How Animal Cultures Raise Families, Create Beauty, and Achieve Peace* (New York: Picador, Henry Holt & Company, 2020), 25.

10 "**This time is rapidly decreased by panic.**" Peter Matthiessen, *Blue Meridian: The Search for the Great White Shark* (New York: Penguin Books, 1997), 9.

11 "**The name of the manta . . .**" Megan Miner, "The Cultural Significance of the Manta Ray in Hawaii," *Hawai'i Magazine*, August 25, 2015, https://www.hawaiimagazine.com/content /cultural-significance-manta-ray-hawaii.

12 **The manta has the largest brain of any fish . . .** Amy McDermott, "Manta Ray Brainpower Blows Other Fish Out of the Water," OCEANA: Protecting the World's Oceans, July 25, 2017, https:// oceana.org/blog/manta-ray-brainpower-blows-other-fish-out -water-10/.

13 "**When by chance these precious parts in a nursing whale are cut by the hunter's lance . . .**" Herman Melville, *Moby-Dick; or, The Whale* (New York: Penguin Books, 2001), 345.

Oncoming

16 **Nash has a book . . .** Joel Sartore, *The Photo Ark: One Man's Quest to Document the World's Animals* (Washington, DC: National Geographic, 2017).

17 **In 2019, seventeen White-Headed Vultures were found dead in Botswana.** Kimon de Greef, "500 Vultures Killed in Botswana by Poachers' Poison, Government Says," *New York Times*, June 21, 2019, https://www.nytimes.com/2019/06/21/world/africa /vultures-poisoned-botswana-poachers-elephants.html.

17 "**Orangutans Face Complete Extinction within 10 Years.**" Ian Johnston, "Orangutans Face Complete Extinction within 10 Years, Animal Rescue Charity Warns," *The Independent*, April 24, 2019, https://www.independent.co.uk/climate-change/news /orangutans-extinction-population-borneo-reasons-palm-oil -hunting-deforestation-rainforest-a7199366.html.

The Smooth Sides of Darkness

23 "**moments when gaps appear . . .**" Pema Khandro Rinpoche, "The Four Points of Letting Go in the Bardo," *Lion's Roar: Buddhist Wisdom for Our Time*, November 29, 2022, https://www .lionsroar.com/four-points-for-letting-go-bardo/.

31 **"Sealskin, Soulskin."** Clarissa Pinkola Estés, *Women Who Run with the Wolves: Myths and Stories of the Wild Woman Archetype* (New York: Ballantine Books, 1996).

32 **The Humpback Whale has the longest known migration of any mammal on Earth.** "Humpback Whale," National Oceanic and Atmospheric Administration, accessed October 4, 2023, https://www.fisheries.noaa.gov/species/humpback-whale.

32 **"Map."** Linda Hogan, *Dark. Sweet. New & Selected Poems* (Minneapolis: Coffee House Press, 2014).

32 **"If we appreciate these successive deaths and rebirths in our lives . . ."** Rinpoche, "Four Points."

The Seventeenth Day

37 **Southern Resident Killer Whale population listed as endangered in 2005.** "Southern Resident Killer Whale (Orcinus Orca)," National Oceanic and Atmospheric Administration, accessed August 9, 2023, https://www.fisheries.noaa.gov/west-coast/endangered-species-conservation/southern-resident-killer-whale-orcinus-Orca.

42 **[Orcas] often carry as many as twenty-five times the number of PCBs statistically known to affect health, mortality, and fertility.** Craig Welch, "Half the World's Orcas Could Soon Disappear— Here's Why," *National Geographic*, September 27, 2018, https://www.nationalgeographic.com/environment/article/orcas-killer-whales-poisoned-pcbs-pollution.

43 **five-thousand-year-old heritage.** "5000 Years of Inuit History and Heritage," *Inuit Tapiriit Kanatami*, November 4, 2004, https://www.itk.ca/5000-years-inuit-history-heritage/.

43 **under researched.** Jamie Vickery and Lori M. Hunter, "Native Americans: Where in Environmental Justice Research?," *Society & Natural Resources* 29, no. 1 (2016): 36–52, https://doi.org/10.1080/08941920.2015.1045644.

43 **Native communities are today more at risk for toxic exposure than any other ethnic group in the United States.** Daniel Brook, "Environmental Genocide: Native Americans and Toxic Waste," *American Journal of Economics and Sociology* 57, no. 1 (1998): 105–13, http://www.jstor.org/stable/3487423.

43 **"The more I think about it, the more scared I get."** Quoted by DeNeen L. Brown in "Poisons from Afar Threaten Arctic

Mothers, Traditions," *Washington Post*, April 10, 2004, https://www.washingtonpost.com/archive/politics/2004/04/11/poisons-from-afar-threaten-arctic-mothers-traditions/89af6e09-c411-4b6f-bc97-4839963e9208/.

44 **only caught seven Chinook in their nets in all of May and June 2020.** Simone Del Rosario, "Chinook Salmon Decimated, Southern Resident Orcas Are Residents No More," *Fox 13 Seattle*, July 2, 2020, https://www.fox13seattle.com/video/735907.

44 **a Superfund cleanup site in Oregon where PCBs were identified as a central contaminant.** Monica Samayoa, "Portland, Port Join Settlement with Monsanto over PCBs Contamination," *Oregon Public Broadcasting*, June 24, 2020, https://www.opb.org/news/article/portland-port-join-settlement-with-monsanto-over-pcbs-contamination/.

44 **A necropsy on an Orca calf that washed up in Norway in 2017...** Laura Geggel, "Dead Baby Orca Reveals Harmful Chemical Levels in Killer Whales," *Live Science*, May 24, 2021, https://www.livescience.com/orca-whales-toxicology.html.

45 **The leadership, experience, and knowledge of these "grand-mothers" has been shown to statistically boost the survival of grandcalves.** Carrie Arnold, "Why Do Orca Grandmothers Live so Long? It's for Their Grandkids," *National Geographic*, December 9, 2019, https://www.nationalgeographic.com/animals/article/orcas-killer-whales-menopause-grandmothers.

45 **In an online presentation, Lori Marino . . .** "Orca Brains and Intelligence—Dr. Lori Marino at Whale Museum, Friday Harbor," *Whale Sanctuary Project*, August 26, 2019, Video, 1:09:49, https://www.youtube.com/watch?v=eaCaPwbKWSo.

45 **"gathered at the mouth of the cove in a close, tight-knit circle..."** "Killer Whale Spotted Pushing Dead Calf for Two Days," British Broadcasting Corporation, July 27, 2018, https://www.bbc.com/news/world-us-canada-44984832.

46 **"She's not always the one carrying it; they seem to take turns."** Travis Lupick, "B.C. Orca Whale Receiving Help from Pod in Second Week Keeping Deceased Calf Afloat," Straight.com, August 6, 2018, https://www.straight.com/news/1112771/bc-orca-whale-receiving-help-pod-second-week-keeping-deceased-calf-afloat.

46 **Tahlequah is a Cherokee word. It means "two is enough."** Robert J. Conley, *Cherokee Medicine Man: The Life and Work*

of a Modern-Day Healer (Norman: University of Oklahoma Press, 2014).

47 **Latest research models predict Orca populations that live off-shore from PCB pollution will collapse in under fifty years.** Jean-Pierre Desforges, Ailsa Hall, Bernie McConnell, Aqqalu Rosing-Asvid, Jonathan L. Barber, Andrew Brownlow, Sylvain De Guise, et al., "Predicting Global Killer Whale Population Collapse from PCB Pollution," *Science* 361, no. 6409 (2018): 1373–76, https://doi.org/10.1126/science.aat1953.

48 **A 2021 study evaluated samples of breast milk collected from women all over the United States.** Guomao Zheng, Erika Schreder, Jennifer C. Dempsey, Nancy Uding, Valerie Chu, et al., "Per- and Polyfluoroalkyl Substances (PFAS) in Breast Milk: Concerning Trends for Current-Use PFAS," *Environmental Science and Technology* 55, no. 11 (2021): 7510–20, https://doi.org/10.1021/acs.est.0c06978.

48 **"Who would want to live in a world which is just not quite fatal?"** Rachel L. Carson, *Silent Spring* (Boston: Mariner Books, 2002), 12.

48 **Thirty-seven to 50 percent of Orca calves still die in their first year.** "About ORCAS," Center for Whale Research, accessed October 3, 2023, https://www.whaleresearch.com/aboutorcas.

49 **a mother Orca offloads most of her toxic burden with her first baby . . .** John Ryan, "What Are That New Baby Orca's Chances of Surviving?," *NPR Network*, June 7, 2019, https://www.kuow.org/stories/what-are-that-new-baby-Orca-s-chances-of-surviving.

51 **a hydrophone dropped into the ocean by Orcasound Lab.** *Orcasound Lab (Haro Strait)*, Live.Orcasound.net, accessed October 3, 2023, https://www.orcasound.net/listen/orcasound-lab.

52 **"There is something infinitely healing in the repeated refrains of nature . . ."** Rachel Carson, *The Sense of Wonder* (New York: Harper & Row, 1965), 101.

The Endling

57 **The Baiji, a Yangtze River Dolphin, disappeared in China in 2006.** "IUCN—SSC Cetacean Specialist Group / Baiji," The IUCN/SSC Cetacean Specialist Group (CSG), accessed October 4, 2023, https://iucn-csg.org/baiji/.

57 **a United Nations report estimated a million species will disappear in the coming decades.** "UN Report: Nature's Dangerous Decline 'Unprecedented'; Species Extinction Rates 'Accelerating,'" United Nations, May 16, 2019, https://www.un.org/sustainabledevelopment/blog/2019/05/nature-decline-unprecedented-report/.

57 **a violent encounter between local fishermen and Sea Shepherd in the Vaquita Refuge.** "Mexican Fisherman 'Dies after Attack on Sea Shepherd Conservationists,'" British Broadcasting Corporation, January 4, 2021, https://www.bbc.com/news/world-latin-america-55540506.

57 **"The harmony between man and sea is lost."** Alan Alexis Valverde, quoted in "Souls of the Vermilion Sea," *Wild Lens*, April 6, 2017, Video, 28:58, https://vimeo.com/212128879.

58 **General Efraín Ríos Montt's scorched-earth campaign in Guatemala . . .** "Genocide of Mayan Ixil Community," The Center for Justice & Accountability, accessed October 4, 2023, https://cja.org/what-we-do/litigation/the-guatemala-genocide-case/.

Act II. Migrations

Epigraph: Báyò Akómoláfé, "Let's Make Sanctuary as Fascism Rises," *Báyò Akómoláfé*, August 20, 2019, https://www.bayoakomolafe.net/post/lets-make-sanctuary-as-fascism-rises.

Four Circles

75 **". . . the simple understanding that to sing at dawn and to sing at dusk was to heal the world through joy."** Terry Tempest Williams, *When Women Were Birds: Fifty-four Variations on Voice* (London: Picador, 2012), 225.

75 **"when the edge of the Moon first enters the amber core of Earth's shadow."** Tony Phillips, "Total Eclipse of the Moon," National Aeronautics and Space Administration, March 30, 2015, https://science.nasa.gov/science-news/science-at-nasa/2015/30mar_lunareclipse.

75 **". . . every sunrise and every sunset in the world, all of them, all at once."** Phillips, "Total Eclipse."

76 **according to the psychological researchers Katharine and Isabel Briggs.** "INFJ: MBTI Personality Profile," The Myers-Briggs Company, accessed October 11, 2023, https://eu.themyersbriggs.com/en/tools/MBTI/MBTI-personality-Types/INFJ.

78 **". . . For her, thunder is silence."** Clarissa Pinkola Estés, *Women Who Run with the Wolves: Myths and Stories of the Wild Woman Archetype* (New York: Ballantine Books, 1996), 310.

79 **Man-made sounds can trigger rising blood pressure, slow digestion, and pump adrenal glands.** Thomas Münzel and Mette Sørensen, "Noise Pollution and Arterial Hypertension," *European Cardiology Review* 12, no. 1 (2017): 26–29, https://doi.org/10.15420/ecr.2016:31:2.

79 **The bang of an air gun . . . can travel in water for months**. Jeff Tollefson, "Air Guns Used in Offshore Oil Exploration Can Kill Tiny Marine Life," *Nature* 546 (2017): 586–87, https://doi.org/10.1038/nature.2017.22167.

79 **One study documented that noise pollution was reducing Fin, Humpback, and Minke whale communication range by as much as 82 percent.** Danielle Cholewiak, Christopher W. Clark, Dimitri Ponirakis, Adam Frankel, et al., "Communicating Amidst the Noise: Modeling the Aggregate Influence of Ambient and Vessel Noise on Baleen Whale Communication Space in a National Marine Sanctuary," *Endangered Species Research* 36, no. 1 (2018): 59–75, https://doi.org/10.3354/esr00875.

80 **A recent study concluded one in three people are regularly exposed to excessive noise levels . . .** Chantelle Pattemore, "1 in 3 Americans Exposed to Excessive Noise Levels," *Healthline*, May 15, 2023, https://www.healthline.com/health-news/americans-exposed-to-excessive-noise-levels.

80 **the hydrophones dropped by the Orcasound Lab into the Pacific Ocean.** *Orcasound Lab (Haro Strait)*, Live.Orcasound.net, accessed October 3, 2023, https://www.orcasound.net/listen/orcasound-lab.

81 **"Silence introduced in a society that worships noise is like the Moon exposing the night."** Terry Tempest Williams, *When Women Were Birds: Fifty-four Variations on Voice* (London: Picador, 2012), 61.

81 **"whoops, croaks, foghorns, and growls."** Sam Hancock, "Fish 'Sing' as Indonesian Coral Reef Restored Back to Life," *The Independent,* December 9, 2021, https://www.independent .co.uk/climate-change/news/fish-noises-coral-reef-indonesia -b1972105.html.

Anatomy of a Seagull

84 **My favorite book as a child . . .** Richard Bach, *Jonathan Livingston Seagull,* 1st ed. (New York: Macmillan, 1970).

92 **"What would happen if one woman told the truth about her life?"** Muriel Rukeyser, *A Muriel Rukeyser Reader* (New York: W. W. Norton & Company, 1995), 217.

Phantom Braking

96 **University of Washington news video clip.** "Worn Tires Contribute to Chemical that Kills Coho Salmon," University of Washington, December 3, 2020, Video, 2:46, https://www .youtube.com/watch?v=vxmojuC_dJE&t=42s.

97 **urban runoff mortality syndrome (URMS) killing 40 to 90 percent of salmon before they could spawn.** Sarah McQuate, "Tire-related Chemical Is Largely Responsible for Adult Coho Salmon Deaths in Urban Streams," University of Washington, December 3, 2020, https://www.washington.edu/news/2020/12 /03/tire-related-chemical-largely-responsible-for-adult-coho -salmon-deaths-in-urban-streams/.

97 **"I can't walk along a street without staring at all the skid marks . . ."** Quoted in Erik Stokstad, "Common Tire Chemical Implicated in Mysterious Deaths of At-Risk Salmon," *Science,* December 3, 2020, https://www.science.org/content/article/common-tire -chemical-implicated-mysterious-deaths-risk-salmon.

97 *Phantom Brake Syndrome.* Zack Z. Cernovsky and Milad Fattahi, "Phantom Brake Phenomenon in Survivors of Car Accidents," *European Journal of Clinical Medicine* 2, no. 3 (2021): 9–13. https://doi.org/10.24018/clinicmed.2021.2.3.68.

98 **Americans have 1.83 vehicles per home . . .** "Average Number of Cars per Household in America," *ConsumerShield,* https://www .consumershield.com/articles/average-cars-per-household.

98 burn 489 gallons of gasoline per year, and drive thirty-two miles per day . . . Lem Smith, "Top Numbers Driving America's Gasoline Demand," API, May 26, 2022, https://www.api.org/news-policy -and-issues/blog/2022/05/26/top-numbers-driving-americas -gasoline-demand.

98 thirty-two cars per 1,000 people. "Our World in Data" (last modified May 20, 2024), https://ourworldindata.org/grapher /registered-vehicles-per-1000-people.

98 Residents of the Netherlands average 4.4 bicycle trips per week. "How Much Do We Cycle Per Week on Average?" *The Netherlands in Numbers 2022*, https://longreads.cbs.nl/the-netherlands-in -numbers-2022/how-much-do-we-cycle-per-week-on-average/.

98 Hongkongers walk an average of 6,880 steps a day. Yupina Ng, "Global Study on Walking Puts Hong Kong a Step Ahead," *South China Morning Post*, July 14, 2017, https://www.scmp .com/news/hong-kong/health-environment/article/2102715 /global-study-walking-puts-hong-kong-step-ahead.

98 Stories from a bare-chested centenarian in a thatched Senegalese hut. Philipp Henschel, Lauren Coad, Cole Burton, Beatrice Chataigner, Andrew Dunn, David MacDonald, Yohanna Saidu, and Luke T. B. Hunter, "The Lion in West Africa Is Critically Endangered." *PLoS ONE* 9, no. 1 (2014): 1–11, https://doi.org/10 .1371/journal.pone.0083500.

99 "We have been deceived by what we thought was knowledge . . ." Linda Hogan, "First People," in *Intimate Nature: The Bond Between Women and Animals,* ed. Linda Hogan, Deena Metzger, and Brenda Peterson (New York: Ballantine Publishing Group, 1998), 16.

99 "a smooth superhighway on which we progress with great speed, but at its end lies disaster." Rachel L. Carson, *Silent Spring* (Boston: Mariner Books, 2002), 277.

100 ". . . corporeally connected aqueous community." Quoted in Henriette Gunkel, Chrysanthi Nigianni, and Fanny Söderbäck, eds., *Undutiful Daughters: New Directions in Feminist Thought and Practice; Breaking Feminist Waves* (New York: Palgrave Macmillan, 2012), 92.

100 "*I am a singular, dynamic whorl dissolving in a complex fluid circulation.*" Quoted in Gunkel et al., *Undutiful Daughters*, 85.

101 "The song around salmon is the river's voice and the way the fish fight to live is our fight as well." Elizabeth Woody, "Why I Love

with Admiration Every Salmon I See," in *Intimate Nature: The Bond Between Women and Animals*, ed. Linda Hogan, Deena Metzger, and Brenda Peterson (New York: Ballantine Publishing Group, 1998), 32.

Hidden Geographies

103 **". . . I was confronted, as far as the eye could see, with the sight of plastic."** Charles Moore, quoted in "Great Pacific Garbage Patch," *National Geographic*, https://education.nationalgeographic.org /resource/great-pacific-garbage-patch/.

103 **Abandoned fishing nets and gear, often cut loose, or left in the ocean when snagged or forgotten, account for more than 10 percent of ocean plastics.** Karli Thomas, Cat Dorey, and Farah Obaidullah, "Ghost Gear: The Abandoned Fishing Nets Haunting Our Oceans," Greenpeace Germany, November 1, 2019, https:// www.greenpeace.de/sites/default/files/publications/20190611 -greenpeace-report-ghost-fishing-ghost-gear-deutsch.pdf.

103 **In 2012, a ghost net ensnared a Gray Whale off the coast of California.** Tony Barboza, "Gray Whale Swims Free after Rescue from Fishing Net," *Los Angeles Times*, March 27, 2012, https:// www.latimes.com/archives/la-xpm-2012-mar-27-la-me-0327 -whale-rescue-20120327-story.html.

105 **an industry where 9 percent of plastic is recycled . . .** Douglas Main, "Think That Your Plastic Is Being Recycled? Think Again." *MIT Technology Review*, October 12, 2023, https://www .technologyreview.com/2023/10/12/1081129/plastic-recycling -climate-change-microplastics/.

106 **a film called *Albatross* . . .** "Albatross by Chris Jordan," *Chris Jordan Photographic Arts*, April 12, 2018, Video, 1:37:43, https:// vimeo.com/264508490.

109 **Sixty-two containers fell overboard, one holding 4.8 million Lego toy parts . . .** Mindy Weisberger, "5 Million Shipwrecked Legos Still Washing up 25 Years after Falling Overboard," *Live Science*, February 12, 2022, https://www.livescience.com/great -lego-spill-25th-anniversary.

109 **"could be from the *Tokio Express*. It matches the drift pattern across the Atlantic."** Quoted by Mario Cacciottolo, "Mapped: The Beaches Where Lego Washes Up," British Broadcasting Corporation, January 3, 2015, https://www.bbc.com/news /magazine-28582621.

111 "The current going rate has something like three deciduous forests buying one ship's peanut." Douglas Adams, *The Ultimate Hitchhiker's Guide to the Galaxy* (New York: Ballantine Books, 2002), 299.

111 Meanwhile, fifteen million tons of plastic enter the oceans each year, plastic production is on track to triple by 2040 . . . World Economic Forum, Ellen MacArthur Foundation, and McKinsey & Company, *The New Plastics Economy: Rethinking the Future of Plastics* (2016), 7, https://www.weforum.org/reports/the-new -plastics-economy-rethinking-the-future-of-plastics.

111 Oil companies push the "individual footprint" narratives . . . Geoffrey Supran and Naomi Oreskes, "Rhetoric and Frame Analysis of ExxonMobil's Climate Change Communications," *One Earth* 4, no. 5 (2021): 696–719, https://doi.org/10.1016 /j.oneear.2021.04.014.

112 The Lego factory . . . builds 1.7 million bricks an hour. Joseph Pisani, "The Making of . . . a LEGO," *Bloomberg*, November 29, 2006, https://www.bloomberg.com/news/articles/2006-11 -29/the-making-of-a-legobusinessweek-business-news-stock -market-and-financial-advice.

112 it takes only 3.5 percent of a population to initiate real change through civil disobedience. David Robson, "The '3.5% Rule': How a Small Minority Can Change the World," British Broadcasting Corporation, May 13, 2019, https://www.bbc.com /future/article/20190513-it-only-takes-35-of-people-to-change -the-world.

112 "Wars will be stopped only when soldiers refuse to fight . . ." Arundhati Roy, *Public Power in the Age of Empire* (New York: Seven Stories Press, 2004), 39.

113 "It's a quiet revolution begun by ordinary people with the stuff of our daily lives." Bill McKibben, *Deep Economy: The Wealth of Communities and the Durable Future* (New York: Henry Holt & Company, 2008), 3.

113 "unprecedented view of results that would take regulations years to achieve." Carol Rasmussen, "Emission Reductions from Pandemic Had Unexpected Effects on Atmosphere," National Aeronautics and Space Administration, November 9, 2021, https://climate.nasa.gov/news/3129/emission-reductions-from -pandemic-had-unexpected-effects-on-atmosphere/.

Screening Form

115 ". . . suggested some women with early breast cancer were diagnosed with cancer that may never have affected their health." Dana Sparks, "Women's Wellness: Mammogram Guidelines at Mayo Clinic," Mayo Clinic, May 9, 2019, https://newsnetwork .mayoclinic.org/discussion/womens-wellness-mammogram -guidelines-at-mayo-clinic/.

116 breast cancer's increase of 242 percent between 1970 and 2014. L. C. Leach III, "Fighting to End Breast Cancer," Health Links, September 10, 2022, https://www.charlestonphysicians.com /oncology/fighting-to-end-breast-cancer/.

119 "Profitability in the Health Care Market Has Never Been Better." Robert Laszewski, "Profitability in the Health Care Market Has Never Been Better," *Forbes*, February 5, 2020, https://www .forbes.com/sites/robertlaszewski2/2020/02/05/profitability-in -the-health-care-market-has-never-been-better/.

119 women of color are "missing almost altogether." Lisa M. Jarvis, "Why Can't the Drug Industry Solve Its Gender Diversity Problem?," *Chemical & Engineering News*, March 5, 2018, https://cen.acs.org/articles/96/i10/why-cant-the-drug-industry -solve-its-gender-diversity-problem.html.

Empty the Tanks

122 the story of an Orca who was only four years old . . . Carl Safina, *Beyond Words: What Animals Think and Feel* (New York: Henry Holt & Company, 2015).

122 Orca vocals can reach 40,000 hertz. Marla M. Holt, Dawn P. Noren, Val Veirs, Candice K. Emmons, and Scott Veirs, "Speaking Up: Killer Whales (*Orcinus Orca*) Increase Their Call Amplitude in Response to Vessel Noise," *The Journal of the Acoustical Society of America*, 1 (2009): 27–32, https://doi.org/10.1121/1.3040028.

122 a sound clip of a 40,000 hertz frequency tone. "40000 Hz," HertzFreq2023, March 13, 2017, Video, 10:00, https://www .youtube.com/watch?v=14qGclqa7c0.

123 Corky's teeth are gone or fractured from chewing the gates and concrete walls that enclose her. "A Summary of the Effects of Captivity on Orcas," People for the Ethical Treatment of Animals, accessed October 7, 2023, https://www.peta.org/wp -content/uploads/2021/06/SeaWorldCruelty.pdf.

123 **Corky is the single Orca who has lived longer than any Killer Whale in captivity.** Mark J. Palmer, "Meet Corky, the Longest-Held Orca in Captivity," International Marine Mammal Project, May 21, 2020, https://savedolphins.eii.org/news/meet-corky -the-longest-held-Orca-in-captivity.

124 **the calf could not sort where to suckle . . .** Alexandra Morton, *Not on My Watch: How a Renegade Whale Biologist Took on Governments and Industry to Save Wild Salmon* (Toronto: Random House Canada, 2022), 6.

124 **Then, each time, she sank to the bottom and made the same call over and over for days . . .** Morton, *Not on My Watch*, 9.

124 **"The first killer whale born in captivity . . . died soon after its birth."** "Killer Whale Calf Dies in Marineland," *Fresno Bee*, November 14, 1978.

124 **"The calf, which weighed 300 pounds at birth, began losing weight."** "Whales Lose 2nd Calf," *Napa Valley Register*, November 14, 1978, 7.

124 **"There was concern about the calf bumping into walls of the tank."** "Whale," *News-Pilot*, November 1, 1978.

125 **". . . wispy newborn voices growing raspy and desperate as the babies slowly starved over a week to ten days."** Morton, *Not on My Watch*, 9.

125 **"with a deep crease on the point of her face."** Morton, *Not on My Watch*, 9.

125 **an "accidental feminist icon" with more than 1.3 million online followers.** Joy Dong and Vivian Wang, "A Chinese 'Auntie' Went on a Solo Road Trip. Now, She's a Feminist Icon," *New York Times*, April 4, 2021, https://www.nytimes.com/2021/04/02 /world/asia/china-roadtrip-feminist.html.

125 **videos she posts to YouTube.** "Fifty-year-old Aunt Traveling by Car," @50SuiAyiZiJiaYou, Video, 4:57, https://www.youtube .com/channel/UCtUhcLRfegq2RMxQH7KP9YQ.

126 **fewer than 4 percent of murder victims under age thirteen were killed by non-family.** Matthew R. Durose et al., "Family Violence Statistics," US Department of Justice, June 1, 2005, https://bjs .ojp.gov/content/pub/pdf/fvs03.pdf.

126 **Men represent nearly 90 percent of homicide offenders.** Alexia Cooper and Erica L. Smith, "Homicide Trends in the United States, 1980–2008," US Department of Justice, November 1, 2011, https://bjs.ojp.gov/content/pub/pdf/htus8008.pdf.

126 **More than twenty thousand phone calls are placed to domestic violence hotlines nationwide every day.** "Domestic Violence Statistics," Domestic Violence Services, Inc., accessed November 7, 2023, https://www.dvs-or.org/domestic-violence-statistics/.

127 **More than one in three women in the United States has experienced rape, physical violence, and/or stalking by an intimate partner.** M. C. Black, K. C. Basile, M. J. Breiding, S. G. Smith, M. L. Walters, M. T. Merrick, J. Chen, and M. R. Stevens, *The National Intimate Partner and Sexual Violence Survey (NISVS): 2010 Summary Report* (Atlanta, GA: National Center for Injury Prevention and Control, Centers for Disease Control and Prevention, 2011).

127 **94 percent of the victims of murder-suicides are female.** "Statistics," National Coalition Against Domestic Violence, accessed October 12, 2023, https://ncadv.org/STATISTICS.

127 **"Before, I thought I was the only person in the world who wasn't happy."** Dong and Wang, "A Chinese 'Auntie'."

127 **She is known for being raped, repeatedly, on the El train in Philadelphia as it was traveling westbound.** Eduardo Medina, "As a Woman Was Raped, Train Riders Failed to Intervene, Police Say," *New York Times*, October 17, 2021, https://www.nytimes.com/2021/10/17/us/riders-watched-woman-raped-septa.html.

128 **"The onus is really on us as a collective . . . we need a world where people are doing the right thing when you see someone assaulted."** Alexis Piquero, quoted by Medina, "As a Woman Was Raped."

129 **"The greatest pain in life is not that there is no hope or dream . . ."** "56-year-old Su Min Drove Away to Escape Her Marriage and Finally Returned Home," *MIN NEWS*, August 10, 2023, https://min.news/en/news/846cd0d1c45f0bc0d870e839d813c1c3.html.

129 **"To take them out of this environment would be inhumane and irresponsible, and we will never take such a risk."** "Researcher Wants to Build Corky, the Aging Orca, a 'Retirement Home,'" Canadian Broadcasting Corporation, accessed October 7, 2023, https://www.cbc.ca/radio/sunday/the-sunday-edition-august-12-2018-1.4776504/researcher-wants-to-build-corky-the-aging-Orca-a-retirement-home-1.4779336.

130 **"To bear witness is not a passive act."** Terry Tempest Williams, *The Hour of Land: A Personal Topography of America's National Parks* (New York: Sarah Crichton Books, 2016), 227.

130 **"A sanctuary changes the cultural conversation . . ."** Lori Marino, *The Whale Sanctuary Project,* accessed June 1, 2021, https://whalesanctuaryproject.org/?s=lori+marino.

130 **ABC's *Nightline* did a segment on Corky.** "Corky Hears Her Family—ABC Nightline 1993," December 10, 2013, Video, 12:46, https://www.youtube.com/watch?v=TzqI2HT3c9U.

130 **no two pods speak the same dialect.** Birgitte Svennevig, "Researchers Find 20,000-year-old Refugium for Orcas in the Northern Pacific," Phys.org, August 21, 2023, https://phys.org/news/2023-08-year-old-refugium-orcas-northern-pacific.amp.

131 **"What we most need to do . . . is to hear within us the sound of the earth crying."** Thích Nhất Hạnh quoted in Llewellyn Vaughan-Lee, ed., *Spiritual Ecology: The Cry of the Earth* (Point Reyes, CA: The Golden Sufi Center, 2016), 1.

My Oceans

137 **"As life itself began in the sea, so each of us . . ."** Rachel Carson, *The Sea Around Us* (Oxford: Oxford University Press, 2018), 14.

137 **In the last fifty years, sharks off the Queensland coast have declined by as much as 92 percent.** Melissa C. Márquez, "Shark Populations Decline in Queensland," *Forbes,* December 29, 2018, https://www.forbes.com/sites/melissacristinamarquez/2018/12/29/shark-populations-decline-in-queensland-what-does-it-mean-for-the-reefs/?sh=77b34f293b91.

137 *National Geographic* **tells me baby coral in Australia's Great Barrier Reef diminished 89 percent . . .** Sarah Gibbens, "The Great Barrier Reef's Corals Are Struggling to Recover Fast Enough," *National Geographic,* April 3, 2019, https://www.nationalgeographic.com/environment/article/great-barrier-reef-coral-not-recovering-climate-change.

139 **"The wilderness once offered men a plausible way of life . . ."** Edward Abbey, *The Monkey Wrench Gang* (New York: Harper Perennial, 2006), 47.

143 **Because already in 2022, solar-powered nudibranches are "too rare to research."** Douglas Main, "Solar-Powered Slugs Hide Wild Secrets—But They're Vanishing," *National Geographic,* July 22, 2018, https://www.nationalgeographic.com/animals/article/solar-powered-photosynthetic-sea-slugs-in-decline-news.

144 **This ship was "laid up for disposal"** *before* **she was purchased by Sea Shepherd.** "MY Steve Irwin," last modified August 9, 2023, https://en.wikipedia.org/wiki/MY_Steve_Irwin.

146 **"Women must write through their bodies . . ."** Hélène Cixous, trans. Keith Cohen and Paula Cohen, "The Laugh of the Medusa," *Signs* 1, no. 4 (1976): 875–93, https://www.jstor.org/stable/3173239.

Obituary

148 **Patriarchy, born in 3100 B.C.E.** Gerna Lerner, *The Creation of Patriarchy* (Oxford: Oxford University Press, 1987), 8.

148 **changing God's pronoun from** *she/they* **to** *he.* Merlin Stone, *When God Was a Woman* (Boston: Mariner Books, 1978).

149 **"mom rage" and the prolific use of toxic positivity.** Barbara Ehrenreich, *Bright-sided: How the Relentless Promotion of Positive Thinking Has Undermined America* (New York: Metropolitan Books, 2009).

Act III. Fathoms

Epigraph: Francis Weller, *In the Absence of the Ordinary: Essays in a Time of Uncertainty* (Santa Rosa, CA: WisdomBridge Press, 2020), 49.

Quieseeds

153 **Dr. Gardner's test concluded my primary strength—as one high in "Naturalistic Intelligence"—was finding patterns and relationships to nature.** Howard E. Gardner, *Frames of Mind: The Theory of Multiple Intelligences* (New York: Basic Books, 2011).

155 **You'll find this neologism only in the online dictionary created by the Bureau of Liguistical Reality.** The Bureau of Linguistical Reality, accessed October 12, 2023, https://bureauoflinguisticalreality.com/.

156 **". . . they evolved a 'language' centered exclusively on their interrelationships."** Rebecca Giggs, *Fathoms: The World in the Whale* (New York: Simon & Schuster, 2020), 153.

157 **women's brains are more interconnected with fiber pathways that zigzag** *between* **hemispheres that "facilitate communication between analytical and intuitive processing modes."** Madhura

Ingalhalikar, Alex Smith, Drew Parker, Theodore D. Satterthwaite, Mark A. Elliott, Kosha Ruparel, Hakon Hakonarson, Raquel E. Gur, Ruben C. Gur, and Ragini Verma, "Sex Differences in the Structural Connectome of the Human Brain," *Proceedings of the National Academy of Sciences* 111, no. 2 (2014): 823–28 (quote on 823), https://doi.org/10.1073/pnas.1316909110.

157 **The right and left brain functions have sometimes been over-simplified . . . but what remains true is that the two sides work differently.** Jared A. Nielsen, Brandon A. Zielinski, Michael A. Ferguson, Janet E. Lainhart, and Jeffrey S. Anderson, "An Evaluation of the Left-Brain vs. Right-Brain Hypothesis with Resting State Functional Connectivity Magnetic Resonance Imaging," *PLoS ONE* 8, no. 8 (2013), https://doi.org/10.1371/journal.pone.0071275.

157 **"a special form of speech called metaphor . . ."** Leonard Shlain, *The Alphabet Versus the Goddess: The Conflict Between Word and Image* (New York: Viking Adult, 1998).

158 **Researchers discovered the whales demonstrated a preference for left-turned movements in shallow waters.** Ari S. Friedlaender, James E. Herbert-Read, Elliott L. Hazen, David E. Cade, John Calambokidis, Brandon L. Southall, Alison K. Stimpert, and Jeremy A. Goldbogen, "Context-dependent Lateralized Feeding Strategies in Blue Whales," *Current Biology* 27, no. 22 (2017): R1206–R1208, https://doi.org/10.1016/j.cub.2017.10.023.

158 **"A medium of communication is not merely . . ."** Shlain, *The Alphabet Versus the Goddess*, 21.

159 **lawyer Raphael Lemkin.** "Raphael Lemkin and the Genocide Convention." *Facing History and Ourselves*, accessed August 4, 2024, https://www.facinghistory.org/resource-library/raphael-lemkin-genocide-convention.

159 **a book founded in 1806 by a racist man named Noah Webster.** Donald Yacovone, "Textbook Racism: How Scholars Sustained White Supremacy," *Chronicle of Higher Education* 64, no. 32 (April 8, 2018), https://www.chronicle.com/article/textbook-racism/.

159 **"When their songs cannot become more ornate and still be remembered . . ."** Giggs, *Fathoms*, 177.

159 **Scientists call them "revolutionary songs."** Giggs, *Fathoms*, 177.

160 **"We live in capitalism, its power seems inescapable . . ."** Ursula K. Le Guin, "The National Book Foundation Medal for

Distinguished Contribution to American Letters," November 19, 2014, https://www.ursulakleguin.com/nbf-medal.

160 **She rested her case by playing Humpback songs before Congress.** Charlotte Epstein, "The Anti-Whaling Campaign," 2008, https://doi.org/10.7551/mitpress/9780262050920.003.0007.

160 **Carl Sagan curated the record and titled it "A Love Song."** Megan Gambino, "What Is on Voyager's Golden Record?," *The Smithsonian*, April 22, 2012, https://www.smithsonianmag.com/science-nature/what-is-on-voyagers-golden-record-73063839/.

161 **In 2023, NANOGrav (the North American Nanohertz Observatory for Gravitational Waves) reported a "major discovery"** . . . Gabriella Agazie, et al., "The NANOGrav 15 Yr Data Set: Evidence for a Gravitational-Wave Background," *The Astrophysical Journal Letters* 951, no. 1 (2023), https://iopscience.iop.org/article/10.3847/2041-8213/acdac6.

161 **"The picture that emerges is a universe that looks like a choppy sea."** Quoted by Joel Achenbach and Victoria Jaggard, "In a Major Discovery, Scientists Say Space-Time Churns like a Choppy Sea,'" *Washington Post*, June 28, 2023, https://www.washingtonpost.com/science/2023/06/28/gravitational-wave-background-nanograv/.

162 **". . . no one could write truthfully about the sea and leave out the poetry."** Linda Lear, ed., *Lost Woods: The Discovered Writing of Rachel Carson* (Boston: Beacon Press, 1999), 108.

Baby Jesus the Girl

167 **Because the headline read** . . . Dan Waidelich, "Want to Leave the Catholic Church? Officially, You Can't," *Washington Post*, October 22, 2018, https://www.washingtonpost.com/religion/2018/10/22/want-leave-catholic-church-officially-you-cant/.

168 **If you decide to leave the Mormon church** . . . "How to Leave the Mormon Church," WikiHow, accessed October 11, 2021, https://www.wikihow.com/Leave-the-Mormon-Church-Gracefully.

170 **Of course, the pilgrimage is still claimed as "Christian"** . . . Olivier Guiberteau, "The Camino de Santiago's Ancient Secret," British Broadcasting Corporation, April 12, 2019, https://www.bbc.com/travel/article/20190411-the-camino-de-santiagos-ancient-secret.

172 **"The master's tools will never dismantle the master's house."** Audre Lorde, *Sister Outsider: Essays and Speeches* (Berkeley: Crossing Press, 2007), 112.

173 **Here is the updated canon law . . .** The Vatican, Code of Canon Law, Book VI, *Penal Sanctions in the Church*, Part 2, Title 3, "Offenses against the Sacraments," Canon 1379, https://www.vatican.va /archive/cod-iuris-canonici/eng/documents/cic_lib6-cann1364 -1399_en.html.

Resuscitation

180 **nearly five hundred life-sized statues at the southern tip of Isla Mujeres constituting the world's largest—literal—underwater museum.** Jason deCaires Taylor, *The Underwater Museum: The Submerged Sculptures of Jason deCaires Taylor* (San Francisco: Chronicle Books, 2014).

181 **"a movement of people in defense of the sea."** "Museo Subacuático de Arte (MUSA)," Jason deCaires Taylor, accessed October 12, 2023, https://www.underwatersculpture.com /projects/musa-mexico/.

181 **Coral reefs are thick arms of the ecosystem, spreading across only two-tenths of a percent of the seafloor, yet supporting over 25 percent of marine species.** Ove Hoegh-Guldberg, Elvira S. Poloczanska, William Skirving, and Sophie Dove, "Coral Reef Ecosystems under Climate Change and Ocean Acidification," *Frontiers in Marine Science* 4 (2017), accessed October 12, 2023, https://doi.org/10.3389/fmars.2017.00158.

181 **up to 50 percent of the world's coral reefs may have died in the last thirty years**. David Souter, Serge Planes, Jérémy Wicquart, M. Logan, David Obura, Francis Staub, eds., "Status of Coral Reefs of the World: 2020 Report," Global Coral Reef Monitoring Network (GCRMN) and International Coral Reef Initiative (ICRI), 2021, accessed October 12, 2023, DOI: 10.59387/ WOTJ9184.

181 **"The afternoon of life is just as full of meaning as the morning . . ."** Carl G. Jung, *The Collected Works of C. G. Jung, Vol. 7: Two Essays on Analytical Psychology* (Princeton, NJ: Princeton University Press, 1972), 114.

182 **To do things in the last half of our lives not only for ourselves, but for society and for the sake of our souls.** "Enjoying the 'Afternoon of Life:' Jung on Aging," Jungian Center, accessed November 12, 2023, https://jungiancenter.org/enjoying-the -afternoon-of-life-jung-on-aging/.

184 **They boosted their size and alliance and defense by congregating into "extensive herds" of more than a hundred.** Carl Safina, *Beyond Words: What Animals Think and Feel* (New York: Henry Holt & Company, 2015), 82.

185 **when they share space, they touch each other a lot—they nuzzle.** Jonathan Amos, "Social Insights from Whale Chatter," British Broadcasting Corporation, September 9, 2015, https:// www.bbc.com/news/science-environment-34197333.

186 **"What we need in these times is attuned and attentive individuals who can sense the distress we are feeling and offer us assurance . . ."** Francis Weller, "Rough Initiations," Daily Good, March 4, 2021, https://www.dailygood.org/story/2701/rough -initiations-francis-weller/.

187 **The ancestors of whales once walked on legs on land.** Charles Q. Choi, "Early Whales Had Legs," *Live Science*, September 11, 2008, https://www.livescience.com/7564-early-whales-legs .html.

189 **"soup can be made from a stone."** Ann McGovern, *Stone Soup* (New York: Scholastic Inc., 1986).

The Shift

196 **This skin-to-skin contact . . .** "Psychologists Say There Are Five Types of Love Languages, but to Newborn Babies, Only One Really Registers: Physical Touch," Stanford Medicine, accessed October 11, 2023, https://www.stanfordchildrens.org/content -public/pdf/magazine/give-em-some-skin.pdf

197 **"Every woman has known the torment of getting up to speak . . ."** Hélène Cixous, trans. Keith Cohen and Paula Cohen, "The Laugh of the Medusa," *Signs* 1, no. 4 (1976): 875–93 (quotes on 880, 881, 883), https://www.jstor.org/stable/3173239.

199 **Black newborns in the United States are three times more likely than white babies to die when looked after by white doctors.** Tonya Russell, "Mortality Rate for Black Babies Is Cut Dramatically When Black Doctors Care for Them after Birth," *Washington Post*, January 13, 2021, https://www.washingtonpost.com/ health/black-baby-death-rate-cut-by-black-doctors/2021/01/08 /e9f0f850-238a-11eb-952e-0c475972cfc0_story.html.

199 **Male primary care physicians spend 15 percent less time with patients compared to women primary care physicians.** Mara Gordon, "Female Doctors Spend More Time with Patients, But Earn Less Money Than Men," *NPR*, October 28, 2020, https://www.npr.org/sections/health-shots/2020/10/28/925855852/female-doctors-spend-more-time-with-patients-but-earn-less-money-than-men.

199 **Women are more concerned with climate change due to value systems more associated with altruism, compassion, fairness, and social justice.** Matthew Ballew, Jennifer Marlon, Anthony Leiserowitz, and Edward Maibach, "Gender Differences in Public Understanding of Climate Change," Yale Program on Climate Change Communication, November 20, 2018, https://climatecommunication.yale.edu/publications/gender-differences-in-public-understanding-of-climate-change/.

Good Grief

202 **Death was the theme of the third of ten weeks comprising my "Good Grief" eco-anxiety group therapy program.** "10 Steps to Resilience & Empowerment in a Chaotic Climate: Created by LaUra Schmidt & Aimee Lewis Reau," The Good Grief Network, accessed October 11, 2023, https://www.goodgriefnetwork.org/10steps/.

204 *They were of a cove in the Dutch Faroe Islands . . .* Joanna Thompson, "Slaughter of More than 1,400 Dolphins in the Faroe Islands Sparks Condemnation Worldwide," *Live Science*, September 16, 2021, https://www.livescience.com/slaughter-of-more-than-1400-dolphins-in-the-faroe-islands-sparks-condemnation-worldwide.

206 **The climate futurist Alex Steffen says climate crisis made us lose our footing in time.** Elizabeth Weil, "This Isn't the California I Married," *New York Times*, January 3, 2022, https://www.nytimes.com/2022/01/03/magazine/california-widfires.html.

207 **They fell in Arizona after their flight across Colorado skies.** Hunter Bassler, "Hundreds of Thousands of Songbirds Dead in Arizona, Southwest Due to Climate Change Issues," *12News*, January 5, 2021, https://www.12news.com/article/tech/science/environment/mass-die-off-of-hundreds-thousands-songbirds-dead-in-arizona-us-southwest-caused-by-due-to-climate-change-issues/75-cc970585-336e-4852-b447-142c43a6abf0.

207 **the emotions of guilt, fear, and regret.** Jia Tolentino, "What to Do with Climate Emotions," *The New Yorker,* July 10, 2023, https://www.newyorker.com/news/annals-of-a-warming-planet/what-to-do-with-climate-emotions.

209 **". . . one of the first mandates given us as chiefs, to make sure and to make every decision that we make relate to the welfare and well-being of the seventh generation to come."** Christopher Vecsey and Robert W. Venables, eds., *American Indian Environments: Ecological Issues in Native American History* (New York: Syracuse University Press, 1980), 173–74.

211 **Audre Lorde's famous conclusion that caring for oneself is "an act of political warfare."** Audre Lorde, *A Burst of Light* (Ithaca, NY: Firebrand Books 1988), 130.

214 *I have always / been a woman.* Caitlin Carleton-Barnes, *They Say* (Portland, OR: Skookum's Tongue Press, 2015).

214 **"Ours is not the task of fixing the entire world all at once, but of stretching out to mend the part of the world within our reach."** Clarissa Pinkola Estés, "Letter to a Young Activist During Troubled Times," *Maven Productions,* accessed October 11, 2023, https://www.mavenproductions.com/letter-to-a-young-activist.

Fog Rescue

219 **"we are all fugitives" and "we are being chased."** Báyò Akómoláfé, "Coming Down to Earth," March 11, 2020, https://www.bayoakomolafe.net/post/coming-down-to-earth.

220 **"This midway point between the worlds of reason and image . . ."** Clarissa Pinkola Estés, *Women Who Run with the Wolves: Myths and Stories of the Wild Woman Archetype* (New York: Ballantine Books, 1996), 312–13.

222 **the need for a new weave of spirituality and the sacred to meet today's global climate challenges.** Báyò Akómoláfé, "Dr. Bayo Akomolafe on Slowing Down in Urgent Times," podcast lecture at *For the Wild,* June 1, 2020, 1:27:24, https://forthewild.world/listen/dr-bayo-akomolafe-on-slowing-down-in-urgent-times-encore-285.

223 **". . . Yet there are times when I am confronted with something beyond our ability to scientifically quantify."** Carl Safina, *Beyond Words: What Animals Think and Feel* (New York: Henry Holt & Company, 2015), 337.

223 **". . . Something needs to die in the process."** Francis Weller, *In the Absence of the Ordinary: Essays in a Time of Uncertainty* (Santa Rosa, CA: WisdomBridge Press, 2020), 17.

224 **". . . The future speaks ruthlessly through them."** Rainer Maria Rilke, "Über Kunst (1899)," *Rilke*, accessed October 12, 2023, https://rilke.de/adventskalender/11.htm.

225 **"Slow down, uncenter and forget yourself for a moment, let the world find you."** Weller, *In the Absence of the Ordinary*, 49.

226 **North America, before it was baptized with colonizer names . . .** Joan Tavares Avant, "North America Known as Turtle Island to Indigenous Tribes," *The Enterprise*, September 11, 2020, https://www.capenews.net/mashpee/columns/north-america-known-as-turtle-island-to-indigenous-tribes/article_450f4f21-6782-52c3-8c43-34c928a81b40.html.

227 *there are names each thing has for itself.* Linda Hogan, *Dark. Sweet. New & Selected Poems* (Minneapolis: Coffee House Press, 2014), 160.

227 **a turtle's heart can beat for five days after death.** Albert Johnson, James Clinton, and Rollin Stevens, "Turtle Heart Beats Five Days after Death," *American Biology Teacher* 19, no. 6 (1957): 176–77, https://doi.org/10.2307/4438911.

FOR FURTHER READING

Bessesen, Brooke. *Vaquita: Science, Politics, and Crime in the Sea of Cortez*. Washington, DC: Island Press, 2018.

Carson, Rachel. *The Sea Around Us*. Oxford: Oxford University Press, 2018.

Carson, Rachel. *Silent Spring*. Boston: Mariner Books, 2002.

Chenoweth, Erica, and Maria J. Stephan. *Why Civil Resistance Works: The Strategic Logic of Nonviolent Conflict*. New York: Columbia University Press, 2012.

Ehrenreich, Barbara. *Bright-sided: How the Relentless Promotion of Positive Thinking Has Undermined America*. New York: Metropolitan Books, 2009.

Estés, Clarissa Pinkola. *Women Who Run with the Wolves: Myths and Stories of the Wild Woman Archetype*. New York: Ballantine Books, 1996.

Figueres, Christiana, and Tom Rivett-Carnac. *The Future We Choose: The Stubborn Optimist's Guide to the Climate Crisis*. New York: Vintage, 2021.

Gardner, Howard E. *Frames of Mind: The Theory of Multiple Intelligences*. New York: Basic Books, 2011.

Giggs, Rebecca. *Fathoms: The World in the Whale*. New York: Simon & Schuster, 2020.

Gumbs, Alexis Pauline. *Undrowned: Black Feminist Lessons from Marine Mammals*. Minneapolis: AK Press, 2020.

Hernandez, Jessica. *Fresh Banana Leaves: Healing Indigenous Landscapes through Indigenous Science*. Berkeley: North Atlantic Books, 2022.

Hogan, Linda, Deena Metzger, and Brenda Peterson, eds. *Intimate Nature: The Bond Between Women and Animals*. New York: Ballantine Publishing Group, 1998.

Lorde, Audre. *Sister Outsider: Essays and Speeches*. Berkeley: Crossing Press, 2007.

McKibben, Bill. *Deep Economy: The Wealth of Communities and the Durable Future*. New York: Henry Holt & Company, 2008.

Mies, Maria, and Vandana Shiva. *Ecofeminism*. London: Bloomsbury Publishing, 2014.

Morton, Alexandra. *Not on My Watch: How a Renegade Whale Biologist Took on Governments and Industry to Save Wild Salmon*. Toronto: Random House Canada, 2022.

Neimanis, Astrida. *Bodies of Water: Posthuman Feminist Phenomenology*. New York: Bloomsbury Academic, 2017.

Roy, Arundhati. *Public Power in the Age of Empire*. New York: Seven Stories Press, 2004.

Safina, Carl. *Becoming Wild: How Animal Cultures Raise Families, Create Beauty, and Achieve Peace*. New York: Picador, Henry Holt & Company, 2020.

Saulitis, Eva. *Into Great Silence: A Memoir of Discovery and Loss Among Vanishing Orcas*. Boston: Beacon Press, 2013.

Schmidt, LaUra, Aimee Lewis Reau, and Chelsie Rivera. *How to Live in a Chaotic Climate: 10 Steps to Reconnect with Ourselves, Our Communities, and Our Planet*. Boulder: Shambhala Publications, 2023.

Shlain, Leonard. *The Alphabet Versus the Goddess: The Conflict Between Word and Image*. New York: Viking Adult, 1998.

Tempest Williams, Terry. *When Women Were Birds: Fifty-four Variations on Voice*. London: Picador, 2012.

Vaughan-Lee, Llewellyn, ed. *Spiritual Ecology: The Cry of the Earth*. Point Reyes, CA: The Golden Sufi Center, 2016.

Weller, Francis. *In the Absence of the Ordinary: Essays in a Time of Uncertainty*. Santa Rosa, CA: WisdomBridge Press, 2020.